L.R. Lennox had a colourful childhood. She grew up in a semaphore tower, with her parents, two sisters and no less than 15 animals. She gained an MA in the History of Art at Edinburgh University, where she dabbled in modelling and pursued painting and creative writing. After university, she worked for Condé Nast Publications, Vogue House. In 2011, she took a creative writing course at Central Saint Martins, gaining the confidence to tackle a novel. She exchanged Vogue House for Vancouver where she wrote *Love Friday*. She is a writer, an artist and a mum to her daughters, Freya and Suki; and her dog, Juno.

For Daddy.
Thank you for believing in me.
'Wish you were here.'

"Be small and perfect and not scared of monsters."

L.R. Lennox

LOVE FRIDAY

AUSTIN MACAULEY PUBLISHERS™

LONDON • CAMBRIDGE • NEW YORK • SHARJAH

A CIP catalogue record for this title is available from the British Library.

ISBN 9781528942669 (Paperback)
ISBN 9781528971232 (ePub e-book)

www.austinmacauley.com

First Published (2020)
Austin Macauley Publishers Ltd
25 Canada Square
Canary Wharf
London
E14 5LQ

My deepest gratitude goes to my best friend and husband, Ben, for his love, kindness, patience and unending support. *You are my rock.*

Thanks to Ro, for our chats, laughs and Grenville Island coffees, and for keeping me as sane during this writing process as I could possibly have been. Our friendship is sewn into the very makeup of this book.

Friday's child is loving and giving.

Friday, January 7th

Daisy Hawkins was born on a Friday, but today, counter to poetic tradition, she felt neither loving nor giving. She was moving out of Elgin Avenue; she was leaving Jesse and entering the world of singledom.

'Are you *quite* sure this is what you want?' Jude asked again. 'It's just…well, it all seems so sudden, that's all.'

Daisy had no idea if she was making the biggest mistake of her life. 'Why do people choose to live in flood-risk areas and then try to stay with their properties as long as possible when floods hit?' she mumbled.

'What? No idea Daise, sorry,' replied Jude. *She must be in shock; she's sounding even more bonkers than usual.*

'No, nor me. Some professor of Risk at Cambridge University was discussing it this morning on the radio.'

'*Rii-ght.* And what does it have to do with you and Jesse?'

'Dunno really. I didn't hear the whole thing. Just made me think…when you're faced with risk from every angle, can you really make a rational judgement as to which risk is less risky?'

'Sorry, I'm lost,' said Jude, brushing dust from her stripy jumper.

'Me too,' reflected Daisy.

Jude being Jude was always there in a crisis. Geographically removed from major flood-risk areas, she offered her services to the crises closer to home. The girls had taken the day off work to empty Jesse's flat of five years' worth of Daisy's clobber. The move was a draining process; Daisy cried flash floods and Jude mopped up on demand.

The girls had been best friends since school. Jude had always been the more settled, balanced and bossy – or rather, in charge – of the two. Now as a mother and wife, Jude was even more in control. She liked to keep things simple and viewed life in black and white, with neat rows of tasks accompanied by tick boxes. She had filled "the most important boxes" with cheery ticks, completing tasks in their "appropriate order". Daisy, on the other hand, had just chosen to side-step the crucial husband box, which was now looking emptier than ever.

She saw life as a noisy thing, in a variety of clashing colours, with black and white being the only pigments absent from her palette. There were no rows or boxes and little clarity, order or peace. Jude insisted on dishing out her blacks and whites, even when Daisy didn't ask. Sometimes Daisy mixed them into her own colourful palette, resulting in an ugly grey slush.

Today, Jude was mentally preparing herself for the technicolour rollercoaster that would be Daisy's single life.

It wasn't Jesse's fault. Jesse was textbook Mr Right. And that was exactly what she had wanted at the time. The nice guy who fulfilled all he promised to fulfil, promises which had attracted her in the first place – the nice guy, whom she chose to leave for being precisely that. She would miss him for the reasons she had left him: for his sweet gestures of love, the security and the routine. He had made her tea, for example, every single morning, *without fail*. This made Daisy's heart both flutter and tremble; her 62-year-old father made tea for her 58-year-old mother every morning, but Daisy was 29 – soon to be 30 – and there were other things she would rather be doing in bed than sipping her lukewarm life away.

Concerns had begun to simmer one evening three months ago. Whilst anticipating another cosy evening curled on the sofa with Jesse, she caught her reflection in the window. Or was it hers? There *someone* stood in a frumpy dressing gown, smudged glasses and cracking facemask – *What a sight!* – slumped over a pan of Bolognese. *Is that a puppy at my ankles? And who's that tugging my dressing gown cord? A child? Mine? Bloody-hell...* Reluctantly, she recognised the woman she was not ready to be. Her heart pounded. She was the "too settled, too soon" cliché. She needed to bubble, to sear, to feel alive. Could she find it in her to leave him? Five years in the bin, with the charred Bolognese. *But I put a lot of love into that.*

The sex thing had been a mounting concern too. She wasn't ready to dump it on the back seat with bags of nappies. She wanted to feel *desired* again. Another was boredom – it had invited itself in like a tactless third party and wriggled between them in bed, and reclined around them on the sofa. It refused to budge, and when she turned a blind eye, it simply lodged in her other eye, making it wander and wonder. At work, for example, she wondered why it had taken her so long to notice Sam in editorial, Ben in transport, and cashier Pablo at the corner-shop? *Well, hello!*

It was clear that something needed to be done, and she was confused and afraid for a while. Her head niggled with questions: *What if Jesse is my one and only shot at love?* And she knew he was a damn good shot.

'What, this Friday? You're moving out *this* Friday? This one coming?' Jesse couldn't understand the rush. He loved Daisy with all his heart. She was *his* Daisy. *Was.* He swallowed. At work, his computer flashed figures but all he could see was Daisy – an erroneous subtraction. *Where did I fuck up?* He dry-gulped sixes and sevens and their sides scratched his throat. He had miscalculated somewhere. His financial exams had put pressure on their relationship, he knew that, but he had done it for *their* future. 'Why invest in something that may never exist?' his scornful face appeared on screen. 'You've lost the best thing you ever had,' it said. *But at which precise point did I fuck up so massively? Which fuck-up triggered the catastrophic fuck-up? Or was it just fuck-up upon fuck-up, destined to explode?* Shards of broken heart splintered his clarity, and he could not see clearly at all. His lips mouthed YOU LOSER, over and over in slow motion; he had no problem seeing that. He dreaded taking his broken heart home to a haunted carcass with only memories and aromas of *The One That Got Away* to taunt and tease for eternity.

It's like a divorce, thought Daisy, as one hand left the side of a bundle of clothes to scoop a runaway tear. An edition of *Nimbus* magazine slipped unnoticed onto the pavement, falling open on her *Musings of a Pisces* column. Turning to her column's pseudonym *Eliza*, Daisy mentally prepped her *Musings of a Pisces* for next month's issue of *Nimbus* magazine:

'Right about the "settling down" stage that biology and society prescribes, I have hit a crossroads. It appeared from nowhere: no warning signs, nothing. And now I'm stalling. Behind me is a queue of other girls, in separate cars but the same boat. I can hear the discordant melody of blown gaskets and engine failure. A burning rubbery smell of panic thickens, as does the grey fog of pressure; it's hard to breathe. You see, none of us know which direction to turn. In the queue there are the lost and lonely, those whose bottom have fallen from their world, some who removed it themselves, with no clue as to what lies beneath. There are dashed expectations and broken hearts. Paths, once so defined, are now barely visible scuffed tracks.'

Marcus True was taking a break from his painting. He shivered on his doorstep and rummaged in his pocket for papers and tobacco. Rolling a cigarette with numb fingers was no easy task, but he enjoyed the absorbing process, and the promise of the warming lick of lighter flame.

His studio, on the top floor of his house, was light and bright with whitewashed walls, but if he stayed there too long his head would throb and threaten to explode and paint the walls red. He was also taking a break from his brother Jasper, the only subject he could paint since the death of their father, and Jasper's consequent plight. Jasper provoked emotional torment, which Marcus then pummelled onto his canvases. He frequently felt trapped with Jasper bounding off the walls inside his studio and mind. When it all got too claustrophobic, Marcus would take himself for a walk. It stopped him going mad.

From his home on Aldridge Road Villas he walked up Great Western Road towards Maida Vale. As he strolled along Elgin Avenue, he noticed two girls criss-crossing with loads on the pavement between a flat and a silver Polo. The girl wearing the stripy jumper was shorter than the other, tiny in fact. As he got closer, he noticed the taller of the two drop something, as she nudged wavy caramel-coloured hair from her face. The escapee was a damp magazine. A sturdy silver ring on her thumb caught his eye. *Is she crying?* She hung her head low, and he could not see her face. He studied the delicate crescent of her neck and her long skinny legs – *like pencils*. He watched the sad figure disappear back inside the flat. Marcus picked up the magazine and stole a glance at the open page. He couldn't help it, the bright purple heading was striking – *"Musings of a Pisces",* he read. The logo signature of the columnist was an equally purple *"Eliza". The shite girls read*, he thought, with a mixture of amusement and amazement. He wanted to wait for the taller girl to reappear so he could return it. Allured by the sadness of the stranger, he felt an overpowering desire to see her face. But the smaller girl appeared instead. Deciding it would be very un-cool to engage in tug of war over a girls' magazine, he returned *Nimbus* to the stripy girl.

'Ah thanks,' said Jude losing herself in the stranger's green eyes. *'Dreamy...'*

'Sorry?' The rollie bobbed in the corner of his stubbly mouth. He combed a hand through his dark mane and cocked his head.

Jude's cheeks flushed. 'Oh, err, nothing... Thanks for that.' Flustered, she grabbed the magazine. 'Have a good day!'

Marcus continued on his walk. *Musings of a Pisces* etched across his mind in *that* purple. Vibrant colours always gave images extra legroom in his memory and when his mind played on those vivid trivial moments, Marcus True felt free.

'I know it's a bit early for this type of chat, Daise, but *that* guy', Jude pointed to a diminishing coated back, 'was gorgeous!' She shimmied her eyebrows. 'Seriously fit. Sexy. Totally and utterly smoking hot in fact. Wow. H.O.'

'Got it Jude. He was hot. And yeah, *way* too early, Jude,' interrupted Daisy, rolling her eyes, before another tear fell.

'Hey, Daise,' Jude opened her arms. 'Come 'ere.' Daisy snuggled into the warm, familiar hug. 'You know it's not too late to change your mind. Jesse would take you back in a heartbeat. Just tell him it's all been a big misunder –'

'No, no,' Daisy interrupted. She filled her lungs with the cool air. 'It's the right thing.' She was surprised by her sudden certainty. Within the crispness was a fading scent of forest and turpentine; it smelt amazing. Inhaling once again, she breathed deeper conviction, 'Most definitely.'

That evening, with her belongings placed in Jude's spare room, along the corridor, and in any available space in the Franklin family home on Ladbroke Grove, Jude and Daisy left baby Millie with her daddy, Will, and headed to *Jazbar*, their favourite bar on the Portobello Road. Mounting need for a drink had allowed no time to freshen up and change clothes.

En route, a black cab's headlight caught on Jude's engagement ring, and a temporarily blinded Daisy envisaged the end of next month's column stretching before her like the Portobello Road:

'Ahead are those who need not deliberate at the cross-roads; the ones who turn decisively left, right or straight on. Those whose lives are on track. The sorted ones. Their eyes are fixed on their journey and ahead to their chosen destination. They don't need maps, as getting lost is not a part of their agenda. The heartily chugging motors belong to the settled lovers: the engaged, the just married, the expectant young mums, the new parents. No one reverses because no one regrets. The white teeth framed by broad glossy smiles and the big, proud diamond rings catch in the headlights of the lost and are blinding.'

Jazbar served the best cocktails and the best mix of music; jazz of course, but hip-hop, indie, funk and soul too. Daisy loved *Jazbar* for its vibe, a conflicting but harmonious combination of edgy, unassuming and glamorous. The walls were burgundy, topped and tailed with white skirting boards and adorned with large silver framed black and white photographs of all the musical greats: Ella Fitzgerald, Louis Armstrong, Barry White, Frank Sinatra, Stevie Wonder, Billy Joel, Bob Marley. The walls were almost entirely swallowed up by musical idols and low-lit guitars, which hung at jaunty angles, as if swaying to a beat.

Daisy had heard that the owner was a singer-songwriter, and presumed that *Jazbar* was his bespoke utopia. It was quite a romantic thought.

Enticed by jazz seeping from the basement bar, the girls wandered to the dimly lit stairwell where Jude almost tripped over an inebriated form slumped at the top of the stairs. His head was tucked into his chest, hiding his face, and his thin body folded in on itself like origami. He needed help. Jude beckoned over one of the staff before the girls disappeared down the stairs.

'Jasper mate, come on. Up you get,' Stephan tried to coax Jasper, the flaccid proprietor of *Jazbar* up from the floor. It was only 8pm, but Stephan already felt exhausted by the prospect of yet another predictable Friday night at work. Forget the bar, managing Jasper was a full-time job in itself.

Sunk into leather chairs, the girls reached up to sip multi-coloured concoctions from fancy glasses. Beneath a chandelier canopy of glass droplets, Daisy thanked Jude once again, for the temporary refuge, 'just until I find somewhere to rent, OK?'

'For as long as you need, Daise,' replied Jude, relieved Will wasn't anywhere in earshot. His Daisy-related charity had been pushed to the max already.

It dawned on Daisy that she was no longer just "best friend". 'I've been *demoted* to *that* troublesome *single* best friend.'

'The *essential* accessory to the settled maternal type,' Jude jokingly reassured. 'Everyone *must* have one.' Daisy giggled. This was new territory for them both.

They spotted Tara Forsyth, another *Sainthill Publications* employee, seated at the table by the fireplace. She was laughing at something her male companion had said. Her black glossy hair bounced up and down as her long neck angled backwards. The girls watched Tara present her décolletage expertly to approving eyes. Her companion plunged beneath the table to manoeuvre his twitch.

'My God!' squealed Jude, 'She's with Simon Pelly! *Slippery Si!* I can't believe it...'

'Why?' asked Daisy, who knew all about Jude's disapproval of her rival Tara Forsyth, and had been fully briefed on her infamous "extra hours".

'Slippery Si is also *my* client you see.'

No, Daisy didn't see. She knew that the two girls had many clients in common. Sometimes she wondered if Jude's hunger for Tara-related fodder was triggered by jealousy towards her ad sales package, which promised better value for money, more legroom. And a firmer hand on the desired position – offers which Jude would never make.

'Look at her fake laugh,' Jude continued; her eyes were mere slits now, but she took it all in. 'She's such a dick. And to gain what? One measly page of advertising, if that. It's pathetic.'

Daisy Hawkins, Jude Franklin and Tara Forsyth all worked at *Sainthill*, a publisher of established magazines covering the arts, fashion, food and travel. Tara worked for the society magazine, *Sabre,* otherwise known as "the posh-totty's bible", where each page celebrated "poshness" and captivated their exclusive market to claim international leadership in the magazine world. *Sabre* targeted the thirty five plus lady of classy leisure, positioning itself as the glacé cherry on the top of the cake of luxury living. Like Jude, Tara was a *Senior Account Manager* – a glorified sales rep. From their respective advertising departments, at either end of the same corridor, the two girls sold pages in their magazines to the same wealthy arts and fashion clients. *Sabre*'s posh and pretentious readers responded eagerly to the advertising, inflating the bellies of Tara's fat-cat advertisers.

Nimbus on the other hand, was a smaller magazine with a smaller circulation, targeting twenty and thirty somethings within the M25. And like its advertising clients, *Nimbus* had smaller editorial budgets to play with. From *Sabre*'s snobby stance, *Nimbus* survived off its leftover scraps of readers and advertisers.

This isn't to say that *Sabre* would turn its toffee-nose away from "inferior" advertising clients, who were willing to risk bankruptcy for a sniff of *Sabre*'s wealthy readers – for money was money after-all. Hence, Tara and Jude's clients sometimes overlapped – Slippery Si being one. But this was where the mutual overlapping ended. Body overlap was Tara's speciality.

Whilst Jude ogled at the live Tara action, Daisy became distracted by thoughts of Jesse. *Is he OK?* She missed him and felt sick with guilt for abandoning him. She pictured him alone in *their* home… Or was he on a vengeful night out, boozing himself into oblivion? *Who'd check he'd get home OK? Should I call? Does he hate me now?* She had broken his trust and his heart. Daisy shivered and felt the familiar simmering of unconsciousness and what felt like butterfly wings scraping the walls of her stomach, and suspected that one of her fainting episodes might be on the cards tonight.

Another cocktail later, something aroused her drowsy eye. Looking over in the direction of the fireplace, she saw flames dance in a shiny cufflink, which decorated a tidy blue cuff. Through tipsy vision she admired polished brogues, matching turquoise socks, a maroon velvet jacket and designer stubble on a handsome, *regal* face. He sipped on a brown drink crowned with cream foam… *Espresso Martini! Good call.* Daisy wobbled to the bar and placed her order.

Tara Forsyth had noticed the velveted gentleman too: Baron Max von Beck. She recognised him from *RAH!*, the Society pages at the back of *Sabre*. She shot him a smouldering look and shimmied manicured fingers; he nodded back a smile. Tara Forsyth liked Max von Beck, for Tara Forsyth liked a challenge, and these days they were hard to come by. Like a lion hunting a gazelle, the thrill of the chase was not diminished by inevitability of the outcome – *and this Bambi*, she thought with excitement, *might be more challenging than the usual*. The baron had a vast number of women chasing him and a reputation for being picky. He maintained what, he argued, were superior standards, getting *any* lady he desired. Tara would take great pleasure in this competitive chase for the pedigreed baron.

She invested no time in the pursuit of "love"; *why pursue something when its very existence is questionable?* She came from a loveless broken home, and had experienced only loveless broken relationships. She associated so-called love with a surrendering of control, incessant compromises, stifling illogical demands and pressures – the inevitable consequence of sharing one's life. *Why would anyone willingly make those sacrifices?* As far as Tara was concerned, love, if it did exist, was a disability, which could reduce even the most career ambitious and composed of women to indolent stay-at-home mums and hormonal wrecks. Time after time, Tara had witnessed the hasty collapsing of personal goals, the shunning of priorities and friends, all to satisfy a "loved one"…who then cheats or dumps – or both – leaving these once strong women in soggy states with the remaining scraps of their life dragging around their ankles. *Err, not for me. Thanks.*

Of love, or whatever it was, Tara wanted no part. She was a strong, independent woman, and hence had no desire to test its existence, or the existence of her own heart for that matter. She feared every outcome, and in this particular case, found bliss in ignorance – the only ignorance she deemed acceptable.

Tara was oblivious as to why she always felt empty. Unconsciously, she attempted to fill her vast loveless gap with the fleeting thrills of challenges and sex, two actions that allowed her control. Sex might be messy, but it was far less messy than love. Hence, Tara's life was clean, controlled and empty; and she tricked herself into believing she liked it that way.

In *Jazbar's* kitchens, proprietor Jasper True lay in a drunken heap on the floor. Around him chefs continued to roll pastry, chop tomatoes, marinade beef strips and caramelise crème brûlées. Stephan dialled Marcus. *A typical Friday night.*

He put the phone down. 'It's going home time, mate,' he informed his boss. Propping him up into a slightly more respectable slump, Stephan rescued the remaining contents of the Châteauneuf-du-Pape wedged between Jasper's thighs. *Poor Marcus*, thought Stephan again, *far beyond the call of fraternal duty.*

Six espresso martinis later, Daisy was snoring loudly. Jude decided it was a good time to call it a day.

They entered the evening chill as Marcus paced up the steps towards *Jazbar's* double doors. He recognised the small stripy-jumpered girl from earlier that day. But it was her same tall companion who caught his eye on ascent. Again, he failed to see her face, which buckled and sunk inside a hood, stolen by greedy shadows. But he recognised those long pencil legs, which dragged the ground reluctantly as if suspicious of their destination – or just pissed, he mused. He recognised the delicately stooped angle of her head. *Such elegant sadness.* At the top of the stairs he hesitated. He felt overcome by an urge to turn around, to say something, to see her face. But Jasper, Jasper needed him. Jasper always needed him. And Marcus was always there.

Jasper had battled with drink and drugs since their father had died of cancer two years ago. Marcus spent every waking moment worrying about the rapid deterioration of his younger brother, and his progressively obstinate refusals to contemplate rehabilitation. Marcus expelled his angst-ridden energy onto his canvases, plunging paintbrushes into Jasper-tinted fears and splashing them onto canvasses like a madman, creating images of Jasper – Jaspers and more Jaspers – his concerns vented, reflected and recorded for analysis in each painted angle of his brother. Or he would sketch with a freshly sharpened pencil, rapidly drawing line upon line, pressing harder and harder until the lead broke and the paper tore. It was Marcus's compulsion and his therapy.

Back home he tucked Jasper into his camp bed, amongst the paints, canvasses and easels in his top floor studio – a far cry from Jasper's own plush Chelsea bedroom. *A typical Friday night*, thought Marcus, as he turned out the light.

In their respective bedrooms, Marcus's housemates stirred. The twins, Beth and Floyd, had woken up once again to a smashed Jasper crashing down the corridor, attacking the staircase with jarring steps, back sliding down the walls, giggling, crying, shouting and dry heaving in the loo... It was uncomfortably familiar.

On Ladbroke Grove, Jude hugged baby Millie against her chest. She stared out through the gap in the curtains at the glowing moon. Daisy's face stared back. She worried about her best friend.

In the next-door room, a pesky cart-wheeler cartwheeled around and around in the inebriated circus of Daisy's mind. She wanted to puke him up, but he resisted. From her bed, she attempted to steady herself by latching eyes on the moon's face. But the orb joined the cart-wheeler for fun and games, and rotated and multiplied across the sky. One shook his head at her, another mouthed IDIOT, grating her head with each curl of lip and biting like a Venus flytrap with each opening and closing. From another, Jesse stared back with sad eyes. She needed water. Her heart raced; she felt a pounding in her chest. As the familiar palpitations grew, she stumbled into unconsciousness.

Half a mile away, on Aldridge Road Villas, Marcus went to bed. As usual he struggled to sleep. He stared out at the moon. As usual, Jasper stared back. Then a familiar sad figure glided across the face. *Who is she?* Marcus blinked for clarity. She temporarily eclipsed his brother, and Marcus felt a foreign serenity before she was consumed by Jasper.

Friday, January 21st

Daisy felt the nip of the early morning air as it seeped across the fields and hedges, down the country lanes, and through the feeble defence of archaic central heating at the Hawkins family home. It was 6am, and already the house was alive with chaos. In fact, wedding or no wedding, chaos never slept in the Hawkins household.

Daisy put her leather jacket over her long cream bridesmaid dress, and reaching her hands behind her to secure her big blue sash, she heard a crunch on her left side – *Fragments of my damaged heart?* she pondered. The last week had felt long. Neither Jesse nor Daisy had been in contact and the silence had been painful. She reached into the right pocket of her jacket and withdrew not a broken heart but a magazine article Jude had given her promoting a new London-specific dating website called *Shine Online*. It was aimed at the settled and sorted who had increasingly burdensome single friends they wished to nominate, and offload onto the website for some professional help. Despite the web being today's *go-to* place for love, she was well aware that Daisy, an old-fashioned romantic at heart, was reluctant to *go-there*. 'It's to help you "connect" with all your single readers, Daisy. *Musings of a Pisces* column needs to get with the programme, embrace the times, *connect*,' Jude had said. *'It's meant to be written by Love, whoever Love is,'* which was immensely worrying, thought Daisy, because if Jude, with her doting husband and beautiful baby, didn't know who Love was, then what help was there for the rest of us? Daisy skimmed her eyes over the article once more:

'London is full of single girls. On the way to work, crammed in the tube or bus, catching eyes and crossing paths with other lonely hearts looking for love. From the focused commuters crossing Chelsea Bridge, or walking along the Strand, or cobbly Brick Lane, or around the stately Houses of Parliament, or across lush Green Park, the shrill wail of lonely hearts unite. I hear you all.

In the evenings, I hear the same cry, seeping from bedrooms and trendy clubs and bars along the King's Road and swanky Notting Hill, and across the cool Shoreditch hangouts and moody bars of London Bridge. London whimpers loneliness. Lost souls sway blindly like balloons, clinging to hopeless hearts with gnawed string. Never has there been a city which so craved me but failed to see me. But I see you all.

By Christmas, I had had enough. Enough of failed attempts to match lonely hearts; of coaxing her to drop guards and him to contact afterwards, of pointlessly paving the way for an exchange of words and not just eye contact; of countless wasted opportunities...of being ignored! I was at my wits end! My ears rang with pain!'

Hence, the Christmas birth of *Shine Online. Promising happiness all year around, not just for Christmas*, mused Daisy cynically. Even Love gave up on good old-fashioned romance it seemed, and pimped itself out on the Internet in exchange for an easier life and greater success rate.

What Jude didn't appreciate was that, of late, Daisy was in fact pretty chummy with her readers, and she didn't need Jude's long-winded, quirky little Love ad to help her connect. Single Daisy now approached her column *Musings of a Pisces* from a different angle, settling naturally into subjects that resonated with all her readers, and via her pseudonym *Eliza*, replying with empathy and sincerity to the letters she found time to. Her job was not to play the role of agony aunt, but rather to offer readers a light-hearted column, which mused on the quirks and varying nuances of life in London from a girl's point of view. Thanks to her experience of married life (sort of), and her growing experience of single life, Daisy was thrilled to discover that she was appealing to a broader spectrum of London ladies and doing a brilliant job at work.

As cringey as Daisy decided the *Shine Online* promotion was, and as irritatingly verbose as Love apparently was, she couldn't help but feel a sense of relief that today, at the Hawkins home at least, Love could rest its ears and celebrate unaided success, for today her older sister Orlaith was marrying her true love, Vinnie Wallace.

Daisy had decided a long time ago that, unlike her sister, she hadn't inherited the nauseatingly perfect gene, but instead an unlucky legend: Apparently Paul McCartney thought of *"Daisy Hawkins"* before *"Eleanor Rigby"*, and for a while it was Daisy Hawkins who *picked up the rice in the church where the wedding had been*. Daisy's parents, hard-core Beatles fans, decided that Daisy Hawkins was a pretty name and that was that. *Am I destined to be one of the lonely people too?*

She wandered downstairs towards the bangs, slams and profanities, to help her mother with final preparations.

'Is the dip OK, Daise? Because if it's not, well then that's just tough. It'll just have to do, won't it? Because quite frankly there isn't any time left.'

Mrs Margot Hawkins buzzed. She always got like this under pressure. She was a whirlwind of panic and fluster, zapping around and around, seeing to absolutely everything but nothing at all. There were pots, pans and various vessels of prepared food on every surface. Margot's hair was cemented around rollers – the result of a generous attack of hairspray – but the cucumber mousse refused to set; her makeup was over-done and the duck rolls were under-done. Her dressing gown cord threatened to dismember the entire kitchen, with each rotation of her body, as she saw to this here, that there, but absolutely nothing anywhere.

'Mum. Mum. Chill out a bit. It's delicious,' Daisy reassured her mother, as she licked the dip from the end of her finger, before shooing her out of the kitchen in an attempt to reinstall some degree of calm.

Left alone, in the chaos of her own thoughts, Daisy wondered what true love might taste like if she ever got the chance to try.

Orlaith and Vinnie had done it. 'You did it,' Will confirmed, 'congratulations, sir.' He took Vinnie's sweaty palm with one hand and landed a manly pat on the groom's shoulder with the other, before returning to hold his wife's small hand.

Jude noted that this was her second Hawkins-induced Friday out of the office. Given any opportunity, her work piled high; the thought of this made her feel decidedly nauseous. Before the birth of Millie and the end of Daisy's relationship with Jesse, Jude had only ever taken two sick days in her career: a healthy statistic which she had been immensely proud of.

Even in her heels, Jude had to tiptoe to kiss the bride on both cheeks. 'You look wonderful, Mrs Wallace!' Jude gushed.

Jude worked the "Prime Minister's wife" look remarkably well. She had dressed her small frame in a tidy fitting primrose dress, and looked glamorous as always with her permanently brushed and freshly highlighted thick blonde hair skimming a neat line just below yellow padded shoulders. Her investment in expensive make up paid off, and the expert application *always* followed two primary rules: never too much, and no crazy colours. (Jude tended to err on the non-crazy side of most things). Her eyes were big and brown beneath a canopy of mascara'd lashes, and framed within an *appropriate* thickness of eyeliner. Pale, glossy, wide lips made way for a broad smile, which in turn made way for a distinctive laugh, reminiscent of a squeaky engine. Jude stood on the taller side of tiny today, in her red-soled Christian Louboutins. With a degree of carefully controlled effort, Jude transformed herself from plain Jane to glamour puss, making sure the former was as buried beneath grooming as she was in her past.

Daisy was a natural beauty – she didn't know it, but she was. She looked fresh faced and her wavy blonde hair was free from highlights and straighteners, and as a result not as wiry as Jude's on those rare occasions maintenance levels fell short or serum levels dropped to potentially hazardous. Both women were slim, but Daisy's slenderness was stretched by her taller physique. She had a pretty nose and an easy smile. Though she wasn't smiling much at all these days.

Oh bloody-hell, not again, thought Daisy, as Aunt Flossie approached, with empty ears demanding a refill of break-up gossip. Daisy swerved towards the music coming from the corner of the sitting room and stood close to the sexy, charismatic guy who masterfully juggled singing, strumming and sipping champagne. *That must be Jasper True.* Daisy recognised the face and voice from a CD her sister had played to her before the wedding. Orlaith had come across Jasper at a friend's party, and wasted no time in securing her wedding in his diary.

He wore grey shoes with orange laces, black skinny jeans and a white T-shirt with a graffiti-style print on the front. He looked strained, noticed Daisy, with thinning brown hair and taut skin wrapped around a slim frame. She wondered how old he was. Life had branded his face and his words, and she guessed he looked and sounded older than his years. She imagined each pore had a rock and roll story to tell. His eye twitched energetically as his sideways grin sliced his cheek with mischief. Each facial shift, each bodily movement was part of his dance with life. It was captivating to watch. He looked both defiant and crushed in the arms of life. He looked bold yet scared, happy yet sad. She wanted to work him out, to know all about him; the sensation was sudden and intense. He was addictively compelling. He looked quite out of place at her sister's wedding, on the edge of the carpet at the fringe of the crowd. His lyrics danced with contagious energy. Somewhere within the triangle of "love", "free" and "soul", their eyes met. Daisy felt her heart flutter on waves of electricity and revelled in the tingling sensation.

Waiters snaked through the sea of guests with trays of canapés and bottles of champagne to refill glasses and re-line stomachs.

'He's awfully attractive, darling.' Mrs Margot Hawkins pointed out the approaching blonde-haired waiter to her daughter. 'Shame he's quite obviously–'

Daisy's father cuffed her gently on the wrist, and then whisked her off into the crowd.

'Gay...' Mrs Hawkins's words trailed off.

'Isn't it just? Very jolly indeed,' Margot's sister, Aunt Flossie, had caught the end of the sentence, and hurried an answer before dipping a lemongrass kebab into the coconut sauce on the head waiter's tray.

'De-jish-us!' Her words came out chewed.

The coconut sauce leapt onto Flossie's turquoise blouse, some squeezed down her cleavage, only to find a dollop of chilli sauce already taking refuge.

'Yes. Delicious...' Margot's eyes followed the broad shoulders of the blonde waiter into the throng of hungry guests.

'You're not serious, are you?' Flossie pursued her sister's gaze. 'He's very clearly not interested in the female sex.'

'I know, I know. Shame really. Maybe he'd be good for Daisy, if he wasn't, you know, not interested, as you say.'

The sisters' eyes locked between bubbly sips. Flossie's two children had married lawyers. She didn't think a waiter, a gay one at that was quite the thing for her precious niece Daisy.

'He would've been ideal for her, just for a bit of fun,' Margot explained. 'Healthy for her, after such a long time with Jesse. You know, a fling type thing,' she took another sip. Their eyes relocked.

'A very mini-fling perhaps,' Flossie couldn't help but stick her nose in. Her niece was nearly 30 after all, hardly a time to be having flings. She could not understand why that stupid, stupid boy Jesse hadn't just got on with it? Asked the big question. Put a ring on it, as Beyoncé would say. What the hell was wrong with young men these days? She glanced over at Orlaith. *Still, one daughter out of two isn't bad, I suppose...*

Flossie's face moved in the rhythm of her thoughts and Margot translated all with sibling accuracy. Flossie had always been judgemental and patronising, and a stickler for social convention.

'You've dripped sauce down your top,' Margot pointed at her sister's Jackson Pollock attempt on her turquoise bosom. 'And by the looks of things, some is making serious headway down your front too.'

Well, that shut her up.

'Another one? You sure?' Head Waiter Floyd hesitated before pouring.

'Quite sure,' Daisy replied, noticing his ice-blue eyes.

He handed her another fizzy glass. 'You OK...? You make a beautiful drunk bridesmaid.' He pictured his mother, lying in her bed, sick, weak and fragile but beaming from ear to ear if he took home a girl like Daisy Hawkins. All she wanted before she slipped away was to know that her children were happy and settled. It had never crossed her mind that her son was gay, and it was far too late to tell her now. She had long lost her ability to cope with any change or big news. Floyd knew that telling his mum that he was gay might well, at this stage, tip her over the edge. She took comfort in oblivion.

Daisy made herself not so comfortable on a box of canned colas behind the drinks table. 'My cheeks ache,' she said forlornly. 'It's exhausting answering the same questions and fake smiling all the time.'

'Sure is.' Floyd popped open another champagne bottle. Platinum blonde hair flopped over his delicate Nordic features. His hair looked soft. Daisy had an overwhelming urge to touch it and ask him what shampoo/conditioner/treatment he used. Yet another waitress sashayed past, again trying her luck with Floyd. But oblivious to her efforts, he only had eyes for a duck roll which he pinched from her tray.

'Smiling when you don't feel like it? Comes with practice. I'm an actor you see, so I'm pretty good at it now. I'm the proud owner of a well-tuned, well-oiled fake smile.' He flashed her one.

It looked real enough to her. She liked the sexy confidence of actors. 'I'm Daisy,' she offered her hand.

'Daisy, the cute bridesmaid,' he said with cheeky charm, as he took her hand.

'Floyd with the *exceptionally* moisturised hands, and the impressively believable smile.'

'That was a real one.' He flashed another; flirting with members of either sex was second nature.

Hmmm, is he flirting? Her radar was rusty but her heart fluttered nonetheless. Her body washed with familiar giddiness, and she felt those butterflies in her stomach gently flexing their wings. Fearful of fainting, she steadied herself on a can of cola, and in doing so, pushed it from its plastic casing, causing both herself and the can to topple to the floor; her ability to reciprocate flirtations were somewhat rusty too.

Jasper True joined Floyd and Daisy, overwhelming them with a rush of energy.

'Yo Floydy!' – and addressing Daisy with an arm pointed at Floyd – 'That guy's the best!'

'Old friends,' Floyd explained, before introducing her.

Female crushes on his gay friend Floyd were a constant source of amusement, thought Jasper, as he tipped his imaginary hat to Daisy and necked a glass when Floyd's back was turned.

'Hello to the beautiful bridesmaid.' His words were charged with charisma. Spasmodically, he squinted at Daisy three times in a row, before twitching his neck to one side then back again.

Marcus...

Suddenly, his brother was in Jasper's head. From the second he had clamped eyes on the bridesmaid, *Marcus. Marcus. Marcus. Why?* Jasper's mind was compressed by a magnetic pull between the two, Daisy and Marcus. *Weird.* He twitched again, to free himself from the faultlessness of this union.

Jasper had always been jealous of his brother and, for as long as he could remember, had always felt inferior. At school, Marcus had better results, more friends and hotter girlfriends; and the same at university. Jasper had nurtured paranoia that he was the lesser of the siblings, the black sheep. The poor younger brother starved of paternal affection. In his eyes, Marcus stole it all. Jasper True's entire life had been darkened and crushed by his perfect brother's oppressive shadow. Paranoia was the only thing that flourished in the shade. And then their father died, which hadn't helped at all, and Jasper resented how much more he needed his brother who was integral to his survival.

But I saw Daisy first! *He* was the one here with her at the wedding, *not* Marcus. Their paths would never cross and Marcus's life would remain incomplete. Perfect Marcus would never accomplish true perfection. And only Jasper would know why. He felt powerful, yet his self-loathing stirred. He felt trapped inside the child he was, unable to be kind and fair to the one person he needed and who kept him alive.

Daisy was entranced by Jasper and his surplus of nervy energy. Unlike Floyd, she noticed, Jasper True was not textbook gorgeous, with his wispy hair, strained skin, peculiar twitch, fidgety energy…but for all those reasons he had a magnetism which was impossible to ignore. In a nutshell, he was off-the-scale sexy.

Behind Floyd's back, Daisy watched him down the glass of champagne before pressing a finger to his lips – *shhhhh!* – his eyes darting over at Floyd. He then winked at her – three times in rapid succession – before returning to his guitar and filling the room with music once more.

Daisy listened. His lyrics were windows to his soul, which opened only briefly before they slammed shut. Tipsily, she wrenched one open, and peeking beneath the protective layers of aura, discovered a body of insecurities. She shuddered. Bewitched by the depth of his layers, his mystery and vulnerability, Daisy's heart felt compelled to flutter. Again she felt the wash of dizziness and the dread of impinging blackout. She wondered if another trip to the doctors, to re-test her fluttering heart, might be a wise idea. She latched onto this thought to steady her rapidly pixelating mind.

'He's a bloody liability that one,' cautioned Floyd, following Daisy's gaze. Besides, having allowed the scene where he introduces Daisy to his mother to gain momentum in his mind, the last thing Floyd wanted was Jasper getting in the way. His mother would adore her. She had remedial qualities, he just knew. With a girl like Daisy by his side, he knew his mother would never have to worry about him. She needed to save energy, not waste it on worries. Perhaps Daisy would add a month or two onto his mum's life, a year…completely cure?

Floyd checked his watch before grabbing the microphone for his big moment. 'The moment we've all been waiting for,' he grinned cockily at Daisy, before switching on the microphone.

Daisy wobbled to her feet, stroked the circular prints of the cans from her dress, and went to stand by her mother.

Floyd gonged the gong. A humming hush descended immediately with more vigour than precision. He instructed the guests to please make their way to the marquee. With an enthusiastic gesture he pointed in the direction of the portaloos.

After diverting a few love-struck ladies, Daisy took her place on her sister's table inside the marquee. Her stomach now barrelled enough champagne to numb lingering thoughts of Jesse and their own wedding that could have been.

It was after midnight. Jasper's bandmates had arrived after dinner to get all the twisters twirling on the dance floor. Slurred words slipped unnoticed past slurred brains, and Jasper's singing was met with disproportionately loud applause.

Since the death of his father, Jasper discovered that he was attracted to bars like moths to light. He had never had a problem locating a bar, nor emptying the entire stash of bottles behind. And even with his friend as head waiter, burdened with his brother's instructions to prevent him from drinking, getting beyond pissed was hardly a challenge.

Will was waiting in the car in the driveway with a snoozing baby Millie. Jude, meanwhile, was rushing around searching for Daisy, trying to recall the last time she had seen her.

Marcus was regretting offering to collect his housemate, Floyd, and his brother from the wedding. He had driven all the way from London and was now caught in the spider web of Hampshire lanes. He was late. Every road looked the same. *Some were the fucking same!* Beth, Floyd's twin and Marcus's other housemate, had a show opening at her art gallery; Floyd's car had broken down, and Jasper no longer had a license, so with the rural trains slumbering, the buck stopped with Marcus. Having figured the opportunity to get his brother home safely was more desirable than a crippled evening spent worrying about his safe return, he agreed to make the journey.

Jude found Daisy in a cold half-heap outside the marquee. The other half belonged to the wedding singer Jasper True. It was dark, but the marquee lights outlined their faces and the debris of bottles and glasses that lay around them. Her head lay on his shoulder. The blonde-haired waiter ran over and reluctantly laid claim to Jasper. With some shakes and gentle prizing, both heaps stirred and found their feet.

Marcus finally arrived in the shadowy drive to witness a small woman lugging high-heels in one hand and a taller stumbling figure in the other. He had seen the duo before. As he watched their silver Polo turn down the drive, his headlights stroked a back seat tear.

Floyd had managed to drag Jasper inside the marquee by the time Marcus entered.

'I'm so sorry,' said Floyd, 'I tried...I just couldn't watch him all night.'

His housemate's apology embarrassed him. 'Please. Don't be ridiculous. I'm the one who's sorry,' Marcus said. Jasper was thirty. Way too old to be babysat. Marcus should have been there. *Or should not have let him go? Trap him? Control him? Are any right?*

'He doesn't help himself,' said Floyd, as the car wiggled down a dark road in the direction of bright lights and motorway. He didn't need the lights to know Marcus's face was saturated with undue guilt. He wasted more words on deaf ears, 'He's not your responsibility, Marcus.'

At the Franklin home on Ladbroke Grove, alcohol defeated insomnia and Daisy slept like a baby.

On Aldridge Road Villas, Marcus listened to the rhythm of Jasper's snores coming from the camp bed in the studio above his bedroom; the safest place for him when he was in this state. This was the *fourth* time in the last ten days that Jasper had needed rescuing and roofing; *Floyd and Beth's patience must be wearing thin.* He wondered at the familiarity of the silhouetted duo, and if they could possibly be the same two girls he had seen last Friday, shifting bundles on Elgin Avenue and later that same night, leaving *Jazbar*. Something about them, or rather one of them, wouldn't let him forget. Captivated by thoughts of this peculiarly elegant stranger, and the cause of her sadness, Marcus stopped hearing Jasper's snores and his own noisy worries, and somewhere between 4 and 5am, he fell into a deep sleep.

Friday, January 28th

Having looked forward to her first quiet evening in her modest rented flat on Sutherland Avenue, Notting Hill – (her "Warren", as Jude affectionately referred) – Daisy's Friday plans were interrupted by two thimble-sized nuggets of blue wax. The previous night's attempts to combat anxiety-fuelled insomnia had led to an over-enthusiastic insertion of the earplugs, which had lodged themselves firmly, refusing to budge all day. Hence, a much anticipated evening alone was stifled by an unplanned visit to Chelsea and Westminster Hospital.

It had been an exceptionally trying day at work. She could hear her phone ring but was unable to translate the muffled words at the end of the line. She resorted to leaving her phone off the hook and putting her work mobile on silent, so as not to irritate her colleagues.

Her boss, the publisher of *Nimbus*, had called her into his office several times that day only to be ignored. Hanratty was an awkward, shy and reclusive man. He looked like a cross between an owl and a tortoise, with a beaky nose, cross eyes and tufts of orange hair. He had tough skin, and the propensity to vanish inside his shell, where he stored the combined wisdom of the two.

'Sleep well, Daisy?' he tried again, knowing full well she had not, by the look of the dark circles cradling her eyes. He knew about the break-up, and the house move and the general unsettled time she was going through, and he was keen to show he cared, understood, supported. He needed her; the magazine needed her and couldn't afford for her to lose her way. Daisy's column, *Musings of a Pisces* was largely accountable for *Nimbus*'s growing circulation. *Eliza,* Daisy's nom de plume and *Nimbus*'s "people's person", was hugely popular with the female waifs and strays across London. 'Daisy,' he tried one last time, with as much volume as he could muster. He rapped his knuckles tentatively on his glass partition, (he never dared leave his office unless he needed the loo). But again, all efforts were met with nothing.

Even after three marriages – albeit failed – and an office full of women, the only thing Hanratty was certain of the opposite sex was that they were a complete mystery, and disconcertingly intimidating.

And it was a mystery to the entire *Nimbus* workforce, how and why he still worked at *Sainthill Publications*. He seemed out of his depth every day, submerged beneath *Nimbus*'s glossy pages of female fashion, sex, periods, contraception and the perplexing world of female emotions.

Hanratty was from the old-school publishing world; an old Etonian who had enjoyed the giddy hay day of advertising, along with his now retired peers. Big money deals were clinched during boozy breakfasts, which slipped into long lunches. He felt baffled by this foreign, restrained world of tedious bureaucracy and powerful women.

After work, and two patience-testing hours, Hugh Grant came to retrieve Daisy. The A&E waiting room had emptied, bar Daisy and an elderly gentleman with a bloody arm. She kept looking over at the door where the doctors and nurses emerged every now and then. When her eyes fell on a spectacularly handsome doctor, who looked uncannily like the famous actor, pristine in his white coat and mouthing her name, she slunk down in her seat and wondered why she was continually picked on as the butt of destiny's jokes. Her friends went to hospital for normal things like having babies. Daisy went to hospital to have not one, but two waxy nuggets extracted from her ear, *by none other than the world's most attractive doctor.* He was tall and delicious, with thick chocolaty shavings of brown hair. Looking straight at her, he mouthed her name again. Seeing as she was the only possible Daisy in the room, she stood up in shame and wobbled her jelly legs over to the very edible Dr Oliver Cranston.

As she lay on her side in the treatment room, Dr Oliver poked long crocodile tweezers down her external auditory canal. He was so close she could feel his warm breath on her cheek; there was something weirdly romantic about the intimate scenario and she imagined stealing a kiss: healing, determined, hygienic. On cue, came the palpitations of her fluttering heart. Loud vacuum cleaner noises destroyed the moment, and the offending waxy articles were triumphantly excavated.

Dr Oliver Cranston was Daisy's new hero. Daisy Hawkins was Dr Cranston's latest NHS statistic, (if her waxy peas allowed her the honour). *That's unrequited love in an ear canal*, she thought gloomily, as she walked out onto the Fulham Road to catch a bus to her new home.

***

An earplug got stuck down my ear.
Was the meaning of life down my eardrum?
The hot doctor sucked it out in a second.
'Is that it?' I asked wide-eyed.
'That's it,' he said.
'But there's another one!' I said, victoriously.
It was extracted before I'd finished the sentence.
Brutal.
I sail the waves of dead-end sagas that trough as fast as they peak.
I drown alone in insignificance.

Friday, February 4th

It was a relief to Hanratty to discover that he was no longer in Daisy's bad books. Her unexplained silence thankfully lasted only a day.

'I understand you've been through a difficult time, Daisy, so to boost morale and keep your wise words flowing, I have a proposition for you,' he said, scratching a lonely orange tuft of hair. Hanratty had a heart, and a pacemaker kept it ticking. He cared about the success of *Nimbus*, his wallet, and his romantic getaways with a sci-fi novel (invariably *Iain M. Banks*). But he also genuinely cared about his employees; and he had a soft spot for Daisy who wrote from the heart in a way that was so alien to him, he was in awe.

'Many of your readers, as you know, experience difficult relationships, and many, I am led to believe, are, err, single.' He paused for composure. 'I understand that London life for a...' *hmmm ...maturing?* '...maturing single lady,' he looked uneasily at Daisy's face, but found zero guidance. He paused, took a glug of black coffee and began again. 'I understand that single life in London, for ladies orbiting their thirties can be...complicated, challenging even.' He cleared his throat, tweaked his beak-like nose, scratched an orange tuft and wiped his dewy forehead, whilst Daisy sat patiently.

'I'd like to offer you a sort of promotion, Daisy. I'd like to dedicate an entire page to you, well, to *Eliza*, and no longer just a column. *Eliza* will have more space to express herself and be more interactive. She will now publicly address readers' individual concerns, and respond to all those imploring emails you get sent, but from now on your support and guidance will be done in work hours, for all to see, and what's more you'll get paid for it. Readers hang off your every whimsical word in *Musings of a Pisces,* Daisy, so imagine the positive reception of what will feel like a one-on-one dialogue, in a sort of Q&A format. We could refer to it as *Ask Eliza*, if you like. You'll have more space now to share your own personal experiences in your compassionate responses, in your cherished whimsical way. See yourself as consoling friend, rather than aloof Agony Aunt.' Hanratty swigged his coffee, with uncharacteristic aplomb. He looked out of his window and swept his arm across Mayfair's cockled horizon.

'I want you to be more *real*, more accessible. I see your page as an open forum, with your *Musings* working alongside *Ask Eliza*, inviting single girls to share experiences, loneliness, wacky female theories on men and dating... You know the ones.'

She shot him a look.

'See your current experiences, if you will, as positive, constructive research for your replies. Expect to confront singletons' concerns on nearing 30; the tick-tock and all that...'

'*Excuse me?*' Daisy stared at him in disbelief.

Hanratty was in dangerous territory yet again. He coughed and shuffled in his seat.

'All I'm really trying to say, Daisy, but not very well I grant you, is that I'm offering you more writing space, in return for greater *Eliza* interaction, and a much deserved review of your salary.'

'Are you attempting to profit from my melancholy, Hanratty?' she teased.

Was she teasing? Reading women was harder than Hindi. His palms started to sweat and he touched his pacemaker.

She smiled. 'A whole page all to myself is what I've always dreamed of. Thank you, Hanratty.'

By the time she had returned to her desk he had sent an email; *'Your challenge is to find true love by the end of the year and celebrate it on your page.'*

She felt a rush of determination and self-belief. This was a challenge she was going to grab by the balls.

The kitchen on the second floor of *Sainthill Publications* was a grubby hovel containing basic necessities: fridge, kettle and a leaning tower of plastic mugs. The kitchen was shared by *Nimbus* and *Sabre* Magazine: competitive titles, despite belonging to the same publishing house.

Tara Forsyth was filling up the kettle when Jude entered to scrub cemented cereal remnants from her bowl. The two rivals danced awkwardly around each other in the confined space. Small talk fell on their various shared clients. Each exchanged word was controlled, so as not to expose any juicy revelations of large budgets or potential ad campaigns.

If Tara was as loose with her tongue as she was with her clients, thought Jude, then the conversation might be a damn sight more interesting.

Jude Franklin was what you might describe as a typical saleswoman. Whether selling vacuums door-to-door, or double-page-spread advertisements in *Nimbus*, the bare bones are more or less the same; smart attire, a finely tuned sales pitch, persuasion and persistence.

She practised her sales pitches at home in front of the bathroom mirror and long-suffering Will, who knew them off by heart and could mouth his wife cues to forgotten lines. He discovered he slept soundly after a good pitch. *Boy had things changed...*

Jude's sales patter was comprehensive to the point of tedious. Her clients – the ones who stayed awake – were generally bored into submission and would hurry her to produce a contract to sign, the large fee a relatively small price to pay for another year of advertising in *Nimbus* magazine and some peace and quiet.

Jude had worked for *Nimbus* since leaving university and had known most of her clients for that same period; they were, despite full ears and empty wallets, incredibly loyal and adoring. Some had even witnessed her marrying Will, and had sat in church dreaming of her maternity leave and their subsequent respite.

Oblivious to the true nature of her notoriously dull pitches, Jude believed she was a bloody good saleswoman. Her consistently high sales figures were confirmation. Secretly, she hoped there was more to her, something alluring... A *"je ne sais quoi"*, that extra bit of magic that secured her the same sales figures as Tara, whilst keeping a firm grip on her dignity, (and her knickers). Occasionally, Jude might offer a seductive head tilt or flutter her eyelashes – but if, and only if, she felt it vital to clinch a deal.

A spread for a spread, that was Tara's ethos. She worked on commission after all, and being blessed with both brains and beauty, she felt obliged to maximise the profitability of both. Over expensive meals at glamorous London restaurants, she hypnotised clients with beauty, charm and wit. Many of her clients were mature gentlemen who ended up spending vast amounts of time and money – the *latter* on *Sabre*, the former waiting for her call. The more impatient and savvy would call her, complaining about the position of their advertisements, without having even glanced at the issue – this resulted in another scheduled lunch on *Sabre,* and another chance to drool over Tara and a plate of costly langoustine.

Clients lucky enough to be granted Tara's "complete sales package" never complained about positions in the bedroom. Married, divorced, single, dating, older, younger – she didn't care as long as they were vaguely attractive and paid duly for advertising. It was business, after all. With her cushiony breasts and lustrous hair, Tara exuded sex appeal. With each stroke of her face, lick of her lips and cross of her legs, she promised sex to the unattractive ones too. She teased sex, sex, sex, from each crafted move, but only delivered to a select few.

She never researched before meetings, and barely knew the name of each client she dined. She couldn't give a toss about their company or advertising needs. After 30 years of practice, her pitch was infallible. She pitched herself; *Sabre*, the international leader, was a mere subordinate.

Seeing this awkward kitchen moment with Jude as an opportunity to stamp ownership of potential new client and artist Marcus True, Tara mentioned their meeting earlier that week, which had resulted in her agreeing to model for life-drawing sessions.

It was obvious to Jude that Tara had a thumping great crush on Marcus True and was not only grooming him for advertising. *Misplaced slutty-ness*, thought Jude; the chances of a struggling artist buying an £8,000 page of advertising were slim to none, even if Tara was first-rate in the bedroom.

For the first time ever, Tara had left her meeting with Marcus with a monumental crush, a challenge, and no sale, in exchange for a lie of generous consequences. Both insulted and aroused by his apparent disinterest in her, and in a desperate attempt to see him again, she blurted, 'I'm a professional life-drawing model by the way, so if you ever need me…' She was astonished by her own delight when Marcus yielded two days later…

Arguably one of his odder decisions, Marcus decided, as he had sent the text to Tara confirming the life drawing session that would take place that evening, but a healthy exercise and an overdue distraction from his habitual subject, Jasper, and the intriguing duo he couldn't rid from his mind of late. He had felt compelled to paint one poignant picture of the two girls; one, petite, supporting her taller elegant friend, and then he painted another, which focused on just the taller girl, her stoop heavy with sorrow. But believing this splurge was a rare and temporary diversion, he decided that only good could come from life-drawing sessions in his studio with a hot, practised – albeit incredibly narcissistic – model. Marcus hadn't seen a female nude for quite some time and supposed Velazquez's *Rokeby Venus* at the National Gallery didn't count. He was somewhat apprehensive.

'Hey, guess what,' said Jude, as she returned to the office from the kitchen, 'Tara's doing a free life-modelling session for a new artist client, in exchange for sex, then advertising, or the other way around. I mean, what the fuck? How desperate is that! What a sad cow!' Jude rarely used the F word, unless she was seriously wound up.

'Urgh, what?' exclaimed Daisy, simultaneously scrunching up her face and raising her eyebrows. 'That girl is unbelievable! She must have *a lot* of sex…' she trailed off, feeling envious as hell.

'Yeah, the bitch!' Jude grinned, energised from the brief slag-off-Tara-session. She tugged on her coat, disappeared down the stairs, and shouted back, 'Off early! Goodbye, my lover! Have to relieve Millie off my mum… Can hear someone wailing and I'm not sure which one! Have a good one! Oh, and check your inbox!'

'Don't kill me' – the words fidgeted neurotically in the subject bar. Daisy opened Jude's email:

'Hot and sexy, talented and creative, witty, talkative, (in a nice, not annoying way), interesting, good for a giggle, intelligent…are a few words that spring to mind.

My best friend is caring and thoughtful, a good listener and basically, before her head explodes, a bit of a catch!'

The colour drained from Daisy's cheeks as she read *Shine Online* at the top of the new dating website that Jude had posted her *profile* to… *Oh Jude.*

With every step of her long walk home through Hyde Park, Daisy weighed up the pros and cons of Internet dating. Loads of friends were giving it a go, some had success stories – one of her friends had even married her Internet lover – but others not so much. Her friend Gaby, for example, had been on a perfectly nice date with what seemed like a perfectly nice gentleman, until she opened an email from him the very next day revealing nothing but a close-up shot of his erect penis. Blown up on her screen, she practically puked and had some explaining to do to her boss. But it wasn't the penis story that put her off, not at all. An unexpected enlarged cock appearing on her work screen would certainly brighten up an otherwise dull day. Quite simply, Internet dating had never been her thing, and because of Jesse, had never before had to be her thing.

However, consumed by thoughts of marriage and men's big privates, by the time she unlocked her door, she was more open minded and decided to give it a go – *Fuck it* – for Jude, for her readers, for her page, for research, for Hanratty and his mesmerising challenge… *But not, I repeat, not for true love.* She refused to believe that a girl like her, an old-fashioned romantic at heart, whose very makeup, she believed, was made up of the likes of Gone with the Wind, and Grease 1 (and 2), would ever find true love on the Internet.

As usual, she penned her thoughts:

'I cringe at the thought of my future Love recounting tales of early cyberspace meetings.

I hope to meet my soulmate the traditional way captured by old movies: on departing library, elegant lady gracefully collides with handsome gentleman. Classical mythology books and a cheeky Mills & Boon slip from her white-gloved fingers. Without delay, the gentleman stoops, lingers beside her slender ankles, before sweeping books off the floor and the lady off her feet, in one smooth move. Think Butler and O'Hara, Bogart and Bacall, Burton and Taylor…

A programmed introduction to a relationship developed in an e-Petri-dish is not for me.'
(Thanks.)

Daisy refused to blow her cover by uploading a photo. After all, she thought, she was a journalist on love and life, and this was her research into modern dating. *Will men be interested in faceless words? Will they bother to read the words to make a deeper judgement?* Let's test the priorities of men, she thought, as she took a deep breath, tiptoed into cyberspace and prepared to make contact with the other side. Naturally, she chose the alias *Eliza.*

Despite the lack of a photo, Daisy was encouraged to discover that only an hour after lift-off, her message box wriggled with testosterone. Enthusiastic men knackered their copying and pasting tools to bank an A-Z of cheesy chat up lines in her inbox. Having forgotten how sweet flattery tasted, Daisy was overwhelmed. She was like a child in a sweet shop, gawping at an extensive mouth-watering display of men to gratify all tastes.

'Sensitive, thoughtful and creative artist' Lucian, *32, Notting Hill,* (also faceless), had sent her three messages in two hours and was proving hard to ignore. *Hmmm, an artist...* Daisy's heart fluttered as her mind marched off on one of its obscure romantic tangents... *I lie naked. Stillness battles with beating heart. His brush strokes nude beige then swells in blushing rose. Like a Renaissance master, his obsessive eye measures my body, painstakingly analysing forms until he sees nothing but perfection. He trims here and cushions there, until I pulse harmoniously on the canvas. In the presence of a genius, I quake with rapturous humility. Vocal morsels of Italian deliciousness – chiaroscuro, sfumato – flow like frothy cappuccino from his cherub lips, whilst Vivaldi's Le Quattro Stagioni colours the background. Burnt sienna and vermillion red drip to the floor. I die in a haze of ecstasy as raw umber cups my breasts...'*

Reluctantly, she admitted, she quite liked the sound of *Shine Online's Lucian, 32, Notting Hill.*

Chat-up lines of any description were not Marcus's style. Nor was Internet dating, but his persistent housemates gave him little choice. With the promise of peace, he succumbed.

Since his father's death and Jasper's deterioration, Marcus had resigned from most things in life, including women. Time spent outside his home was invested in Jasper – supporting, consoling, rescuing and pleading him to go to rehab. He would return to his studio with a sweat, alcohol and often blood-drenched brother, tuck him in like a child, before turning to canvas to vent his complex web of emotions, all embraced by heartache. With the eyes of an artist and the mind of an anatomist, acquired during years of medical training, he dissected Jasper's body like a surgeon: magnifying and shrinking hands, feet, torso, cheek, the whole face in profile and head on. Rotating the body in his mind's eye, he produced both unrecognisable snapshots and uncanny likenesses, depending on his disposition. Zooming in and out, he recorded Jasper's transformation from child to adult, capturing the adult in the child, the child in the adult, and the mockery of

31

progression. Whilst Jasper's young eyes chirped with peace and hope, older ones appeared to dart wildly and weep with regret over self-afflicted premature ageing.

Marcus felt sick at the knowledge that he was painting "his best work yet" and occasionally tried to appease his guilt by donating some profit to charities. His paintings fetched ballooning prices and were celebrated amongst the experts for their psychological penetration. Galleries were chomping at the bit to represent him. Marcus had accepted a request to partake in a Christmas exhibition, *Artopsy; Symbiosis of Art and Science*, at the Natural History Museum. Along with a privileged few, he had been selected to represent contemporary young British artists – an honour for which Jasper was to thank, for without him, his inspiration would wane. But Marcus resented the guilt-laden notoriety and found it impossible to appreciate this exclusive invitation. He had not asked for any of this: not the dead father, nor the time-consuming, substance-abusing brother, nor the fame, nor the money.

It was an unhealthy co-dependent relationship as far as Floyd and Beth could see. They hated seeing Marcus in this destructive vortex. He was 32, high time for a girlfriend, or decent sex at the very least. With this in mind, the twins wrote Marcus an effusive *profile* for *Shine Online*, hoping to snare some lustful lassies.

Every now and then it did concern Marcus. His friends were in steady relationships, some married, some with children. Had he been left behind? He felt lonely at times, and fearful of being alone forever: *'an old man found dead in his studio...been dead for weeks... The stench of rotting corpse was repulsive.'* And children...yes, he felt the yearning when self-control lapsed. But Jasper was child enough.

Since Marcus's current life had embraced agoraphobia and introversion, he felt more comfortable concealing his face and name on *Shine Online*. An ardent admirer of Lucian Freud, whose work encouraged him to capture life's ugliness and imperfections, Marcus chose *'Lucian'* as his alias. If he did have a little boy of his own one day, he thought, and if the Mrs agreed, he would call him Lucian. Fuelled by this domestic vision, and spurred on by the twins, he fired off a brief, *'Hello, you sound lovely,'* to (an also faceless) *Eliza*, who just so happened to appear first on the "new arrivals" page and sounded nice enough. The doorbell rang. He looked at his watch; Tara Forsyth was bang on time for their first life-drawing session. As Marcus slipped away to answer the door, Beth hijacked his laptop and fired off another two messages to Eliza, so she would be in no doubt of his interest, and at the very least feel sorry for the lonely, intense artist and feel obliged to respond.

'Well hello there, Marcus,' Tara smiled coyly. She leant against the doorframe and seductively sucked the last life from her cigarette, before dropping one butt on the floor, and wiggling her other inside and up the stairs to the studio, as Marcus led the way. She hoped he noticed the fur coat slipping down her back, revealing absolutely nothing underneath: a tantalising aperitif to whet his taste buds.

Marcus's apparent disinterest captivated Tara: this was a rare phenomenon. With her legs akimbo, she lay on a blanket on his studio floor, licked her lips and plotted her next move. She suspected it might be like a game of chess she was destined to win, the challenge amplifying the pleasure of the victory. Her legs widened further in a smile.

'Why do your knees hate each other so much?' Marcus teased.

Embarrassment slammed them together.

'Not completely together,' he laughed. 'Open a bit… There. Good angle. Thanks, Tara.' He sketched her in charcoal and temporarily erased Jasper from his mind.

There was something about him, Tara pondered. *Something unnerving.* She felt…*what was it…humility?*

Most men turned into salivating puppies in her dominating presence, but not this one. She extinguished the absurd idea that he wasn't attracted to her. *Of course, he was!* She tilted her head to glance down her body to check the lighting was flattering her curves. When Marcus requested, she return her head to its original position, she did so *immediately*. Her face flushed; what the hell was wrong with her? What was it about Marcus? He was aloof and sexy – a bewitching combination. She felt like a schoolgirl with a crush, an altogether unfamiliar experience.

In Daisy's Warren, she widened her drowsy eyes and opened her laptop as *Shine Online* flashed on her task bar; *Lucian was online.*

'Hello there, Lucian,' she typed, hoping her words sounded confident and sexy. His reply was immediate. She thanked him for his three messages. He blamed his housemates for two. With both out of their comfort zone, and neither wanting to waste the other's time with mindless chit-chat, and with no clue of what else to do, they agreed to meet up the following Friday to catch the final evening of the Hyde Park funfair.

'Great. It's a date,' wrote Marcus awkwardly to the stranger. Fuck it, why the hell not? he reasoned.

Fuck it. For research, Daisy figured.

'Good night, Eliza. Sleep well.'

'Sleep? What's that?'

'Apparently, it's a place where normal people go to when they close their eyes. To be honest, I'm not the best person to ask.'

And conversation didn't end but changed tract; it relaxed, found a natural, easy course, as the two insomniacs united on common ground. Withholding details, they touched on the anxieties that kept them awake, Marcus's miscreant brother and Daisy's recent break-up. The conversation flowed and they moved onto their passion for painting and writing.

From their bedrooms, they both looked out of their windows at the starry blackboard of the sky, and Lucian, the self-confessed astronomer geek, led Daisy's gaze to the planets and constellations that kept him company whilst he painted the nights away. Daisy was captivated. He brought the night sky to life. She had no idea that an astronomy lesson, at whatever ungodly hour of the night, could be so mesmerising, nor that computer chat with a faceless man could be so utterly romantic. Daisy's heart fluttered as the rabble of butterflies flapped in her stomach like never before.

They talked unreservedly in a dreamlike timeless space, free from expectations, pressures and inhibitions. Conversation flowed until magic broke with morning and they reluctantly called it a day.

Feeling the heady mix of pleasure and palpitations, Daisy rested her dizzy head on the pillow and placed a hand on her thumping heart. As the psychedelic rainbow wings transformed into twinkling blacks and whites, she slipped into unconsciousness, where she had fallen so many times before.

Marcus felt the sensation of internal warmth. Eliza had sparked something, that was for sure, but what it was he couldn't tell.

An icy bird-singing dawn seeped through his shutters. He closed his eyes to visualise the face and hear the voice behind the words.

He fell into a peaceful sleep.

Friday, February 11th

Daisy met Baron Max von Beck and Leibe, his white German Shepherd, on her walk to work through Hyde Park. This was not the first time she had noticed them; the polished pedigree chums were distinctive.

Max was tall and slender, a princely dandy figure, impeccably uniformed in clean jeans, brown brogues, a creaseless shirt – blue to match his blood – adorned with gold cufflinks. A signet ring stamped the air with nobility, whilst his feet stamped the ground with their Jermyn Street hallmark print. Stylish to military precision, he ambled rather than marched, clasping hands behind his velvet-jacketed back. His shoulders ever so slightly curved inwards and he looked down as he walked buried in contemplation – or, Daisy wondered, to protect his eyes from the London riff-raff.

He certainly had much on his mind. His parents' pressure on him to marry had escalated and life was becoming increasingly difficult. He felt burdened by responsibility to keep his lineage as pure and nourished as his ancestors had. Generations of beady von Beck eyes bore down on him like owls, from the heavy branches of his heraldic tree.

He could not silence his parents by marrying just anyone – he spotted a tall female silhouette wandering his way – *like her*.

Fortunately, he had already found his noble needle in a haystack of commoners, although securing his diamond heirloom, which was the size of the Zugspitze Mountain, on her finger was another matter altogether.

Thin and acerbic, Luise von Meyer was his needle. Having captained the winners of the notable national women's polo tournaments, she was a striking figure, with her fantastically long legs that allowed her to hop on and off a horse with sensational ease. Drooling men were as jealous of her horses, as women were of Luise von Meyer.

She approached life like she approached polo – a game both on and off the field. She was shrewd and calculating and knew exactly how to play Max von Beck. She was destined to marry him – of this there was no question – but she had a few more winning moves to play.

Luise was born of noble birth, so the "purity" of both family trees would remain unblemished. Both sets of parents approved of the match and failed to understand why Max was taking so long to climax the courting. 'Where are the boy's balls?' Freifrau von Meyer would shriek at her husband, 'do I detect traces of weak blood?' They were clueless to the fact that their precious daughter was simply refusing to play ball.

Luise saw marriage as the end of fun and games. According to Luise, where there was a chase, there was a challenge, an interest and a real relationship. Within the confines of marriage, however, the chased is eventually demoted to the caught and rendered impotent; the challenge is annulled, and the relationship dies, and the huntsman inevitably turns hungry attentions elsewhere. Consequently, Luise concluded that all marriages were fucked, cursed from "I do". Which is precisely why she did not… *Yet.*

Her weapons were silence and unpredictability, and her tactics were as follows: show up unexpected, with either warm hugs or frosty detachment, arbitrarily alternate love and hate, return texts and calls sporadically with fluctuating delays – keep him guessing and wanting. The longer Luise left Max hanging, the more firmly lodged she knew she would be in his mind. Skilfully combining a girly dependence with ruthless independence, she wrapped Max around her finger, whilst his noble tootsies ambled on uncertain ground. She mashed his masculinity and toyed with his insecurities.

18 missed calls over the week! She transformed him from baron to court jester. He pictured her lithe body entwined around Argentinean polo players, called "Santos" and "Eduardo", and took his anger out on a stray pebble, kicking it across the park.

'Ow!' exclaimed Daisy.

She caught eyes with the perpetrator and recognised the beautiful martini drinker from *Jazbar*. Her heart fluttered and her legs turned to jelly.

As they drew closer, Max apologised; she was surprisingly kind to the eye. He hid his Rolex beneath his cuff and asked if she had the time to prolong the moment. He was boosted by the thought of Luise watching him converse with a pretty girl in the park.

Jealousy was Luise's Achilles heel. Jealousy meant she cared. Since *"Mission Marriage"* had got underway, Max avoided pretty women altogether. But today he was furious. He intended to drop this *liaison* casually into conversation… If the erratic bitch ever bothered to return his calls.

Daisy was relieved to have checked the time only moments before, for when she glanced at the face this time, her watch mouthed, 'No chance honey, keep dreaming.' Indeed, handsome gentlemen asking her for *anything* were part of someone else's script. She pinched herself.

When Daisy Hawkins entered her teenage years, she discovered three things simultaneously, 1) boys, 2) her special heart, 3) Love. From then on they became intrinsically linked: her merry threesome.

For years, only Jesse made her heart flutter. Random acts of romance would trigger palpitations causing butterflies to surge in her stomach and through her veins, tickling her body with quivering wings until, sometimes, she fainted. This is how she saw it anyway; the doctors had failed to offer an alternative explanation.

Falling out of love was equally provocative of fainting, but the episode felt different. When her heart began to tremor with doubt and fear, and when pain displaced pleasure, she suspected Jesse was the wrong man for her. Her butterflies exchanged their playful tickles for scratches and scrapes.

The soft flutters had returned – and been well exercised – in the weeks after leaving Jesse, when she began to notice other guys again. And wow, there were a lot to notice! Each time someone caught her eye and her butterflies stirred and her heart thumped faster, she felt it was a sign that she must be in love. Twice at her sister's wedding, with Floyd the waiter, and Jasper the wedding singer; with the gorgeous guy she caught eyes with on the bus; with the bohemian barrister at the coffee shop; with the seriously cool yoga instructor with the tight ponytail; with the hotty on the tube, (who gave his seat up, not once, but twice: first to an OAP and then to a pregnant lady); with the taxi driver who helped her with her bags (who she automatically kissed on both cheeks by way of a thank you); with the man wearing stripy socks who rescued her hat from a puddle; with the suited businessman who noticed the homeless man, sat down next to him on the grubby ground and handed over the contents of his wallet; with the retail assistant, Tyrone (according to his badge), who slipped her refund past the "no receipt, no exchange policy". Distracted by what else Tyrone might slip her, her heart fluttered, and she gripped the counter for support.

And again, just this morning, as she walked to work minding her own business…And it was only 9am.

My heart is special. It rules my head. Emotions infiltrate the mainstream and render rationale redundant; head loafs in subservience. I fail to ignite fight. (Do I want to?)

Someone pumps the bellows, sparks inflame. Heart-shaped wings stir. Butterflies are wingmen – they glide and tickle. Butterflies are foe – they scratch and jolt.

Colours turn to black and white, clarity to fuzz. The tremors torment and the flutters thrill. Either way, I prepare for flight into black.

Over the past week Daisy had updated Jude on *Shine Online's* shiniest member *Lucian, 32, from Notting Hill.* Jude heard all about their initial conversation which had gone on and on for hours until some ridiculously early hour of the morning. Jude had been delighted. She hadn't seen her best friend's face light up so bright in ages.

When Daisy arrived in the office that morning with the news that she had cancelled her date with Lucian, Jude struggled to justify the depth of her disappointment.

As did Daisy.

'But I had a good feeling about him!' exclaimed Jude.

So had Daisy.

But she had chickened out. She always knew she would find Internet dating a struggle, but she didn't think it'd be quite such a head fuck. Her initial conversation with Lucian a week ago had felt magical, as had all their conversations since – they had *worked* in that detached time and place. In the context of the real world, however, she was determined that they could not. They had enjoyed conversations so unreal that when she switched off her laptop, there was nothing tangible to prove that they had actually taken place outside her imagination. Their conversations floated around the blurred edges of reality.

'Daise,' Jude interrupted her thoughts, 'may I just say, this is yet another perfect example of you over-thinking everything.'

'I over-think. It's how I'm programmed. Don't diss it, I make a living out of it.'

Daisy tried to make light of her decision, which seemed to be having a far greater effect on them both than she could ever explain.

'I don't even know what he looks like, do I? Really, if you push aside all our words, he's just a total stranger.'… Albeit a stranger whom she felt comfortable chatting to, and who made cyberspace feel like the cosy café down the road… A stranger whom she felt close to already, whose black text brimmed with colour, whose letters spelt warmth and intimacy… A stranger who could make her heart flutter into unconsciousness with a single word.

She was scared of losing what they had. The magic that thrived in their special world was too good to jeopardise by meeting.

'And how did he take it?' asked Jude pointedly, hoping he'd given her a bollocking for messing him around.

'Yeah, he was totally cool, didn't care at all.'

Daisy recalled last night's chat – (as per usual, far from what most people would describe as cool. But rather, artistic, creative, romantic, where both felt free to express themselves. She had become so protective of their conversations that she was reluctant to divulge details even with her best friend). After an uncharacteristic pause in their dialogue, Lucian had replied, in his unique style, which now seemed so familiar, *'OK. Let's stick to what we're best at, painting pictures with words.'*

Instead of her date, Daisy spent the first half of her Friday evening in *The Toad and Tankard*, the "old man's pub" on Artesian Road, just off the Ledbury Road, with Jude and some other colleagues, where a rotund burlesque lady with ruddy cheeks called Brenda stood behind a heavy maple bar, serving oaky beers to regular locals.

Daisy ordered a second bottle of red wine, and thought of Lucian and the night that could have been.

She had never known that *regret* tasted like corked red wine, but, looking over at burly Brenda, she didn't dare complain. The girls left *The Toad and Tankard* and headed to *Jazbar* in search of better wine and younger men.

Marcus spent the evening leaning against a white wall in Beth's *Gemini Gallery* on Walton Street, South Kensington. The usual throngs of art lovers, buyers, critics and socialites were there. He alternated big gulps of champagne with small talk; the latter of course, depended entirely on the former. He thought about Eliza, their ridiculously easy and enjoyable conversations, and the evening that could have been.

A signet ring glinted in firelight. *My God!* Daisy flapped her hands to cool her heart.

As a general rule, Jude was opposed to hasty judgments, unless there was good reason. As she witnessed Daisy's eyes froth with infatuation for Max von Beck, she felt *now* presented good reason. She had seen Max many times in *RAH!*, the social pages at the back of *Sabre*, and each time he had made her cringe. His arrogance and egotism were almost tangible, and perhaps the only things about him that were real.

'He looks like a complete knob-end,' warned Jude. But it was too late. Max was on his way over. She glanced at Daisy – *bugger* – Love had struck.

From another table Tara Forsyth watched the sickening scene unfold: the gorgeous Max von Beck *flirting* with weirdo *Nimbus* columnist Daisy Hawkins, who scribbled her far-fetched musings from her far-flung planet. Tara had never been arsed to read her column properly – besides, it was for the loser dreamer type. She watched Daisy smile when he touched her arm and tuck hair behind her ear self-consciously. *Daisy Hawkins attempting to flirt!* Such an unlikely union, it was laughable.

Daisy skipped home with a royal date stamped in her diary and the hope of a Valentine's card on Monday.

Usually, Max would have hailed a cab home to Notting Hill's Chepstow Place. But tonight he chose to walk away conflicting feelings of guilt and justice. He thought of Luise – spoilt, untrustworthy Luise. 'A date with Daisy is justified vengeance,' said one foot, as it stamped away the guilt of the other.

Once inside his home, he popped a pill to calm his thumping head; as he washed it down with a glug of sparkling water, he firmly reminded himself that Daisy was nothing more than a temporary painkiller to him.

Friday, February 18th

Valentine's Day had come and gone like a 24-hour bug, contagious to an unlucky few. A selective contagion that had swept through *Sainthill Publications*, picking off the lonely hearts. The hallway had transmogrified into a florist. Daisy received a card from her father, and a rose from Jude, but was gutted that there was no royal delivery. Max was far too superior for such a grossly commercialised event, she reasoned, and he would look so out of place in Clintons. Instead, Daisy looked forward to Friday evening.

Polish the matrimonial silverware, prepare the Coldstream Guards, groom the stallions...for tonight I shall be plucked from the servants' quarters, for my royal date with Baron Max von Beck!

Max von Beck was not just anybody. He was a Somebody, wanting a special Someone. Daisy gulped. *Could I, Miss Daisy Hawkins, possibly be a Somebody's Someone?* She wanted to fall to the office floor, span the celestial sky with outstretched arms and thank the delusional Lord (or whoever might be up there orchestrating this circus), for his outlandish matchmaking.

She was ignorant of the sprawling nature of the German aristocracy; chunky peanut butter spread meanly to the crusts. The von Beck clan perched on a crumb of the crust. But in her spellbound state, she was going on a date with an emperor. Suddenly panicky, she searched the Internet for advice on "German etiquette".

She hadn't stopped to think whether *she* actually wanted to go out with Max, or whether he would be good for her. Her thoughts and wants became reflections of his. Overcome with humility and gratitude towards him, she searched some more, hoping to find who she could be for him – she felt she *owed* it to him to be exactly who he wanted. And Max was the kind of guy who knew exactly what he wanted. There was no room for error; she couldn't fuck this up.

'I hope you're aware,' said Jude, sitting back in her chair and crossing her legs beneath her desk, 'things that appear too good to be true, more often than not, *are*.'

'I hear you, you strange guru lady,' Daisy lied, not looking up from her computer; she had heard nothing of consequence. 'I'm going to call you Buddha from now on,' she thought for a second, 'or Juddha, if you'd rather.'

But Jude didn't share this childish, jovial mood. She had seen the arrogant way *Max von Mega-Dick* had spoken to Daisy at *Jazbar*, and how she had looked and sounded small beneath the weight of his presence.

It was obvious that Daisy was not adapting well to single life. Jude could see that she was lonely, floating rock-free, searching for admiration and reassurance. All confidence and self-belief had jumped ship, leaving her wreck exposed and susceptible. She was convinced she was falling in love at the speed of knots, and basing these strong feelings on meaningless pursuits, from flimsy flirtations to the selfish attentions of the baron. Her friend was pimping quality love to unworthy customers and for what in return? For a transient, artificial feeling of strength and security, onto which she erroneously attached a significance and longevity, and mistakenly translated as true love. It was a sorry thing to witness.

Jesse had been Daisy's rock. Now she was a lost limpet, looking to glue herself to the next available Jesse replacement – but Max was no Jesse. If Jesse had been a rock, Max was sand, (*an exquisitely fine grain, admittedly*), but equally useless for building on. It was no surprise, Jude reflected, as she glanced over at Daisy looking sensational in her scarlet dress, that Max von Beck had taken a shine to her. Daisy was a natural beauty…and naïve enough to be a pawn in whatever ugly game Max was playing.

'He's a wanker, Daisy!' Jude practically shouted across the office, hoping for some reaction. But again, Daisy failed to so much as glance up from her computer screen. Daisy had switched off from hearing sense, and was falling into her own world. It was a slippery slope.

As Jude was being uncharacteristically unsupportive and increasingly annoying, Daisy turned to her loyal readers instead and typed her current *Musings*:

'We expect a perfect love story – and why not?

Childhoods are sprinkled with fantasy. After bedtime reading, glass-slippered imaginations dance down yellow brick roads to the magical land of sleep. All that glitters really is gold, and all the clouds are silver – not just the linings. We are born into a world of tooth fairies, the Easter bunny and Father Christmas, where beautiful princesses marry handsome princes. We are guided through a fairytale that promises a happy ending. (Sleeping Beauty got her man, as did Rapunzel and Snow White).

Whilst they live happily ever after, we are expected to grow up, and unravel reality from fantasy, as if by magic.

The Peter Pan within us protests. "But look at our real Cinderella. Fantasy can survive in the hostile kingdom of reality. If it can happen to Miss Middleton, then it can happen to me!"'

(Please?)

5.30pm: Daisy brushed her hair and applied a fresh layer of nude lip-gloss.

'Well, have fun then, I guess,' muttered Jude, reluctantly.

Preoccupied with herself, Daisy put on her coat.

'That lip-gloss looks shit by the way.'

'Oh crap. Does it?'

'*Knew* that would get your attention! I was obviously joking, you idiot. It's gorgeous. You're gorgeous. Now piss off.'

'Oh. OK! Phew! Bye then.' Daisy grabbed her bag and disappeared, via the mirror.

'Don't say I didn't warn you!' Jude shouted as the door slammed.

Daisy was delighted that Max had suggested they catch the final evening of the Christmas funfair, where she and Lucian had previously planned to visit.

Max couldn't quite work out what in God's name had prompted him to suggest this blue-collar event – it couldn't be further from his idea of fun. But with the guaranteed distractions he hoped it would be less awkward and less expensive than a dinner; Daisy was neither a girl he wished to dine nor waste hard-inherited cash on. Tonight was nothing more than a move in a game…like *Tiddlywinks*, and Daisy was nothing more than his *wink*. His strategic game play was in retaliation to Luise's moves. After he had mentioned the "pretty girl" in the park, Luise promptly began returning his texts. Max looked forward to her returning his calls too. Luise's game was proving most educational, and right now he was a more adept player than she.

'Me and Jude have been wanting to come for ages!' exclaimed a flustered Daisy, as words barged past quality control to banish the awkwardness of silence.

'Jude and *I*,' Max corrected.

The correction struck her like detention. She felt like his freshly whipped horse, and hung her head low in shame.

Making it clear he was not a hand-holder, he led the way through the food markets. He stopped for a mulled wine, (*in a polystyrene cup!*), and looked disgusted when Daisy nibbled self-consciously on a German sausage, and even more disgusted when she called it "dinner".

'Supper,' he corrected.

Ouch! She was whipped again.

Daisy admired the stalls and rides which circled a skating rink that spun with smiles.

Max watched with disdain as the plebeians threw themselves haphazardly around on the slab of ice.

Daisy could think of nothing more romantic then being escorted around the ring by a handsome prince… But she gathered it was not his thing.

Nor was it his thing when she said, 'I'm just going to the toilet.'

'Loo,' he corrected, 'or lavatory, if you prefer.'

Crack went the whip. *Ouch!*

'I, I, was just reading the toilet sign,' she stammered. 'Don't shoot the messenger,' she said, under her breath.

However, whilst peering into a stall of aromatic herbs and spices she discovered that it was his thing to enquire whether she was of "good stock". But not his thing, apparently, to ridicule the seriousness of the enquiry.

'Are you kidding?' she blurted.

Nope. (Whip – *Ouch!* – sorry, 'No'). *Apparently he was not.*

Her mind – the disobedient thing – wandered to Lucian, and the funfair date that could have been. *But* she persevered, and aimed instead for a princess-like dignity. She shut her mouth but it wanted to spring open with festive cheer. At Santa's Grotto, she watched grinning children and giggly first-daters and noticed one man standing with two blonde friends. The blonde friends had their backs to her; they were a man and a woman of a similar height. The other man was looking down at a bag he was holding with a goldfish inside. For a fraction of a second everything in her body was willing the man to look up; so strong was this sudden urge to see his face. But Max whisked her away, following his nose past the vagrant who hovered at the funfair exit.

'*Big issue*, and a festive Brucey Bonus! *Biiiiiig Issue,* madam?'

'Come on, Daisy, don't linger by beggars,' said Max. 'It's not a good look, is it now?'

But Princess Diana would have... The homeless man looked freezing. His coat was vast but he was twig-like. Ignoring Max for the first time, she stepped closer and held out a hand containing the few pounds in her pocket. He opened his coat. She gasped. Inside was row upon row of little fish in bags of shallow water. They appeared to swim in sequins as the bags reflected the colourful fairground lights.

He leant towards her, 'Just an extra pound love for yer fishy Brucey Bonus.'

They looked sad. Daisy scrabbled for more coins.

Max fidgeted with impatience, 'Do hurry up, woman.'

'So sorry, yes,' she stammered, and to the beggar, 'that one, please.' She pointed to the tiny rose-gold one.

In true ungentlemanly fashion, Max walked her all the way to his door on Chepstow Place. To Daisy's surprise, he kissed her and asked her in. 'The funfair starts in the bedroom.'

Slightly taken aback, she pointed at her pink fish in the water bag and blurted, 'I should really take her home...she's drunk way too much.' She laughed alone, loudly and awkwardly.

'But I want to show you my big dipper!' Max protested. Beneath all the pomp, he was just a big kid who was used to getting his own way.

Daisy wanted to be a princess not a concubine. *I'm sure Kate Middleton didn't put out on her first date.*

Max's smile drooped, (as did his dipper). 'Fine. Whatever,' he muttered, slipping his key in the lock.

Debating whether or not to apologise for having wasted his time, she instead mustered all sluttyness she could and began, 'but the second date is *quite* a differe _'

Prince charming slammed the door on her sentence – *Frigid Bitch.* Inside he switched on his phone, and Luise's texts flooded in.

As Daisy walked home she attempted to sew true love into apocalyptic terrain. She named her pink fish Juliet, for that night she wanted to be Juliet and for Max to be her Romeo. They were star-crossed lovers.

Inside her Warren she plopped Juliet into a fresh bowl of water, and placed her on her shelf next to her jar of waxy earplugs. She switched on her laptop, hoping that Lucian would be online. She wanted to tell him about her date with Max. She wanted to tell him she was in love!

She was relieved that they had moved on from the online dating awkwardness, and were now nothing more complicated than online best buddies and insomniac companions. She concluded that she had been right all along: sewing romance into cyberspace was too great a challenge for her to realistically take on.

But Lucian was not online.

As she lay in bed, seeds of thought brushed on Max, but unable to find any substance to grip onto, they drifted to Lucian, where they took root on fertile soil. She wondered what he was up to... Her mind meandered down paths of possibility. One pictured Lucian with a beautiful girl, one of really good quality sexy stock, who represented all she felt her new self lacked. Daisy tossed and turned and failed to find sleep at the end of this path. So she changed direction. This one took her to Lucian's sofa, where he sat with his housemates watching telly.

'*Television,*' Max cracked his whip and pixelated her vision. *Max!* Her prince...

But once again, failing to find substance, her mind wandered from Max's realm to Lucian's sofa, where he made room for her and they sat together watching telly. And she slept.

A few roads away, Marcus pictured the girl who had caught his eye earlier at the funfair. He had spotted her through the crowds. What made him pick her out of the sea of people? The scarlet flame, which licked the gap in her coat? But the area was vibrant with colour. Her height? Like the taller of the silhouetted pair he'd painted on his canvas…but she was not so tall that she really stuck out. *No.* Her elegance? Amongst a clumsy mob he had witnessed grace in motion. Like the girl who dropped the magazine some weeks ago now – what made him think of her now? Her hand maybe, which brushed hair from her face? He rewound the rise and fall to play again in slow motion, zooming in and out with the expert surveillance of an artist and the analytic eye of a medic. Or the hair? Both the magazine girl and the funfair girl had such similar-looking caramel hair, which coiled like calligraphy. He recognised the envelope hand of the funfair girl whose palm of secrets was guarded by a silver thumb ring…uncannily similar, surely, to the hand of the girl who left *Jazbar* with her friend? Inevitably, he dreamed that these girls were really one and the same, and wondered how this was born from such fragile evidence, and if he had finally, seriously, lost the plot.

Through the fairground crowd, he thought he had felt someone looking at him. He felt an "aura", so he turned. And there she was. With those long pencil legs… *Felt* someone looking at him? *Felt her aura?* He knew how bonkers that sounded.

Again, he had not managed to catch a glimpse of her face, for when he looked, she was being dragged by the wrist, head down, through the crowds by a man – *her boyfriend? What a cunt!* Her stooped posture suggested that she was not happy. He was reminded of the sad magazine girl, and Jazbar's girl, and the teary girl in the back of the car at that country wedding. Yet another intriguing, faceless, stranger. *Like Eliza.*

With thoughts of calligraphy hair, pencil legs, envelope hands and Eliza all playing in his mind, his thoughts focused on writing, and his respect for Eliza's diction; his appreciation of her turn of phrase, how each of her words lured him in, and how just one could make the world seem better. Eliza, to Marcus, *was* writing; after all that's all she revealed of herself. And bizarrely, these girls, directly or indirectly, all reminded him of writing, be it slender pencils or curly Japanese script. He felt teased by the numerous coincidences. They crushed his mind and the only release was painting, but his canvas supply was empty. He searched his studio – he was usually military about keeping them stocked… What had happened to him? Desperate to paint, he turned to the upper section of his studio wall and began work on a fresco. He recorded the hustling, bustling fairground. He painted the lights, stalls and haphazard smiling crowds. Off to the centre and cushioned between figures, he painted a scarlet slither of a tall female with long legs and hair-sweeping fingers revealing a silver dash to mark the ring on her thumb. There was no smile in this section of the crowd – no eyes, nose or mouth either, just a faceless oval. Neither had he seen her face, nor could he trust his imagination to do it justice.

Standing back to peer into the decorative strip of studio wall, his eyes fell immediately on the female slither radiating an aura so familiar, so intense it was hard to look away. *How had he captured that?* He could hear her breathing in the crowd and was captivated by her faceless stare.

Friday, February 25th

It was 5pm, and outside the office the rain was pouring.

Daisy took the liberty of cutting the afternoon short by spending half an hour in the office loo, getting ready for another date with Max. She glanced out of the window. It looked cold and wet. She did up the orange buttons on her cream cardigan and zipped up her jacket. She coated dry mascara clusters with a fresh waterproof layer and warmed in the memory of their second mid-week date. He had taken her to the cinema and, *'Wait for it,'* she told her reflection, *'he said he loved me! That's right, LOVED ME!'* Unfortunately, however, she had choked on popcorn and failed to return the sentiment – although she *knew* she felt it.

Max had suggested they meet after work at the Animals in War memorial on the edge of Hyde Park and walk together back to Notting Hill. The heavily laden bronze mules always made her sad, but not today...

Off her lead, Leibe ran excitedly through tall wet grasses, disappearing then reappearing to check on her master. She barked at words and tasty smells seeping from one random purple tent within a cluster of trees. On investigation, she was riveted to find two figures with white blond hair similar to her own white coat. Her tail wagged like a flag. Max whistled as Daisy obediently headed through the trees to fetch her.

'Have not saints lips, and holy Palmers too?'

Daisy heard a familiar male voice.

'Ay, Pilgrim, lips that they must use in prayer,' came an unfamiliar female voice.

As a bored Leibe whipped past Daisy en route to her master, Daisy disobediently strayed further from Max's ankles.

'Come on, Daisy, for goodness sake! Nothing to see there! Just two unemployed thespians.' On catching a clear view of the tented picnic scene, Max beckoned Daisy and looked up towards the heavy clouds. *Why on earth have they pitched a tent; are they homeless or just insane? This is Hyde Park, for Pete's sake, not the Brecon Beacons!* 'This type just feed off welfare,' he scoffed, 'so if it's a decent picnic you're after, Daisy, then good luck!' Feeling that he had endured quite enough of this nonsense and wet weather, he led Leibe – the most faithful and loving female he would ever know – back home to Notting Hill. What did he care if Daisy failed to follow? Well, his libido did. He had been hoping for sex tonight, in return for his declaration of love.

Daisy was delighted to discover that the voice belonged to Floyd, the charismatic wedding singer.

'Thus from my lips, by yours, my sin is purged.'

She watched him touch his lips dramatically.

'Then have my lips the sin that they have took.' The honey voice belonged to a girl who sat inside the opening of the pink tent with her long legs protruding. From the little Daisy could see, she noticed the girl was also blessed with Floyd's features and colouring: faultless skin, platinum hair and pointy delicate impish features. She stretched out of the tent to embrace her role, and taking more of her in, Daisy concluded that the two must be siblings.

'Sin from thy lips? O trespass sweetly urged! Give me my sin again.'

Floyd – *Romeo* – flung himself towards Juliet and pouted his cherub lips.

Juliet pouted back.

'You kiss by the book!' Daisy blurted, purposefully interrupting the scene. Had she prevented a weird, inappropriate sibling moment?

'Well, hello!' said Floyd looking over at Daisy lurking behind a tree. A smile spread across his face. 'The beautiful bridesmaid.' He beckoned her over and introduced his twin sister Beth.

Beth, Daisy noticed, was alluring. *Very*. Like Floyd, but a female version; her ice blue eyes were equally piercing, the points of her nose, ears and chin were softer; her lashes even thicker, her voice softer and sweeter, and her wrists even prettier. She looked as fragile and valuable as fine Scandinavian porcelain.

She handed Daisy a glass of Glögg, whilst explaining that their sensitive skin was intolerant to the sun. So, just as their tent was for wet weathers, their picnics were too. 'And the fresh air helps me learn my lines,' Floyd added, thinking again how delighted his poor mum would be if he took a "Daisy Hawkins" back home.

'This Juliet is bored already,' he complained, as he passed Daisy a script.

'*Preoccupied* would be more accurate,' corrected Beth, turning to Daisy. 'I'm busy preparing for an exhibition at my gallery, for a very good friend of ours. And it has to be perfect. He's a perfectionist, you see; knows exactly what he wants.'

It was warm inside the tent. Daisy took off her jacket and cardigan, whilst Beth topped up her glass. Floyd leant his head on his sister's lap. The twins were close. Daisy shifted uncomfortably, as she witnessed a series of *suggestive* sibling gestures. *Very close.* Her imagination was cheap to run, requiring only the smallest amount of fuel, and gained pace with every sip of hot spicy Glögg. The bond between them was demonstrated through their tactility – a gentle touch of the hand here and a soft stroke of the wrist there. The tent was alive with chemistry, but Daisy's senses were smudged by alcohol and she could fathom neither source nor target of flirtations. Indeed, she had fallen for Floyd at her sister's wedding – that much she knew – but in this enchanting purple tent, she found *both* of them intriguing…*and attractive.* Floyd strummed the guitar and they talked, giggled and flirted.

Daisy was quite sure she was not a lesbian, although she had kissed Jude once at school, but it was more of a peck than a kiss. And she had wondered what Tara Forsyth from work would look like in her underwear…and out of her underwear…*but who hadn't?* Surely, these did not constitute full-blown lesbianism? If she were, then Beth would certainly be her type.

Daisy could feel the magic mystify her senses. She wanted to go, but she wanted to stay; she was trapped between the two, a willing captive.

'What brought you to this neck of the woods, fair maiden?' slurred Floyd.

'Err,' she scratched her head. 'Shit, Max!' She had been completely brainwashed by these two woodland pixies.

As she leant over to kiss Beth goodbye on the cheek, Beth turned her head and their lips met. Daisy giggled with embarrassment, 'I must be drunker than I thought.' Her heart did not flutter, she noted, with some relief; her life was confusing enough. Then turning to Floyd, he gripped her long fingers with determination and pulled her towards him, planting a kiss with cupid lips. 'Mmm, you *do* kiss by the book,' he said, approvingly.

Flustered, and with heart all aquiver, she put on her jacket, forgetting all about her cream cardigan with orange buttons, and wobbled in search of her other love, Max, with two surprise kisses lingering on her two guilty lips.

Floyd Clansey had fallen in love with the prospect of his fragile mum's rejuvenated face if he was to introduce Daisy as "his girlfriend".

Beth watched Floyd plot tactics. She read his thoughts, like only twins can, and shook her head.

'No, you don't. Not Daisy,' Beth warned, feeling the urge to protect the loveliest girl she had ever met. 'Don't be an arsehole; you'll break her heart.'

'Hers? Or do you mean yours?' asked Floyd, reading his sister with equal accuracy; she had a look of love that he had not seen before in her.

She pinned him with narrowed icy eyes. 'Maybe both.'

'Not even to save Mum's?'

He had a point. The thought of their dying mother was too much to bear. Daisy – their sacrificial lamb. She hoped that young hearts were easier to mend.

Luise von Meyer opened Max's door.

'Yes?' she said, already frosty with impatience.

'Who is it, darling?' shouted Max from up the stairs.

Daisy's words stalled. The walk had neither sobered her up nor prepared her for a nasty surprise of freakishly tall proportions, sprouting from polo boots in all jodhpured glory.

'*Look.* We didn't order a pizza, and we aren't interested in Jehovah's witnesses. Is that any help?' snapped Luise.

Silence had a time and a place and this was not it. She had been standing on the doorstep a while now, just gawking.

'A girl who doesn't appear to speak, Maax!' Luise yelled up the stairs. Obediently, he joined them at the door.

'Oh, it's you,' he said, glancing sideways at Luise. Beads of sweat cultivated on his top lip.

He now realised that telling Daisy that he had "loved" her was a reckless and rancorous move in the game; she was now at his door – uninvited – *Scheiße!* The blunder was on the back of 24 tormenting hours of Luise's silence, throughout which he was haunted by sweaty, fleshy images of her infidelity. Paranoia had polluted his caution, and now he was paying the price.

Turning to Luise, he whispered, 'The dog walker, darling, nothing to worry about.' Miss Polo raised threaded eyebrows and snorted horsey-style. She turned pursed lips and went up the stairs, tight jodhpurs hugging pursed behind.

Max wiped his top lip. 'I lost you to Bacchus's picnic in the park. Now is no longer a good time, Daisy,' *(i.e. if you could kindly fuck off),* 'Something's come up.'

Six foot two up, thought Daisy, as she drooped a finger up the stairs, 'Who…?'

'Who…her? Who is she?' He cuffed his nose and looked down, *chef? Masseur? Maid?* 'Mai–' he began, before changing his mind, 'cousin. Yes. Mai cousin. *My* cousin. She is exactly that. Delivering my polo equipment. She's a professional, you see, a player. Like me. Nothing to worry about.' He wasn't ready to dispatch Daisy quite yet. Checking the coast was clear behind him, he pecked her cheek. 'I'll call tomorrow, now run along like a good girl. Go on, shoo.'

Obediently, she shooed.

His beautiful, polo-playing, cousin. *Hmmmm.* Did she buy it? Her head told her she was mad if she did, but her heart piped up, 'Yes, he told you he loved you, so quit the paranoia.'

She misheard her head and misinterpreted her heart's cautionary palpitations. She passed out as soon as she opened her front door.

Friday, March 4th

At 9pm an orange dash caught Marcus's attention, and it wasn't the one he had just painted on his canvas. He looked at Romeo, his scaly funfair purchase, and realised it was high time that fish left the quarantine of the studio to brave it in the big wide world (of downstairs).

In the kitchen, he emptied Romeo into a bowl of fresh water. He swam around searching again for his pink lover; they had parted in such sweet sorrow. Around and around he swam, searching optimistically. 'All these woes shall serve, for sweet discourses in our time to come.' But Romeo's words amounted to nothing more than empty bubbles; Juliet was nowhere to be seen.

Then several orange discs caught Marcus's attention – orange buttons belonging to a cream cardigan flung on the arm of the sofa.

Floyd and Beth entered the kitchen. Marcus turned to his housemate, cradling the fish bowl, 'My little gift to you, Floydy. Romeo, meet Romeo. Along with belated congratulations on landing the part. You'll make a fine Romeo. Always thought you'd look good in stockings.'

Floyd looked delighted. He loved presents and the attention that surrounded them.

'Plus,' teased Marcus, 'it's healthy for you to think about someone other than yourself, even if he's only a fish. Here's his food, smells amazing, tastes delicious.' He placed the stinky, flaky fodder next to the bowl. 'He's handsome too. Healthy competition. You guys might just get on.'

'Handsome, you say?' Beth got up to take a peek.

'You'll catch all the guys before I even get a look in!' complained Floyd.

'Nothing's fair in love and war.'

'Couldn't have put it better myself,' said Floyd, angling Beth a look whilst considering his plan for Daisy.

'Err, it's a *fish!?*' Marcus rolled his eyes.

Romeo's googly eyes stared through the glass at the two white blondes. The siblings ogled back, before Floyd became distracted by his own reflection, and Beth yawned and clouded over the makeshift mirror. 'Gotta-skate, little fishy. A thousand times goodnight!' She leant forward to kiss the glass bowl. In doing so her dressing gown fell open and both breasts fell out. Unperturbed, she tucked them back in, before neatly folding the cream cardigan and replacing it tidily on the sofa, and taking herself to bed. Floyd, also unperturbed, left for his beauty sleep moments after.

No wonder Romeo looked shell-shocked, thought Marcus. 'You'll get used to this little circus,' he cooed. He quite understood how peculiar the eccentric twins might appear to anyone unfamiliar with their weird and wonderful ways. Their appearance alone was curious. If Marcus hadn't grown up with them, he might have wondered if they had stepped out of a Tolkien novel.

Admittedly, fighting over a fish was a new one, thought Marcus as he plonked himself down on the sofa next to the cardigan and ordered a Chinese takeaway. But the issue of Beth and her lack of self-consciousness was recurring; her casual approach to nudity and her carefree exposure of body parts in front of her brother was the norm in their home. And the fact that neither seemed in the least bit perturbed. This possibly had something to do with the fact that Beth was bi-sexual and Floyd was gay, and both were refreshingly body-confident. (And the fact that Mrs Clansey – to save on water and halve the tediousness of bath time – had bathed the twins together for perhaps longer than advisable, so their nudity was a normal occurrence and simply not an issue whatsoever).

It was not the first time Marcus had seen Beth's breasts; they had a habit of revealing themselves, but they failed to titillate Marcus as they had done 16 years ago, when he had squished them like stress balls in a clumsy teenage fumble, all curious fingers and thumbs. They had been each other's first, second and third, until Beth realised she quite enjoyed sex and Marcus was not the only one who could offer it. Offerings came in all sorts of shapes and sizes, some large, some not so large, and some non-existent – but with breasts to compensate. As she matured, she developed a perfect body and was never short of attention. Both sexes were captivated; she could simply sit back and enjoy the ride – which she did, quite a bit, until recently. Now she was looking for something more.

Their mum, Mrs Clansey, knew she had a daughter who "enjoyed" both female and male "friends" – this she could swallow (with her pills and a bottle of wine). But she was convinced that her son was as straight as Cupid's arrow, and she literally felt she lived for the day he would bring home a special girl, then marry, and produce longed-for grandchildren… She often discussed her dreams with her friends who visited regularly with muffins and flowers and oodles of gossip. The doctors had failed to provide her with groundbreaking treatment, so she looked to her son for an alternative remedy.

As for his constant lack of a serious girlfriend? 'Well,' Mrs Clansey explained, as her friends sat on her bed expectantly, 'with looks like his, what on earth is the rush? I mean, ladies, for Heaven's sake, give the boy a break! His time will come.' But she could read her friends doubtful and worried faces: 'your time is short.' And she would shift in her wall of pillows and smile to disguise the trauma. It was hope that kept her going.

The doorbell rang. Marcus was hungry. He tipped the delivery guy, switched off the downstairs lights, and headed up to enjoy his Friday night takeaway and paint the night away.

Friday, March 11th

'Eliza, Eliza let down your hair, so that I might climb the golden stair!' Upon hearing these words, her heart fluttered. She wrapped her long fair hair around a hook beside the window, and dropped it down to the prince, who caressed his manly hands around it and began his climb to her tower room. Her hair snapped and her heart followed suit. He landed in a heap on the floor, before storming off in search of another maiden to pluck. (One who preferably wore jodhpurs and spent a considerable amount more on hair products).

Last night Daisy had what she could only describe as a nightmare. She spent much of her day analysing it and musing over it on her page. She couldn't wait to chat with Lucian later and get his thoughts on the matter. At this precise moment in her life, on this sunny March morning, she struggled to think of a single person she knew whose views she valued more.

After work she met her sister in a crowded Mayfair bar, had a couple of drinks and a refill of married life anecdotes. She made it home at around 10pm, dropped her bag on the doormat, and before she had even taken off her coat, had reached for her laptop and emailed Lucian. Both had come off *Shine Online* weeks ago. Having swapped email addresses, they now met on more relaxed terrain as just friends, who were comfortable exchanging dating advice. *Just friends.* She had to keep reminding herself.

To Daisy's relief, he responded immediately, and she told him about her dream. (She couldn't think of anyone else she wouldn't be embarrassed to tell.)

'So what do you think it means then?' she asked, hoping for his reassurance.

'That you need medication,' he replied, feeling somewhat downtrodden that he was now officially nothing more than Agony Uncle.

'Seriously, please Lucian.'

'That maybe you should consider another shampoo?'

'Please?' she pushed.

Marcus hated analysing dreams. *What the hell's the point?* They didn't mean anything. *'It's pretty simple. You need to consider another boyfriend,'* he typed. *'Your emperor, baron, prince – whatever he calls himself – doesn't sound like Prince Charming to me.'*

She paused for thought before replying, *'He was too good for me anyway, completely out of my league.'*

Marcus had heard the whole tale from the surprise appearance of the "cousin", to Max's sudden weeklong silence, and Eliza's sightings of the couple driving around Notting hill in her pimped up black Land Rover. 'Cousin,' she had scoffed, 'bollocks to that.' Reading between the lines, Marcus found further evidence of Eliza's unique heart; vulnerable, and naïve in its loyalty, and still committed to a man she claimed she could never be good enough for.

From their respective bedrooms, they peered out beyond the amber and mauve canopy of the city's night sky. *'Imagine you are one of those stars, falling to the ground like star-flakes. Each one of us is a star-flake, totally unique, settling on the face of the earth. No one star outshines the others. Each possesses special qualities. This wanker, your "prince", is definitely not too good for you.'*

Christ, I love his words! Full of sense, wisdom, kindness; they were revitalising. Her heart skipped a beat, then settled on a faster pace.

'Get rid of him, seriously.' He paused for a moment, before adding, *'But before you do, could you ask him to introduce me to his "cousin" with the great bum and the kick-ass Land Rover?'*

Without pausing for thought, she replied: *'No way! You're all mine.'* And when he didn't reply immediately, she felt awkward and changed tact, *'Sorry, I've been miserable... Hope it hasn't ruined your Friday evening.'*

'We're all miserable bastards from time to time.'

'I'm a miserable bastard? Well, thanks very much.'

'Well, you're human at least I think you are. And that's humans for you and that's life unfortunately...it is what it is. Every emotion and feeling, the good and the not so good, is OK and totally normal and all just part of the unpredictable ebb and flow of life.' Lucian told her about Michel De Montaigne, a French diarist, whose essays on humanity had reassured him during an all-time low following his dad's death. *'It was like having a friend. Even though he was writing long ago, he's so relevant that you feel like he's writing right now, just sitting next to you. He said that the greatest thing in the world is to know how to belong to oneself. So fuck this "prince", and fuck working out how to fit in his life, and how to belong to him. If he won't allow you to be you, and love you for you, then fuck 'im. Or don't. In fact, that would be a very bad thing. Montaigne definitely said that too actually – and you don't mess with Montaigne.'*

Daisy giggled.

'When Montaigne thought depressing thoughts,' Lucian added, *'he turned to his books. So, for fear of sounding even more like your Agony Uncle, or your mum, or dad, go to bed, get lost in a fictional world and read until you can barely keep your eyes open and allow yourself to drift off. Failing that, come on over and we can attack a canvas with our frustrations, it's very therapeutic... But ideally stick to Montaigne, his advice is better than mine. You'll find him in the History section of the library if you're curious – probably better suited to the Self-Help section if you ask me.'*

'Well, then he could sit next to me,' replied Daisy. *'If I were a book, I'd be in the Self-Help section, upside down and back to front, making a shitty job of helping myself.'*

'Maybe I should look you up and leaf through your pages?'

'Maybe I'd enjoy that.'

'I can assure you, you would.'

Friends. Just friends... *'And you, Lucian, where would I find you in this little "cybrary" of ours?'*

'Well, let me think... I guess my body would sit comfortably in the Art section, with my spine pointing towards Travel. My cover is rather shabby, but a fair approximation of who I am. I think the blurb on the back over-promises, and the

plot is pretty weak past chapter one. But I guess that's the case with most best-sellers, so hey, who am I to criticise!'

'Well, I'm a sucker for shabby covers. And if the blurb is good then hey, sold again. The middle bit's so overrated anyway, I find.'

'And if I'm not shaping up to be a page-turner after chapter one…?'

'Then I'd plod through one more chapter before passing you onto a less fussy friend. Hate to say it, but most bestsellers are one-minute wonders.'

'Let me get this straight. If you found my dog-eared edition and took me home, you'd happily pass me onto a friend after you'd had your wicked way with me? And you enjoy one-minute wonders? Hmmm Eliza, think I'm falling in love here!'

She laughed at his frivolous remark, but her heart took it seriously and she felt the pulse rock her body again. His attacking-a-canvas-with-paint offer sounded seriously tempting now.

When the dawn began to break, they reluctantly drew their conversation to an end, which invariably took about an hour.

Marcus switched on the radio to fill the silence that always flooded the room once their conversations ended. He felt an urge to work on his sketchy wall scene of the girl at the funfair. His little finger padded yellow and turquoise dots to illuminate the scene, and highlight various figures in the crowd. But again, he could not bring himself to paint the face of the girl with the flame of red dress and protectively made sure the oval remained free from paint splatters. Her face required more than imagination and a delicacy of touch.

He waited for Jasper's call. But it never came. Jasper almost always required his brother's help at some point during a Friday night. Marcus switched off the radio and was met with nothing but unsettling silence once again, but this time it was ominous.

Eliza was occupying his mind too. Perhaps, if he could forget about her company and what her voice might sound like, what she might look like, and if she would always remain his faceless friend, then perhaps he might get some rest. How right Montaigne was when he said that 'nothing fixes a thing so intensely in the memory as the wish to forget it.'

He lay in his bed thinking and waiting.

In her bed, Daisy considered Hanratty's challenge to find true love by the end of the year. Not just any love: TRUE love. Good old reciprocal TRUE love. She wondered how she could represent and contain true love in her column – in the unlikely event of meeting his challenge. Immediately, she looked to Lucian. Then and there, in her sleepy state, she knew she needed him, in some way, to help her meet the challenge.

Who needs Montaigne when you have Lucian as a friend? she pondered dreamily. '…you feel like he's just sitting next to you. And he's so easy to relate to, it's as though he knows you.'

Feeling comforted, she drifted into a peaceful, dreamless sleep.

Friday, March 18th

Today was Daisy's big 30.

She hated the attention of birthdays and knew that 30 required more attention than its predecessors. The egotistical 30. She didn't feel ready to leave the sanctuary of the 20s and enter the pressure zone of the 30s. She felt totally unprepared. Her life was unsettled. Boxes were nowhere near to being ticked. 30 made a mockery of her. 30 made her feel like a failure.

If she wasn't getting older, Lucian had stated earlier in the week, then she wasn't alive. *'Aging is living.' Damn, he was good!* He had a way of stating the obvious, but making it sound completely brilliant, and a knack of detecting positives. His words bolstered her, but the feeling was transient.

At work, she had sworn Jude to secrecy and was grateful for Hanratty's terrible memory – he never remembered his employees' birthdays – so she avoided the pressure of having to tell her readers, or *Muse* her heart out about – *how had Hanratty phrased it?* – 'the singleton's concerns on nearing 30; the tick-tock and all that.'

And the big 30 itself? Well, she thought, what better way to celebrate than attend to matters of her ageing heart? Having still not heard from Max, Daisy felt justified in finally accepting a date with the persistent and charming Floyd Clansey.

Marcus was proving to be more of a challenge than Tara Forsyth had predicted. He was clearly single. There was never any evidence of female presence, no whiffs of perfume, no earrings by the bed, no knickers, no makeup stains on towels. When she peaked into his room on the way to and from the studio, she noticed the laundry basket over-flowing, boxer shorts scattered all over the floor and his bed in a permanent state of undress. In his bathroom, damp towels hung haphazardly on railings and hard bubbles clustered on the top of the toothpaste tube. *What woman would be happy living like a student again?*

A couple of times she had heard Marcus's housemates tease him about an "Eliza" and had witnessed the sparkle in his eyes, but an Eliza never showed up, and sounded more like fantasy than reality – some desirable film or comic book heroine, perhaps. Otherwise, there had been no mention of a love interest of any sort whatsoever, female or male. *Asexual perhaps? No!* It was too tragic a waste to contemplate.

Perhaps the problem was his brother? By all accounts he was a total fuck-up. He had a bed at Marcus's, which he apparently used when he needed "looking after". *The guy was 30!* She could not understand why Jasper refused to go to rehab to flush out his predictable post-public-school addictions.

The brothers were clearly loaded. Marcus's house was located in a prime spot in Notting Hill; his TV was vast and his sound system looked like the cockpit of a jumbo jet. Indications of a small fortune decorated his home. He wore a designer watch and carelessly splattered paint on expensive shirts and trousers. Tara concluded that Marcus could easily treat the *child* to a decent rehab, and her to a decent dinner.

So what then was the problem? She looked at herself in the mirror. It was Friday night and she was at her flat on St Luke's Road in Notting Hill. Unusually for Tara, she had no plans. She had "reserved" Friday evening for her date with Marcus. She had put it in her diary a while ago, estimating the amount of time it would take for him to fall in love with her, locate his balls and ask her out. She had kept her evening free right up until teatime, having decided that eleventh-hour invitations were more characteristic of an eccentric artist. Teatime had come and gone. *Nada.*

Again she squeezed her thigh in the mirror. Again her skin pocked. She steadied herself. She hadn't noticed it under Marcus's studio light and hoped he hadn't either. She slapped on some cellulite cream, which had been ready and waiting for the inevitable. She hoped the burning would singe the dimples away. People had warned her to expect physical changes around 30, but she hadn't believed them. She was born toned, not pulpy like most babies. She twisted to scrutinise her profile. Beneath her tummy button, she was slightly cushioned, noticeable only under harsh light and self-scrutiny. She did 50 sit-ups a day… Maybe her 30-year-old body required more?

She folded up her "borrowed" cream cardigan with the orange buttons. Having felt a little chilly in the buff during her last sitting, she had pinched it from Marcus's sofa, presuming it was one of his housemate Beth's less offensive purchases. She popped it in her cupboard, hoping her designer wardrobe would resist contamination.

Her phone beeped a text. *Better late than never!* But it was from her client Slippery Si. She let out an exasperated moan, before reading the text, *'At Jazbar with a friend. You'll like him.'*

At Jazbar she met Slippery Si and his Hugh Grant lookalike friend, 'Doctor Oliver Cranston' – by far the most tempting option on the menu, which had suddenly jumped from zero to three Michelin stars.

Si had told Oliver that Tara Forsyth slept with her clients in exchange for advertising space. Since Si had never himself got lucky, he begrudgingly introduced his friend, and seeing the two hit it off, Si unpicked his feet from an unwelcome footsy snarl-up and slipped away.

Still starving after polishing off a delicious main course, Tara led Oliver to St Luke's Road, where they polished off each other for dessert.

Beth had searched everywhere for the cream cardigan Daisy had left in the purple tent in Hyde Park. She could have sworn she had put it on the sofa. She had lovingly washed it too and had planned to give it back to Daisy later that evening. *Where had it gone?* She left the house one cardigan down, but one brother up, and went to meet Daisy.

At the sushi restaurant Daisy was greeted by not one but two Nordic beauties. She sat next to Floyd and opposite Beth. She knew the twins were close but was it "normal" to bring your sister along on your date?

So here they were once again, lost in that hypnotic Bermuda triangle of flirtations… Daisy looked again at Beth sitting there unashamedly in all her loveliness. And again she looked at Floyd, looking at his sister. Sibling or no sibling, you would have to be blind not to notice Beth's intriguing beauty... *Right?* And she noticed that Floyd definitely looked at Beth more than he looked at her.

Beth directed all glances and conversation her way. 'Here, let me show you,' she offered, when she noticed Daisy struggle with her chopsticks. 'Oh you're holding them at the wrong ends!' Daisy received gentle touches during the chopstick lesson.

Their dinner was rich with booze and their "threesome" was rich with a curious energy; Daisy's imagination had ripped its reins and was running wild and free: why had Floyd asked her on a date, if he only had eyes for his sister? Was he shy off stage and needed someone to lean on...a "voice"? Did he go everywhere with Beth, or just on dates with Daisy? Was Beth Daisy's competition? *WTF!* Or had she got the wrong end of the stick for the second time that evening?

There was some clarity at least: firstly, Daisy's heart fluttered again for Floyd, and only Floyd. Secondly, the less he seemed to notice her, the more she yearned for him. Thirdly, it was a weird dinner that she didn't want to leave, with an odd vibe she found entirely compelling.

Marcus spent the evening at Jasper's Chelsea flat. He had not heard from his brother in a while and the silence had shifted from puzzling to downright worrying.

He had buzzed the buzzer but got no reply. The door was bolted. He noticed the window had been smashed in and glass shards had sprayed all over the floor. He climbed through, tearing his hands and trousers on the blades. Through the mist of cigarette smoke he saw cocaine scattered everywhere like gunpowder. The bed was a mess of dirty strewn sheets. His heart pumped in his throat. *How long had it been like this? Please let him be alive.* He ventured through to the sitting room. So many empty bottles. Two naked girls – *prostitutes?* Dazed and confused, the girls scurried for clothes and headed for the door where they hovered awkwardly, before emptying Marcus's hand of money and scarpering into the night.

He slapped Jasper, who lay naked between the bottles. Jasper's nose twitched but his eyes remained closed. Marcus wanted to kiss him for being alive. His baby brother. But instead he slapped harder and alcohol juices dribbled from his mouth. Marcus was torn between anger and relief. He slapped again and kissed him on the cheek. His lost baby brother.

He called Dr Oliver Cranston. No answer. He scooped Jasper up and took him away from the hellhole to his safe haven on Aldridge Road Villas.

Marcus was relieved his housemates were preoccupied with their new interest Daisy, whom Beth had been talking about a lot recently. An empty house demanded no explanation.

From beside the bed, he stroked his brother's brow and listened to the snoring sound of magnificent life. He craved Eliza and her soothing words, but knew she would be out for her birthday. He imagined her with her "prince", smiling appreciatively as he wiped his feet on her. They chatted most evenings these days, he reflected: sometimes exchanging one-liners to touch base, others to share discourse that flowed into morning.

Jasper's snoring hushed the loneliness of silence, and Dr Oliver's call failed to come.

Early the following morning, with freshly cleaned pipes, Oliver dressed in the murky light of Tara's bedroom. In the bathroom he felt for the taps, splashed his face with cold water and combed his hair with wet fingers. He felt around for a moisturiser and applied a cream to his face. It tingled terribly.

It was the first time he had ever paid for sex and he hoped he'd left enough. Si had not advised him on payment. He had no reason to buy advertising space, so he left a substantial looking wodge instead. With a scorching face, he quietly closed her door.

As he walked towards Chelsea and Westminster hospital, he noticed a missed call on his phone from Marcus. The unsociable hour of the call confirmed that the cause was Jasper – *again* – and Oliver felt the pang of anxiety that only Marcus's missed call could muster.

Friday, March 25th

Marcus applied the finishing touches to his latest portrait of Tara in her pink pants. He thought she looked like a panther with her swathes of black hair, wild eyes and poised pounce in her repose. He enjoyed the motion of his final sweep over the gentle convex of her tummy. Since Tara was vain and insecure, he smoothed over the pretty crimping on her thighs to avoid any dramatic backlash. He called the painting *Pink Panther*.

Standing back, he took a photo of the portrait on his phone and texted it to Tara, as she had requested. He saved it in his phone under her name so it would appear whenever she called. Seconds later a photo of Dr Oliver flashed on the screen in his blue scrubs. Having been updated on the worrying events of last Friday, Oliver was calling to discuss Jasper strategies.

The Trues and the Cranstons were family friends. Marcus and Oliver had played together as children. They attended different secondary schools so lost touch during their teenage years, but reunited again at Edinburgh University Medical School.

Oliver liked Marcus for his kindness, generosity, philosophical ways, sound cynicism and eccentric tendencies. He envied Marcus's wisdom, emotional depth and sensitivity, and the creative angles from which he viewed life.

Marcus liked Oliver for his cheeky wit, his humorous egotism and loyal friendship. He admired Oliver's magical touch with women and his social dexterity. Whenever they hung out, it was never long before they were engulfed by a flock of pretty ladies – a marvel that Marcus mistakenly credited to Oliver.

Marcus struggled through his medical training because his heart was not involved. He was working towards a goal he did not want. He wanted to paint. That's all he had ever wanted to do. He became a doctor to justify the amount his parents had spent on his education and to see smiles on their faces. When he had told his dying father he was a doctor, a smile spread across his face, giving meaning and worth to every hour spent with books and patients.

Oliver struggled through the training because he lacked Marcus's ability to focus and study. And the women didn't help – colleagues, patients, and all those who had a penchant for men in uniform proved a terrible distraction.

The day before their final exams, during a break in revision, Marcus walked the corridors of the medical library and offices in search of Oliver, an enthusiast of impulsive study breaks. He heard noises coming from the dark, quiet corridor that led to one of the main offices. Marcus drew closer. Male groans interspersed with female screeches. He lingered by the door, unable to decide whether these were noises of pleasure or pain. As he weighed up the potential consequences of bursting in, the door flew open, hiding Marcus behind it. He stood still and listened to giggling, kissing and the frenzied manoeuvring of clothing. He saw a flustered Doctor Amber disappear down the corridor, straightening her skirt, before bundling up messy sex hair and forgetting to lock the office door. *Married* Doctor Amber had been a senior tutor throughout their training and was highly respected for her qualifications and teaching expertise. Marcus felt the disappointment and repulsion of a child having just heard his mother at it with… '*Oliver?*'

'Fucking hell, Marcus!' As Oliver jumped with fright, a baton of papers slipped from his hand. Marcus watched them unfold into the next day's exam papers.

So Oliver Cranston cheated his way through his final exams, Marcus lived with his secret, and Oliver lived with the knowledge that Marcus, at any time, could bring his career to a pitiful end. Therefore, he made his services available, ensuring Jasper had access to hospital facilities and professional advice whenever needed. He also bought much of Marcus's art, but was getting sick of haunting faces of Jasper looming down at him. Oliver had shifted some of his Jasper collection from his flat and onto the hospital walls, but the patients and staff had started to complain. A 30 year old dying of substance abuse and the burden of life hardly promoted an air of health and optimism. Oliver had started to give up hope of Marcus ever painting any other subject. Anything would be a welcome change.

As their phone conversation progressed, the two friends discussed the spasmodic withdrawal pains of Jasper, his continual resistance to rehabilitation (*"incarceration"*), and arranged further tests on his decaying body.

Marcus's eyes fell on *Pink Panther*, still on the easel, and the conversation switched to art. Familiar with Dr Oliver's weakness for the female nude, he mentioned his latest portrait of Tara.

'*No, it's not of Jasper… It is NOT of Jasper… Correct… Well, believe it… I think it's a beauty… Yes she is too… Nude, yes… Well, not completely. Pink pants… Lace… What a surprise…*' On request, Marcus texted the portrait to Oliver, quoting the usual mate's rate.

'*SOLD!*' came the reply moments later. '*Marginally more expensive than the real thing but should age a damn sight better!*'

Other than the first word, Marcus could make no sense of the rest.

Small world, Oliver thought, as he excitedly cleared space on his bedroom wall in preparation for the *fox* that was Tara Forsyth. He had liked her a lot, but her failure to return his calls for more fun and games was vexing.

Meanwhile, a confused Daisy was picking her way back home from the Coronet Cinema through the streets around Portobello Road. Panicky in Max's absence, and her new itchy 30-year-old suit, she had accepted another date with Floyd – and Beth apparently. Again, she was perplexed by the paradox of Floyd's regular invitations and apparent disinterest demonstrated in person. Had he rested his hand on her knee for mere respite…before reaching over to his sister's? Had it even been his hand at all?

Unbeknown to Marcus, Eliza had spent another evening with his housemates – a very small world indeed.

Friday, April 1st

Work was not going well today. Motivated by her fascination in love and her passion for writing, Daisy rarely worked this close to deadline.

Jude began work on another apple, her fourth that day, and Daisy's thoughts were again interrupted by white teeth crunching down on Golden Delicious, before she forced herself back to the work issue. The problem causing today's bout of writer's block lay with her *Ask Eliza, Q&A*'s. She struggled with her duties, and spent more energy nurturing resentment for the whole damn column than offering satisfactory advice and guidance.

Her readers had noticed. *Dear Eliza* complaints had begun to arrive in bulk: *'Are you sure you should be telling a depressed girl to quit her job and go travelling? Is that really wise, considering the current jobs market?' 'Is running away always the answer?' 'Are you suggesting it's better to escape reality than confront it?'...*

Stop! STOP!

But they kept flooding into her inbox.

She considered telling Hanratty she was resigning from *Ask Eliza*, to concentrate solely on *Musings of a Pisces*, but guilt got the better of her; she could not abandon her readers and leave them high and dry. They needed *Eliza*. Old *Eliza*, she corrected. And so did she.

Requests for advice became nagging, needy voices she felt unequipped to silence. *Ask Eliza* had become a burden. Her reservoirs of counsel from which she had dipped so freely were drying up. She didn't know what to think anymore, and had no frickin' idea what *Emily from Hampstead* should do about her cheating boyfriend, or what *Erin from London Bridge* should do about her husband's affair with the nanny, or what *Genevieve from Islington* should do about her commitment-phobe partner, and least of all – she thought of Jesse – whether *Jane from Wandsworth* should leave her adoring boyfriend, who was more of a pal than a lover...

Stop! Stop!

Yet another appeared in her inbox, *'Should I drink soya, dairy or rice milk?'* Oh FFS! A pint-sized Dr Oliver Cranston appeared on her desk. Her heart fluttered before he suddenly vanished, failing to dispense any medical advice. Minor medical research of this nature had never before been problematic, but now Daisy looked to an imaginary vanishing doctor for advice. Things were going from bad to worse.

'I'm in love with somebody I've never met. Is that possible?' For the first time in a while, Daisy felt equipped to answer this one with certainty – *'Yes, Martha, it sure is'* – and had no idea why.

She was no better at fixing her own problems these days, Daisy reflected, than she was her readers'. Thoughts dawdled to Max. He had finally broken his silence with texts and calls; he alternated intimacy and warmth with frosty detachment and was always too busy to see her. His unpredictability was emotionally draining. Again, Daisy thought about him with Miss Polo, and her heart twitched with nervous energy and refused to settle. She didn't know how to play his game, but could not find inclination to quit trying.

'That's love for ya,' her deluded heart told her, breezily.

She pondered on the mysterious Floyd too, whilst absentmindedly digging a nail into the proud back of the L on her silver LOVE ring, then circling the O, plunging into the steep crevasse of the V, and nailing the rake of the E. *How can such a simple arrangement of letters have such a complex meaning?* Jude had given the ring to her for her fourteenth birthday, and she had barely taken it off since. She loved it. *LOVE'd it.* But attaching value to anything in life, she realised, was a risky business. She took off her ring and looked at the exposed white band of skin that had lost out on years of life – scars, bruises, warts and all. *Would my body look like that, if I'd shrouded it in protective metal armour?* But Daisy failed to admire more than the shallow beauty of the soft milky surface. That band of skin had a lifetime of protection, but it was just *surviving*. She decided that she would rather live and risk the scars of life and love than just survive, and in doing so she justified the anguish Max and Floyd induced.

Is pain always a part of love?

Thoughts turned to Lucian. She contemplated his lack of complications and steady friendship. Her heart tremored in the knowledge that one day he might not be there when she needed him. She feared that if she met him in the flesh, their friendship might develop into more – *had it already?* She might love like never before, (a rich, deep once-in-a-lifetime true love), and live like never before, and subject her heart to scars like never before, and die inside like never before. Keeping Lucian at a cyber-arm's length, Daisy reminded herself, was necessary, as surviving without a true love was surely better than dying.

Wasn't it?

Or is true love worth the risk?

It was 5.30pm. The office started to empty. Jude began work on another apple, as she waited for an email confirming a sale. Daisy had struggled to begin work on anything that day. And the crunching had not helped one iota. It would be a long Friday evening in the office, catching up on lost time, and filling up her whole damn page as best she possibly could, even if it involved her pinching answers and generic advice from a more mature, stable Agony Aunt, whom she could research online. Either that or publicly humiliating herself by dying right there on her page, in front of the angry, jeering mob of readers who she could no longer describe as supportive fans. She felt that no one right now, other than Lucian, understood her or had her back.

Back in the Warren much later that evening, she considered her work issues, and looked back to the time, not so very long ago, when all she had to do was *Muse*; when she got paid for doing what came as naturally to her as breathing. She was a Pisces through and through, and was born to muse. Star signs had always intrigued Daisy.

She went online.

'*I'm a Pisces,*' she announced to Lucian, surprised she hadn't mentioned it before. '*A fish through and through. Pisces is undoubtedly the only sign worth any time or consideration,*' she had typed, teasingly.

'*Well, it's a great coincidence it just so happens to be yours, isn't it?*' He was extremely sceptical about astrology or any superstition; '*it's all a load of bollocks*', being the precise words he used. '*People like to see themselves belonging to something. I am a "textbook" Cancer, but the descriptions are so vague, I could just as well be a textbook Leo, or Gemini or rat, dragon, earwig, or newt for that matter. But hey, horses for courses... Let's agree to disagree; I'll shake your fin with my claw.*'

He was a big fan of fish though, he told her. '*I had one tattooed on my wrist in Japan when I was younger. I had no money for canvasses, so turned to my body instead. Back then I was more open-minded to superstition, and I was told that fish were lucky and represented good fortune – but then my father fell ill.*'

'*Oh shit...I'm sorry.*'

'*But hey, now perhaps, just perhaps, I see good fortune in a coincidence! You feel an affinity with the scaly creatures, and I have one swimming on my arm – what the hell are the chances?*' he teased. '*And, come to think of it, a real one in my kitchen–*'

'*Me too! Another coincidence.*' Daisy looked at Juliet, swimming circles in her bowl, next to the jar of waxy earplugs.

'*You have a fish in my kitchen too?*'

'*No, you dick, in mine.*'

'*Aha, I see! Well, if this isn't a "sign", Eliza, then I don't know what is.*'

She ignored his gentle sarcasm. '*Mine's called Juliet.*'

Now that caught Marcus by surprise.

'*She swims around searching for her Romeo.*'

Marcus drew a sharp intake of breath. He thought about Romeo, who he always imagined was in constant search of her Juliet.

'*They're like us, Lucian – just two lost souls swimming in a fish bowl.*'

Marcus reminded himself that he didn't believe in signs, however uncanny the coincidence. Whilst Daisy expected her days to be filled with the mysterious and abstract, odd coincidences and serendipity, Marcus did not. Hence, he was amazed to discover that not only were Pisces and Cancer the "perfect match", but that he was researching the Internet for "Cancer compatibility" in the first place. What the hell was Eliza doing to him? Being a Cancer, and "instinctively intuitive", (*apparently*), Marcus realised he did not need to study Pisces characteristics, because when he did, he discovered what he already knew, that she was '*alluring, caring and loving, and inclined to dream about her ideal lover and attempt to turn fantasies into realities*'. All spot on.

Friday, April 8th

It was 7pm. At Jude's house on Ladbroke Grove, Daisy held Millie in her arms. Supper was in the oven and smelt superb, not a trace of panic; all was organised and the atmosphere was tranquil, as was the norm in the Franklin home. As Will opened the white wine, Daisy counted four glasses for three heads. *A bloody blind date*, thought Daisy.

'Sorry, I'm late,' puffed city-boy Felix Renfrew. 'Straight from work.' He glanced at Daisy and loosened his tie. *A bloody blind date*, thought Felix.

'Daisy, Felix, Felix, Daisy,' introduced Will awkwardly, handing each a glass to soften the blow. He looked at Daisy as if to say, 'Nothing to do with me, Jude's idea, promise!'

Both felt the flush of embarrassment before the rush of disappointment, as neither felt a tickle of chemistry. Daisy grabbed Millie for moral support, whilst Will and Jude faffed in the kitchen, leaving the three of them alone like a perfectly defective family.

Supper was ready and they took their places at the table. Daisy smelt the chorizo before Jude produced the stuffed marrows from the oven. *Oh no*. Daisy's heart quaked as she recalled a dish called *Cupid's Marrow,* which she had read about in last month's edition of *Nimbus*. Apparently, if *Cupid's Marrow* was served during a blind date, *'love was guaranteed to grow.'* Daisy recalled the packet of marrow seeds attached to the page – *'Grow your own Love! Free love for every reader!'* – and the testimonies – *'Love's best fertiliser!'* *'Like the magic beans!'* Her eyes clamped on the oozing tomato beneath the cheesy breadcrumb topping. It looked identical to the dish in the article: *Really frickin' cheesy*.

'Cupid's Marrow...' she blurted. The girls caught eyes and neither knew whether to laugh or cry.

Will looked nonplussed. 'What's Cupid's Marrow?'

'No, I said *stupid*, not Cupid,' prattled Daisy. Stupid being the only word she could think of that rhymed with Cupid.

'Yes, she said *stupid marrow*. Sorry, Daise, I completely forgot you hate it. Stupid *me* more like!' Jude snorted and waggled her head in imitation of a klutz.

'Marrow. *Yuk!* Who likes marrow? *Stupid old marrow!*' blurted Daisy. It was hard to stop now.

'All right, Daisy, that's a bit rude,' said Will, sensitive to his wife's feelings, and fearing a repercussion. 'Jude spent ages making this.' But surprisingly Jude didn't look fussed at all.

Felix slid uncomfortably on his seat. She had *definitely* said 'Cupid', not stupid. Women around his age were all nauseatingly keen, with nothing but marriage and babies on the brain.

As Daisy glanced down at Millie for support, she noticed her little head was nuzzled right into her breast as if she was feeding. *OMG! Not a good look!*

Was it better that Felix heard *Cupid's Marrow* or hadn't? Daisy wondered. If he had, then Daisy was the desperate girl whose best friend was eager to palm off. If he hadn't, then she was just downright rude – *'stupid marrow!' Who the hell says that at dinner parties?* And with Jude's baby pressed against her breast, she was radiating crazy desperation. She may as well strap a loud ticking clock to her forehead! She returned Millie to Will in more of a throw than a pass.

A few big gulps of wine later, Daisy reassured herself that she didn't fancy Felix Renfrew anyway, so actually she didn't care what he thought of her. Her heart had declined to flutter, so there was zero chance of "chemistry", and she was a firm believer of chemistry at first sight if there was to be any chance of love.

Jude dipped into her cauldron to serve second helpings to only herself and her husband, whilst Felix hoped he could resist whatever magic lurked in his first. Fearful of falling under her spell and waking up married to a nutcase, he twitched until 10pm, when he made his excuses, 'a meeting first thing', and scurried away towards the safety of his beloved bachelor pad, the city and the lads.

Having learnt a long time ago that life was less complicated if he simply didn't ask, a bemused Will took himself to bed. In the kitchen, the girls cleared the table, and giggled at the shuffling awkwardness of the evening, and Jude's appalling attempt to match-make.

'Felix is a sweetie though, Daise.'

'Don't you mean a sweaty?'

'Yeah OK, he was a bit sweaty.'

'Very sweaty.'

'OK, very sweaty.' She stacked the plates in the dishwasher. 'I thought he'd be perfect for you.'

'Ree-ally?'

They caught eyes and laughed.

'Oh bugger, he's so utterly, hilariously, obviously not perfect for you, is he, Daise?' When the hysterical laughing subsided, she added, 'Not sure I know what you are looking for anymore.'

'Join the club,' mumbled Daisy, refilling their glasses.

Conversation turned to Tara. Daisy heard the revelations from Jude's kitchen dalliance with Tara that morning, who was simultaneously "carrying it on" with her client Marcus True, whilst "teasingly flirting with his lesbian housemate", and *Sabre* was yet to see "a sniff of advertising".

After what felt like a thousand words on the matter, Jude declared she had just one more word to say, *'absolute slut!'* As Daisy opened her mouth to say 'that's two,' Jude added, 'She's so desperate, it's embarrassing,' which triggered another thousand-word torrent. Daisy's mind wandered to a peaceful place, to Lucian…

'JUST. LIKE. YOURS. DAISY, are you listening? I said Tara was wearing *your* cream cardigan today, the one with the orange buttons.' Predictably, Jude suggested that Tara nicked it from the back of her chair at work.

Come to think of it, thought Daisy, she hadn't seen it in a while. Led astray by Jude, Daisy supposed she could easily have left it at work. She had left the office just after Tara that afternoon, but distracted by a pair of pink lacy pants that crept above Tara's skirt, she had failed to notice her cardigan.

When the conversation reverted back to Daisy's love life, Jude produced her Daisy File from the D section of her bookshelf. 'Shame,' said Jude, as she crossed out sweaty *'Felix Renfrew.'* Uncrossed was *'Floyd.'* Jude could only remember one male waiter at Orlaith's wedding, who had an obvious preference for men, and couldn't recall another, but she listened to Daisy's update, nonetheless.

'Well, perhaps he's shy?' suggested Jude, trying to justify why a man should include his sister on dates.

'Nope. I thought that at first, but nope. Floyd's an actor with more confidence than he knows what to do with. I honestly think he's *in* love with her.'

'His sister?' Jude snorted. 'Don't be ridiculous! You've been watching too much weird shit on TV.' She fell about laughing. 'But maybe, may-bee, his sister's in love with *YOU*?'

'Now who's being ridiculous?' replied Daisy, although flattered by the thought. 'She's a bloke magnet!'

'They're not mutually exclusive, you know.'

'True,' Daisy said, full of thought. 'But nope, I just don't buy it.'

So they gave up on that conundrum and moved onto the increasingly unpredictable Max von Beck, labelled simply *'Dick'* in Jude's file. She couldn't wait to defile his name with a big red cross and was frustrated by the hold-up.

'I love him,' was Daisy's only explanation.

Jude was familiar with the vulnerability of Daisy's heart. 'If I had your heart, I'd save it for one special guy who truly deserves it. Just because it's big, you don't have to pimp it out willy-nilly. You need a quality control transplant. What about Lucian? He's been nothing but patient and supportive, albeit from the other end of a computer screen. Why won't you meet him, Daise? Seriously, I don't get it.'

Lucian. Thinking of Lucian again was like inhaling fresh air. Struggling to find an answer, she looked at her watch.

With her red coat on, Daisy disappeared into the night. Jude's words echoed in her ear; *'Why won't you meet him, Daise?'*

She was still scared. *Yes, that was it.* Now more than ever, in fact. Scared that their chemistry only fizzled in the written word; that he might be disappointed with the way she looked or sounded, that she would fail to make him laugh in person, that he might never show up; (her dalliance with Max had so severely injured her self-confidence that she now doubted every part of herself, inside and out). She imagined Lucian, the recluse, who might not function in the real world. Or worse, she imagined he was just a figment of her crazy imagination. She was scared of losing her mind. She was scared of losing a friend, scared of heartbreak, and dying inside.

In *The Toad and Tankard* on Artesian Road, Dr Oliver was celebrating being off-call with Friday night bevies and a chat with his old buddy Marcus.

An oiled Tara, in her pink pants, reclined on her canvas next to Marcus on the leather sofa. Even from behind her bubble-wrap screen, she didn't fail to attract male attention; grown men dribbled lager and choked on cider.

Marcus breathed in his surroundings and admired the eclectically eccentric bunch. The pub air hung heavy with the smell of rotting tobacco and wet dog. The moody lighting, from orange tasselled lamps, fell on the regular throng of old men and the Friday night friends chattering in ankle-high boots, shoulder satchels with PVC buckles, round lenses with thick glasses, and eyeliner framing eyes young and old, toggled duffle coats, flower clips pinning unkempt hair, 20s-style hats and polka dot dresses with ribbons at the waists... A taste of East London, in a pocket of Notting Hill. *I love this pub*, thought Marcus, as he un-tacked a taco from the sofa.

Oliver cast disdainful eyes over the foreign lip marks on the rim of his pint glass, the knives and forks that wouldn't recognise a dishwasher if one slapped them in the face, and the manly barmaid Brenda, whose steely service came with a whole load of attitude but no hint of a smile. *Such a dive!*

'Ah, before I forget,' Oliver reached into his bag. 'Jasper's latest scans, can you give them to him for me?' He handed Marcus the transparent envelope. Holding the scans against the lamp, Oliver pointed out his shrivelled lumpy liver; it was becoming worn out and scarred. He pointed out bulging juicy blood vessels around the stomach and oesophagus, 'That's what will kill him,' he said. 'That's why he has been vomiting blood. He's pushed his body to the limit and has the insides of a sick old man. Maybe the next bleed will finish him off. Sorry mate, I know that sounds harsh – but nothing his sober self doesn't know already.'

As Oliver headed to the Gents, Marcus texted Jasper to say he had his scans. When a coherent reply came moments later, Marcus knew Jasper was amidst one of his crazed detox sessions – not necessarily a good thing. Jasper was an extremes junkie, and this was just another part of the same enslaving cycle. Bouts of detox alternated with drink and drugs.

It infuriated Oliver to see Jasper blowing his inheritance on empty advice from phony doctors who all too readily prescribed homeopathic "remedies" at extortionate prices. 'It's nonsensical,' he spluttered, having returned from the Gents via the bar. 'I've told your brother on numerous occasions that the pills contain chalk and bugger all else.' He had a bee in his bonnet about this. 'Homeopathy is only effective for susceptible patients with more money than sense.'

'Well then, Jasper's the perfect client,' replied Marcus, with irony. 'He's never in a state to cater for logic. But thanks, mate. For trying, I mean. Appreciate it.'

'Last orders!' bellowed Brenda from behind the bar. The pub shook.

The two men put on their hats and coats and walked outside, with Oliver eagerly clasping the sides of his new painting; he had been waiting too long to get his hands on Tara again.

As Daisy walked along Artesian Road, she saw the eclectic bunch spill from *The Toad and Tankar*d. Her eyes were drawn to two tall men, their faces hidden in the shadows cast by their hats. They patted backs as if to depart. As she approached, she noticed one of the two carrying a reclining nude on a canvas beneath bubble wrap. She wore nothing but pink pants. They were hard to miss...*just Like Tara's!*

As Marcus wandered along Sutherland Place towards Aldridge Road Villas, he noticed a figure in a red coat walking just ahead. For several moments he watched her appear then vanish as she dipped in and out of streetlights, before being swallowed by the darkness at the end of the road.

Once home, and in his studio, he looked at Jasper's scans. Finding inspiration in the bulging forms and weaving veins, he placed the heart scan behind a sheet of acetate and stencilled the cloud shapes and rivers. Jasper became a view from an aeroplane, flying above the clouds. By probing so deep, Marcus could look out to a whole new world, finding freedom in entrapment. He called this piece *Vice Versa*.

He marvelled at the vast body of work his brother inspired – *obsession must be hereditary*. He planned to complete *Vice Versa* over the weekend and add it to the collection for his upcoming exhibition, *Portrait of a Boy* at Beth's *Gemini Gallery*.

He looked at the *Fairground Frieze* across his wall, eyes stalling again on the piercing look of the faceless girl, whom he had named Eliza. Then he cast his eyes over his growing collection of the two silhouetted figures, she shorter girl with her taller friend, whose face was always hidden, cowering in darkness, or too abstract for detail. Her anonymity was mesmerising, her presence spellbinding. His Eliza collection was growing.

He went to close the shutters but changed his mind, as the moon was a perfect crescent, like two arms embracing one lone star. He thought of Eliza and wondered if she was looking at it too.

She was everywhere he turned.

Everywhere but nowhere, really.

He hoped that one day Eliza would want to leave the security of cyberspace and meet in person. Be it tomorrow or in his final days, he would be there for her.

But if all they ever had was what they had right now, he'd die a happy man.

Friday, April 15th

'I'm taking you to an exhibition called *Portrait of a Boy*,' Max told Daisy in the back of the cab, before turning to the driver and barking 'Walton Street'; he barely opened the glass screen for fear of catching something.

Tonight had been a long time coming. Daisy had practically given up hope of ever seeing Max again, and her heart leapt when his call came. She was nervous and excited. *Had he dumped Miss Polo? Too high maintenance?* Well, she could've told him that ages ago. She was flattered and overjoyed to be on Max's arm once again. Previous upset was now forgotten.

Daisy wore the same wrap-around scarlet dress she had worn with Max the night of the funfair, but that evening it had never had the chance to shine. As she unbuttoned her coat – seductively, she hoped – to reveal her low sweetheart neckline, a waft of her sexiest perfume escaped. Sitting directly opposite, Max choked, screwed up his face and opened the window, as if she had farted. Mortified, Daisy closed her coat and shrunk inside.

The taxi stopped in front of *The Gemini Gallery*. Daisy recognised the name – *Beth's Gallery!*

Neither Floyd nor Beth was overjoyed to see Daisy in tow of the dashing Baron Max von Beck. He had a natural sophistication, Floyd noticed glumly, that not even Hollywood roles could buy.

Daisy felt as if she had been busted mid-adulterous romp. She had seen much of the twins lately and blushed as she made introductions. Her heart tremored and fluttered. In Max's aloofness, she had been getting closer to Floyd – they had kissed several times now. Despite Beth's constant presence and Daisy's warped speculations, Floyd had a charm that was hard to resist, and Daisy had accepted an invitation to their mum's upcoming birthday as "his date".

Naïvely thinking love was about ownership and belonging, she didn't know who she belonged to – *Max or Floyd?* – nor if either actually wanted her anyway.

Max found meeting *nobodies* rather tedious. He had little patience for people he had no intention of seeing ever again. He perked up when Daisy introduced 'Curator Beth' and wondered if her bust, perfectly framed in a low-cut number, was up for grabs too.

Sabre photographer Weenie appeared. Daisy knew of her from *Sainthill Publications*, and Max knew her from the high society events they both attended. Max turned to pose, leaning as far from Daisy and as close to Beth as he could. Weenie captured the moment.

Max hoped he would *only* appear alongside "Curator" Beth in *RAH!*'s pages. It was good PR. He couldn't afford to be seen with Floyd, his sexuality could do without the hassle – or Daisy, Luise would lop his balls off. He shivered at the thought of Luise seeing them together in her favourite magazine. 'I subscribed to a fucking magazine, not a cheating boyfriend,' she would scream.

Max looked at Daisy, perfectly pretty and sweet, but a "nobody", bless her. He felt something akin to disappointment. He was fond of her in the same way he was fond of Leibe. The two were similar in their adoration and loyalty, he thought, although Leibe was a pedigree and had softer hair. Again, he felt, *what was it, sadness?* before pulling himself together and refocusing his mind on the mission of the evening: to do the gentlemanly thing and tell Daisy their little fling was finito. Luise was finally ready to wear his ring, so Daisy was no longer needed. *Besides*, he reminded himself, *it hadn't meant anything anyway...*

In the courtyard at the back of the gallery, Daisy cooled her flushed cheeks in the evening air. Preoccupied with the shock-awkwardness of the evening, she failed to notice the solo artist of the exhibition, who passed her as she returned inside.

So distracted by the attention he was receiving, Marcus too, failed to notice Daisy Hawkins as he entered the courtyard. He hated his own exhibitions and never felt comfortable in the limelight. He preferred recognition for his work from the safety of his home. He had little time for small talk and felt itchy in more than one person's gaze.

He noticed Jasper in the shade at the back of the courtyard. It was Jasper who was the real star of the show, thought Marcus, for his face loomed down from the walls at prospective buyers. It was horrid putting a price on your brother – selling him off in scraps like that. Still, Jasper didn't seem to mind, he relished notoriety. He watched Jasper take sips from his symbolic glass of water; face scrunching like it was poison, whilst chatting up three flirtatious star-struck blondes. *Such shallow adoration.*

Marcus thought about Eliza and her depth. She seemed so different to other girls – increasingly so, the more he got to know her. He wished she were here to support him through the evening, but sensitive to her reluctance to meet, he knew an invitation would've fallen on deaf ears – or rather, blind eyes.

Inside, Beth, Floyd and Max were still chatting. Daisy left the attractive trio alone to flirt and compete, feeling more comfortable admiring the beautiful rawness of the walled horror show. The exhibition, *Portrait of a Boy,* seemed to tell a story of degeneration. It was riddled with contradictions. Paintings of the same boy, from angelic child to tortured adult, the journey captured by an array of haunting faces. *Screaming with pleasure or pain? Who is the boy? Why does he cry and rot? Why does the artist hate him so much?* By the looks of things his paint-smudged fingers had dug, dragged, stabbed and scratched in areas of the canvasses. *Or did the artist hate?* There was love in the soft caresses of the brush, love in the careful detail, love in sentiment, love in the arrangement of the display – for if she walked in the opposite direction, the story was not about degeneration at all, but rather of regeneration. So there was love in the hope of recovery, in the offer of a choice. Lucian often reminded her that life always presented choices, even if sometimes they weren't obvious. There was love in the vast body of the work, love in the artist's loyalty to his subject, love in obsession, love in addiction... *Love in addiction?*

She stood before *Echo*, the largest canvas of all. The canvas licked with flames; reds, yellows and oranges, against a calming grey-blue background. The two large eyes of the boy burnt holes in the canvas. They stared out and she stared in. He seemed to occupy real space, yet there was something ghostly and transient about him. There were no tears, yet echoing cries were somehow audible. Daisy was hypnotised by the burning intensity.

Marcus stood amongst the crowd pondering, once again, on the extraordinarily fickle nature of human beings. When you're at the bottom, no one could give a damn about you, but when you're a star of a show, everyone wants a piece of you. The flock bleated at him from all angles.

And then he noticed her.

Lips still moved around him, but everything fell silent.

He was engrossed by the back of her slender neck that supported a dishevelled knot of hair, by her stray ringlets that cascaded in elegant loops and twirls. She stood so close, staring into Jasper's ghoulish eyes... *Such a striking image!*

His heart swelled.

Her head turned.

Their eyes locked. Eyeball to eyeball, pinning each other to the spot. Both stared into new depth, and neither could help but fall.

As Marcus made his way through the crowd to reach the fallen girl, another man got there first and shook her into delirious consciousness before dragging her away. From the gallery door, Marcus cast eyes along the length of Walton Street, but the two figures were nowhere to be seen.

At a white-clothed table in a Knightsbridge restaurant, Daisy reached under the table to catch a little box that had toppled from Max's jacket as he went to the Gents.

When she peeked inside, a diamond ring winked back.

She could barely eat a thing, and feared she might pass out again – the thought made her panic more. She had already embarrassed him enough – he had made that quite clear. *Could he really be about to propose? A bit soon, no? Even for a die-hard romantic like me.* Every time he moved, she wondered if he would end up on one knee.

The girl was a mess. What the hell was wrong with her? *Infatuation? Love? Probably both.* Either way, her conversation was atrocious and her swaying made him feel seasick. Tonight was clearly not the night to tell her their affair was over. He couldn't risk another ugly fainting episode. Had the creamy scallop vermicelli not been so damn scrummy, he would have taken her home immediately.

In her Warren, Daisy looked at herself in the bathroom mirror. What did she expect? All pasty and white like that. Of course he wasn't going to propose tonight.

She removed her eye-makeup and washed her face.

What had made her faint, she wondered, as she cast her mind back to that moment in the gallery. She remembered losing herself in a pair of eyes... *But whose? The eyes in that painting entitled Echo?*

Or did the eyes belong to someone else?

If so, then who?

What happened after Echo?

Zilch. Blank. Nada. Zero recollection.

Suddenly, she found herself back in the fish restaurant, peaking inside a box.

The ring!

But even with an imaginary drum roll, she failed to trigger excitement.

The ring!

She could not understand why her heart tremored rather than fluttered and she felt nauseous. Was this not what she had dreamed of for so long? *Straight out of a fairy tale!*

Drum roll... The ring!

But again, no flutter. She must be very ill indeed. She wanted Lucian, his advice and reassurance, but he was not there. Instead, she went to the loo and puked.

Friday, April 22nd

Jude and Daisy were catching up with some school friends in a pub off Kensington Church Street.

The waitress circled the table, scribbling dessert orders onto her notepad.

'The ice cream, please,' said Daisy.

'An apple, please,' said Jude, ordering off the menu.

'An apple?' said the waitress.

'An apple?' repeated Daisy. 'That's all?'

'Good point,' said Jude, 'make that two, please.'

'What's with the apple obsession?' asked Daisy, not for the first time. 'You'll make yourself sick.'

Jude's answer remained the same. 'Can't seem to quit that health mission I started. I crave them all the time.' She shrugged and avoided eye contact, as was the norm recently.

'Anyone would have thought you were pregnant,' said Daisy, as the two apples arrived. She looked radiant though, it had to be said. 'Guess there are worse addictions to have,' she added.

'Shall we go straight on from here together?' Jude suggested, changing the subject. Tonight the girls were meeting Orlaith and Vinnie for drinks in Soho. The happy couple were freshly wind-burnt from their honeymoon on the Channel Island of Alderney.

'There's something I need to do first,' Daisy replied, trying hard to not look suspicious. 'I'll meet you there, OK?'

Jude raised eyebrows inquisitively. Thankfully, her gob was full of apple, otherwise there would have been endless questions; *What? Where? Shall I come?* If she divulged her whereabouts, Jude would never let her go. Ramming the last spoon of ice cream into her mouth, Daisy hurriedly left cash on the table, got up and waved goodbye to Jude and the others, and escaped interrogation free.

Daisy's walk to Max's house on Aldridge Road Villas was fraught with tension. She would apologise for the state she was in and her terrible company last week, for fainting, for embarrassing him, etc. etc. etc. If she played her cards right, he might choose tonight to propose. Even with the imaginary drum roll and a trumpeter, Daisy could feel no flutter. The rabble of butterflies began to gnaw at her sides. She held her stomach and tried to ignore the pain and the rake of giddiness.

Outside Max's house, Daisy composed herself. Looking down at her hands, she noticed the day had lodged itself beneath her nails. One particular finger on her left hand seemed more important now than the rest. 'This is your big moment,' she whispered to her finger, before polishing her nail with the cuff of her shirt, in the hope it could carry off a whopping, great, sparkly diamond. Next, she looked at her reflection in the gold doorknob, but her skin wrapped the convexity, and her face distorted into a stranger's. She zoomed in on one eyeball and dusted eye shadow from the soft bag of sallow skin beneath; gold was not her colour, she looked positively jaundiced.

The door opened and Daisy came face to face with a jodhpured camel-toe (*yuk!*) and a manicured hand adorned with a familiar diamond ring. (*Hey! That's mine, you bitch!*). Daisy's eyes traced up a slender, tanned wrist, a cashmere arm and a long neck to the fairy tale wrecker, Miss Polo.

Daisy's heartbeat stalled. The ring had never been for her after all. *Of course.* This was way more in tune with the story of her life. She felt so stupid.

'Have you come to polish the knobs today?' Miss Polo asked.

'Who is it, darling?' Max's words descended the stairwell.

'Nobody!' she yelled back.

Oh right, yup, I'm a nobody. The word slapped Daisy on the face. She felt dizzy, like she had been spinning for days and could not find strength to defend herself. As she walked away, she braced herself for the painful sinking of reality. It was "The End". Her deformed fairy tale bubble burst, and she left Miss Polo to polish her royal knob all on her own.

She felt the pain of rejection but mistook it for heartbreak. She felt the tears of relief but mistook them for grief.

As usual, Daisy found comfort in Lucian's words, later that evening:

'Cocoon yourself in love and you will feel strength and protection,' he wrote. *'There's nothing more important than the love for yourself. Don't get carried away like my housemate though, he's a textbook narcissist. He struggles to allocate love for anyone else.'*

'He sounds Charming. Just my type.'

From his studio, Marcus imagined Eliza's sad eyes. He glanced at his group of paintings: his *Eliza collection*. He imagined the same sad eyes on his painting of both the stooped girl with her friend and the faceless girl who was being dragged from the fairground across his wall. Suddenly, his fairground belle started to spin like a ballerina in a musical box. Around and around she went, exposing different sides as she turned; the girl who wiped away tears on Elgin Avenue metamorphosed into the girl who left *Jazbar* later that same day, into the girl at the fairground, into the girl at the gallery with the beautiful face and the cavernous eyes, into which he dived so deep. Around and around the figures spun, faster and faster until they merged into one. Then the spinning began to slow, slower and slower, until he was back with his fairground *Eliza*, but in place of the featureless oval, he saw the beautiful face and sad eyes of the girl at his exhibition. For a moment there, his Eliza and the gallery girl became one.

'Who was the girl in the scarlet dress? The one who fainted?' Marcus had asked after the exhibition. 'That's *our* Daisy,' Beth and Floyd had replied. Daisy, Floyd's token girlfriend, and Beth's unrequited love interest. *Their* Daisy. Loud and clear. The twins weren't used to sharing.

He looked again at the photograph in *RAH!* in which two pages covered his exhibition. Scarlet fabric licked the side of one photograph, which he now knew was the hem of Daisy's dress. The most beautiful girl he had ever seen had been edited from the photo. Again, he thought about her eyes, and the depth into which he had fallen... How much further if her faint had not broken their connection?

Had she felt it too?

Without the scarlet tongue of Daisy's dress dancing with verve, the photograph would be insipid, Marcus thought, dominated by a "Max von Beck" who poured his empty aura into Beth's gallery space and drowned in his own self-importance. *What a cock.*

He thought about what he had just told Eliza: *'Cocoon yourself in love... There's nothing more important than the love for oneself.'*

But what the hell did he know about love? Who was he to preach, now that Daisy had blown apart his theory with one look – for in that moment they had caught eyes, with his feet frozen to the gallery floor, he had fallen deep. One feeling had absorbed him completely and rendered all others irrelevant. It consumed in entirety. Fuck the love for oneself, because in that instance, it was *the most* important feeling he had ever had, the only one that existed, the only one that mattered.

'Do you believe in love at first sight? True love, not just any old love,' Lucian asked Eliza.

'I sure do,' came her immediate reply.

But why was she so certain? Teleported to the evening of *Portrait of a Boy*, Daisy thought of the moment she stood in front of the painting, *Echo*. That moment, or the next? One of them made her believe. She can't have experienced love at first sight with a painting, so what happened after? She shook her memory for where her eyes fell next, but again she remembered nothing but fuzz. Somewhere behind the impermeable black and white pixelated membrane, had she experienced true love at first sight?

It dawned on Marcus that a sad girl with a freshly fractured heart should not be contemplating love at first sight. To change the subject and make up for his insensitivity, he typed, *'If I was with you, I'd give you a hug, or buy you a drink at the very least.'*

'Don't underestimate the power of your words, Lucian. Most of them are pure filth, but some are as embracing as a hug, others are as intoxicating as alcohol, and the rest are so full of wisdom that they linger with me for hours, days, weeks.'

'Like a bad smell?'

'Like a best buddy, guiding, reassuring and supporting me.'

'I'm blushing.'

'You should be. In return, I could do with some of your wisdom. Please.'

'OK. I'll have a rummage around my massive trunk of wise words and find something appropriate.'

'And whilst you do that, I'll just lie back and imagine your massive trunk.'

'You should! And maybe, just maybe, if you play your cards right you can have a rummage around yourself one day.'

'There! Pure filth.'

'You love it! But not as much as you'll love this, pure gold this is. It's a quote, which was on a china pot my folks had at home when I was a kid. I've never forgotten the words. They belong to an American poet and philosopher called Thoreau. "Happiness is like a butterfly; the more you chase it, the more it will elude you. But if you turn your attentions to other things, it comes and softly sits on your shoulder".'

Later, in bed, Daisy pressed her hands to her tummy. She considered the rabble that could flap insanely in her stomach and make her black out. She considered just one butterfly, Thoreau's, Lucian's, sitting softly on her shoulder and it was a soothing thought. She slept soundly.

Fuelled by the flirty banter that had occupied much of the evening, Marcus began work on a new painting that he called *Butterfly Echo*. He painted a girl in a scarlet dress standing before a set of hungry eyes. He was comfortable capturing ugly sadness, not beauty, so she faced away from the viewer and into the painting. If he had tried to capture Daisy's face and the compassion in her eyes, his hand would have stumbled with the pressure of responsibility. He knew that if he tarnished his vision in *Butterfly Echo*, he could risk losing her from his mind forever.

He cast tired eyes out of his studio window. The fragile beauty of sunrise in the city had only ever been captured accurately by masters. Such beauty was quite intimidating.

Friday, April 29th

Today Miss Middleton was marrying her prince. Daisy had *mused* and *mused* about the pending day in her column; it was all her *Musings of a Pisces* readers wanted to hear about. England was happy today.

From the kitchen, Daisy could hear a report of the fairy tale romance from the office radio. The correspondent spoke with fervour and did not miss a thing. Daisy listened to the names of the guests as they arrived at the church, the details of Kate's dress, the pride on the face of Prince Harry, and the splendour of Pippa Middleton's derriere. Jude was currently having a royal gathering and Daisy had been invited, but slow progress on her *Ask Eliza Q&A's,* had hampered her celebrations. *Damn her.* Eliza was proving to be a massive pain in the ass.

She leant against the mottled kitchen surface in the empty office, (empty bar Hanratty, and a few others playing work catch-up), and wondered what she could possibly reply to *'Roberta, 23, who wanted to be Robert',* but didn't know how she (*he?*) could tell her (*his?*) boyfriend.

And then there was the twins' mother's small birthday gathering this evening, and Daisy had agreed to be Floyd's date, and she was apprehensive about her big moment.

'Good-bye, Daisy,' said Hanratty, as he scuttled past the kitchen door. Stretching his neck backwards, he said, 'The recent response to *Musings of a Pisces* has been excellent. Tremendous effort, dear.'

'Thank you, Hanratty. I just wish *Ask Eliza* was flowing as easily.'

'Hmmm, yes,' he scratched an orange tuft. His hair looked like sea grass today. 'The last issue…well yes…oh dear. Let's talk about it another time, shall we?' His eyes darted, his neck withdrew into its shell and he bumbled off home.

She dunked a sugar lump in her tea and popped it on her tongue and sucked. In the sweet sap she found the determination to quit *Ask Eliza*. She couldn't do it anymore. Simple as that. The pay rise for the extra column had been short but sweet.

Tara Forsyth's perfect breasts peered around the doorframe – breasts with attitude. The rest of her body followed suit until Daisy shared the kitchen with a whole body of attitude. It was stifling.

Tara had chosen to spend her day away from the crowds and in the quiet haven of the office. London had gone quite mad. The exhaustive reporting had made her nauseous, but she was spurred on by fact that later today the wedding would be done and dusted and maybe, just maybe, the whole of England, and the rest of the Commonwealth, might just be able to consider moving on to subjects that actually bore some importance.

Girls like Tara Forsyth intimidate girls like me, thought Daisy. *Cat woman meet girl next door*. It was never going to be a match made in Heaven.

Two mandatory smiles were exchanged.

Daisy dodged ruby talons and a whiff of sexuality as Tara reached for the kettle.

A crisp-fitted white shirt tucked into a navy skirt, which perched like a bonnet on two long legs – cellulite-free no doubt, assumed Daisy. She wondered what it might be like to be Tara, if she wore fake eyelashes, permanent mascara, breast-cupping bras, thigh-high stockings, cheese-grater pink thongs; and what it might be like to be fancied by men and women alike.

Tara caught her staring. Daisy went the shade of Tara's nails.

'Were you OK?' asked Tara. 'You fainted.'

Hmmm, which time? Daisy furrowed her brow.

'At the exhibition? You know, Marcus True's *Portrait of a Boy*. Ring any bells?'

Oh God! Tara Forsyth saw me faint! Well, that's embarrassing. She hadn't even realised she was there.

'Oh yeah. Totally fine. Thanks.'

'It was impressive, you know. You triggered an avalanche of avocado canapés. I almost cheered. They had already circulated twenty times and tasted revolting – increasingly bad with each round.'

'I did?' *Change the subject.* 'Incredible artist. Who was the boy in all the paintings?'

'The artist's brother barely recognisable in them though. A tad psycho-obsessive if you ask me.'

The boiling kettle interrupted the conversation and Daisy made a hasty exit.

Marcus had spent the day in his studio, worrying about Jasper's behaviour and performance at Mrs Clansey's birthday gathering. Mrs Clansey's condition was slowly deteriorating; her party was supposed to be a civilised intimate affair, where she could be surrounded by her nearest and dearest whilst enjoying Jasper's most melodic and least offensive songs. Background music. The problem was Jasper didn't function in the background.

Fortunately, Marcus had his December exhibition to focus on too, *Artopsy; Symbiosis of Art and Science*. The collection Marcus planned to exhibit would be inspired by the medical scans and X-rays Dr Oliver Cranston had recently been collecting for him. Marcus found layers of interest in the images. Using various tools and materials, he had begun to work into some of the scans – experimental preparation for the final paintings. Oliver had also handed Marcus "goody bags" from meetings promoting new medical equipment. Twisting metal meshing and plastic tubing, Marcus noticed their resemblance to veins and arteries, and considered attaching bundles of the materials onto the flat painting so they would "exist" in the time and space of the viewer. He toyed with the idea of artistic resuscitation.

Marcus had always been intrigued by the paradox of life and death – polar opposites, yet utterly entwined. In his work, the diseased organs – which caused pain to the dying subject – offered pleasure, in the form of curiosity and visual appeal, to the viewer.

This body of work would be another attempt to depart from the subject of Jasper. There was, however, the same element of catharsis. He felt life at its most extreme in the face of death. The depth of empathy he felt in the face of pain reminded him he was alive. He glanced at his *Eliza collection* and the mass of

Jaspers. Marcus was drawn to sadness, but he liked the fact he could turn it into something beautiful. He painted over some scans in vibrant joyful colours and they became underwater photographs of tropical reefs. The tissue and arteries looked like marine flora swaying with life beneath the sea.

At 6.30pm Marcus left for the party. His red bow tie nipped at his throat. He thought of Daisy. Tonight she was Floyd's "date". It would be a miracle if he got a formal introduction at all. His bow tie nipped some more.

The modest marquee was brimming with red, white and blue. The colour theme poured into the cocktails and the canapés were miniature versions of British classics. Mrs Clansey was thrilled to share her birthday party with such an elevated and romantic event as the Royal Wedding.

Mrs Clansey looked tired but content. She wore a blue cashmere and silk dress with a chunky pink necklace that looked far too heavy for her fragile frame. She sat on a throne-like chair, propped up with cushions, surrounded by her adoring family.

Marcus handed her a bunch of ice blue flowers and Floyd filled her glass with bubbly champagne.

'Marcus,' she gratefully took the flowers with one hand, and presented the back of her other, onto which Marcus gently planted a kiss. 'Looking absolutely dashing as always,' she spoke softly. 'And Floyd, where is your girlfriend we've been hearing so much about? I can't wait to meet her.'

Nervously, Daisy entered the gathering of unfamiliar faces. Habitually, she felt for her silver thumb ring, but it wasn't there. She felt vulnerable and panicked. Her secret source of comfort was missing. *Think Daisy, think. When did I last have it?* Last night, bowling with Floyd and Beth. She had removed it when her thumb rubbed in the hole of the bowling ball. *But then where did I put it?*

Daisy spotted her date in the crowd; the platinum hair was hard to miss. He was talking to a taller dark-haired gentleman; she only saw his back, but it was a damn striking one: beautifully dressed, perfectly proportioned and crowned with a thick mop of chocolatey hair.

As the two men separated, Daisy's eyes followed Floyd as he made his way over to Beth, who defined elegance in a backless white dress. She watched carefully as Floyd placed his outstretched hand on the groove of Beth's back, before leaning in to plant a kiss on her cheek.

'Hello, bro. You scrub up all right. Makes a change,' Beth teased.

Daisy could not hear the words, but having allowed her mind to wander to a murkier place, she misinterpreted the series of gestures, and imagined an exchanging of misplaced sweet nothings.

'Thanks, sis, wish I could say the same for you,' Floyd winked.

The whispers and winks were all part of their secret code language! Suddenly, Daisy was a spy in the MI6, hungry for meaning. Engrossed, she pigeon-stepped towards them.

Unfortunately, the length of her dress demanded larger strides and less pointy shoes to avoid her tripping. This conflicted with her MI6 duties. Her toes caught on her hem, but thankfully her fall was discreet. Daisy made the snappy decision to dive beneath a nearby table until any minor disturbance had subsided.

'Hello, I'm Joshua, are you all right?' asked a young waiter who was also under the table. He was retrieving sushi rolls that had tumbled from his tilted tray.

'Hi, I'm Daisy. Thanks for noticing…I think. I'm fine, thanks. I save tripping for special occasions, like birthdays, weddings, bar mitzvahs.'

He smiled.

'I don't recommend you wear a long dress with pointy heels,' she added. 'The two should never go together.'

'I'll bear it in mind. Like slippery trays and sushi. Big no-no.'

'Precisely.'

Squelching the last salmon nigiri onto his tray, Joshua left Daisy to 'hang for a little longer' under the table.

Daisy spotted Floyd and Beth, who had relocated to a different area. Folding her hands around the table-leg, shuffling the table above her like an umbrella, she shifted it ever so gradually through the crowd towards them.

'Where's Daisy? She here yet?'

Daisy recognised her name and Beth's voice. She planted her table.

'I haven't seen her yet.' *(Floyd's voice)*. 'Mum is desperate to meet her, of course.'

'Of course. Poor Mum. You shouldn't be treating Mum or Daisy like this. Honesty is always the better option.'

'But Mum, think of Mum's health. Daisy's totally perfect for –'

'For your little lie?'

'Anyone would think you were jealous, sis…'

'Yeah, you know I am.'

'Well, save me the lecture.' His eyes fixed on a heavy silver ring, which dangled on the end of a chain around his sister's neck. 'Or I might just have to take back my present. Which I have to say, looks seriously cool.'

From beneath the table, Daisy saw Beth look down at the chunky silver ring at the end of her necklace. She watched as Beth tossed it in the palm of her hand before admiring a wrap-around inscription.

Daisy gasped – *My thumb ring!* – and misinterpreted Floyd's 'present' as one of incestuous Love.

Daisy's suspicions were confirmed: Floyd was using her. She was only his "date" to disguise his true love for his sister! *'Anyone would think you were jealous, sis…' 'Yeah, you know I am.'* Beth wanted her brother all to herself. Had he stolen Daisy's ring knowing it was hers, or had he been oblivious? Either way, the inappropriate sentiment behind the gift remained the same. On Daisy's finger it had symbolised innocent young friendship, on Beth's it symbolised the opposite.

Appalled, Daisy inched her way across the floor to the exit, gently nudging away anyone who disrupted her course. There she found Joshua, who helped her to her feet.

As she attempted to exit, Joshua heckled her back.

'Dip the palm of your hand in a pot of paint – red, white or blue, and print here please,' he pointed at a large silver sheet of card. 'It's a Happy Birthday card for Mrs Clansey,' he explained. She could not find the strength to argue, so shoved her entire hand – ('Err, just your palm') – into the nearest paint and pressed it against the sheet, before she raced home.

Having fielded bemused looks on the District line, it was only when she was back in the comfort of her Warren and scrubbing her hand in her basin that she understood why her journey had been besieged by nervous glances. In fact, she was amazed to have made it home at all, for tonight London was full of security staff and police officers on the lookout for any post Royal Wedding trouble. At best, she could have been mistaken for a careless vet who had forgotten to scrub after delivering a calf, at worst a serial killer about to be caught red-handed. She could have spent the night in prison, before detectives were able to confirm that her red hand dripped with paint, not blood, and her crazed look was one of foolish naïvety, not of a psychopath.

It was all too much, and she passed out on her bathroom floor.

Marcus had glimpsed Daisy, but only briefly, early on in the evening, as she made her way through the crowds towards the twins. His heart had raced and so had his footsteps, until he was thrown off course by one of the twins' cousins. By the time he had exchanged pleasantries and made his excuses, Daisy had apparently vanished into thin air.

At the end of the night, he pressed his own painted hand onto Mrs Clansey's birthday card. Immediately, his eyes fell on the most elegant hand with long fingers that fanned like a butterfly wing on the silver sky. He wondered if it was Daisy's.

At about 4am, Daisy came around. Her head felt woozy. She dragged her body into her bed, between the cool sheets. In the charcoal sky inside her eyelids, she followed the flight of a solitary yellow primrose butterfly as it fluttered towards her with the gift of joy and peace on its wings. She recalled the quote Lucian had told her – *'Happiness is like a butterfly.'* Peace sat softly on her shoulder whilst sleep wrapped itself around her.

Friday, May 6th

It was 9am. Daisy's walk to work through Hyde Park was lovely. Spring was nudging over to make room for summer and the melee was sublime. Respectful of its forbearer, summer edged in gracefully and was made to feel most welcome. April had been the hottest on record, Daisy had heard earlier on the radio, and May promised to maintain the scorching standard. But there would be thunderstorms and heavy rain too. Daisy felt the warmth of the rays through the damp air, and her mind flitted to Lucian. She hoped he might be around to chat later. Their busy lives had kept them apart over the week. And she missed him.

At 11am, she was distracted from *Musings of a Pisces* by another text from Beth. Daisy had no intention of seeing either freaky twin for some time. Again, she did not respond. *What to say? Where to start? How to throw an accusation into their cosy little threesome?* In one text, Beth had mentioned that their housemate had spotted her at their mum's party. Daisy wondered how this was possible since she had never met, nor even heard much mention of any housemate.

She would miss Beth and her pixie splendour, but she could do without Floyd and his lies (even though she had given him a piece of her heart), and it was impossible to see one twin without the other. It could never work. She sat at her desk and became distracted once again by thoughts of what life might've been like with him – *and Beth*. Jude encouraged her to stop over-thinking and to turn a blind eye, but Daisy, with her active imagination and excellent vision in both eyes, thought that a terrible waste. She knew she could never be Beth for him. She looked at the hard peach on her desk… If Beth was a fruit, Daisy thought, she would be the sweetest, ripest peach. If Daisy were a fruit, however, she would be ripening, but never quite ripe enough.

She dry-wretched into her bin.

Her screensaver of a Barbados beach popped up. She imagined herself following Floyd along the sandy beach. She watched herself exaggerate strides to keep up, and noticed that her footprints were never quite in line with his. He noticed too. Then she saw Beth following, and watched her exaggerate her strides until her footprints imprinted perfectly within his. Daisy imagined him wishing that the beach could continue into the path for the rest of his life, with his sister's footsteps always in his, together forever…

Ah, stop! This was getting too weird, even for Daisy.

She would rather have a lonely duped heart than live her life in shoes she could never fill…

She wretched again.

She considered sending Floyd the dry-cleaning bill for her red splattered dress, the repair bill for her ruptured heart, and another for her ring's priceless sentimentality. She wondered how to go about converting heartache into pounds sterling.

The loss of her ring was particularly painful. In hindsight, she wished she'd leapt up from beneath the table and claimed ownership, but she had been too stunned by the creepiness of the whole damn scene to think straight.

Since Marcus's brief sighting of Daisy at the party he had not shut up about her. He had voiced his hopes of an introduction, but the twins had not heard a squeak from Daisy since, so they persuaded him instead to focus his attentions on Eliza and *FFS* ask her out.

Marcus gave it some more thought during his dinner with Claudette Harper, owner of an eminent Shoreditch gallery, who had expressed interest in his work post *Portrait of a Boy*. As Claudette Harper banged on about art, Marcus drank Dutch courage in preparation to ask Eliza on a date. He had been meandering along the patience path for months now; the more he got to know Eliza the more reluctant he was to apply pressure, for fear of her turning her back on him and diving into the cyberspace abyss. He found encouragement and support in a handful of clichés such as "what will be will be," and "good things come to those who wait." He hoped Eliza would be around to chat later. He missed her.

After dinner, his hopes were realised. He heard about the odd twins, Eliza's lost ring, and the betrayal of another boy. Eliza, as usual, mentioned no names, and Lucian, as usual, never probed.

'My housemates are twins. They're close, but not that close,' Lucian said. *'You've been hanging out with some strange people, Eliza.'*

They looked out of their separate windows at the glowing moon.

'The May moon looks pretty damn excited at the prospect of summer, don't you think? Bet Summer's a right hottie,' remarked Eliza.

Marcus was reminded of some lines from a poem by Thomas Moore called *The Young May Moon*, although his memory was a little disjointed.

'The young May moon is beaming, love,' he wrote.

A poem. She furrowed her brow. She wished she could impress him by firing off the next line, but unfortunately, she didn't have the foggiest.

'When the drowsy world is dreaming, love,' he continued.

Tis never too late for delight, my dear.'

'I'm well up for a spot of delightful mooning!' Damn. That was the best she could do.

The moon beamed encouragement, and swept up in the moment, Marcus finally suggested a date.

'A real-life date?' She hesitated. *'You and me? Us two loners?'* To live is to love and to love is to risk dying a little inside. *'I have a thousand What Ifs. What if we don't work? On the outside, I mean. All exposed and vulnerable.'*

'We'll never know if we don't try it out.'

'In the flesh. Eyeball to eyeball.'

'Warts and all.'

'Genital warts included?'

'Sure. If they become an issue I know a good doctor.'

'But I'm scared.'

'But I have a good feeling.'

Me too, considered Daisy. *I would rather "live" a short life than "survive" a long one. 'OK, let's do it.'*

'Yes. Let's.' Marcus was over the moon.

Excitement at the prospect of finally meeting in person at this stage of their hither-to exclusively e-relationship was overwhelming. Both embraced the risk and arranged to meet the following Friday.

A twin, a self-absorbed, weird twin…? Marcus pondered. *Hmmm…*

But Floyd denied any knowledge of "Eliza".

'Apart from Eliza Doolittle,' Floyd replied to Marcus, 'the only other one I'm aware of is the one you can't shut up about.'

Friday, May 13th

Bloody typical. Daisy's date with Lucian fell on Friday 13th. The black omen crushed the day like an elephant. It was a case of bad planning, thought Daisy.

Unlike Daisy, Jude sensed good vibes. She had high hopes for her friend's date and was bracing herself to say goodbye to *Dating Daisy*, and begin a new, happier chapter. *Dating Daisy* had given Jude a purpose outside her mundane motherly and wifely duties, and for that she was thankful. Looking over at Daisy as she sat at her desk with head entrenched in *Musings*, Jude realised she had actually enjoyed riding the emotional rollercoaster and finally living out those crazy dating days – albeit through her best friend.

Again, Daisy contemplated Hanratty's challenge to find true love by the end of the year, and how she might celebrate love in her column if the situation happened to arise. Again, she thought of Lucian. Her mind wandered to happy places, like Spanish orange groves and Tuscan vineyards, where a lone butterfly kissed her shoulder, the sun kissed the leaves, and his lips kissed hers…until the one butterfly multiplied, and colourful wings of all shapes and sizes tickled her tummy. She felt sick with nervy excitement and wondered if she would be able to make her date at all.

Whose idea was it to call it a "date" anyway, for fuck's sake? The word was laden with undertones. "A drink" would have been better – she would even have settled for "a coffee" – way more chilled and far less expectant.

Still, Daisy thought, she was grateful for the familiarity of the meeting place. Remembering – from the little information exchanged on *Shine Online* – that they lived in the same leafy neighbourhood, they had arranged to meet at *The Toad and Tankard*, a shared favourite for its general scabbiness and lack of pretence.

She considered her attire. After much deliberation, due to indecisiveness rather than overwhelming choice, Daisy decided to wear her ole' fave, the scarlet dress. It always made her feel comfortable, and dressed down with her leather jacket, would be totally fine for *The Toad and Tankard*. More importantly, with the bow at the side, it was easy to unwrap in an emergency – usually of the bloating rather than sexual kind, she considered gloomily.

Jude told Daisy that she looked 'très ooh-la-la, mademoiselle!' in the scarlet dress, which Daisy translated as a big thumbs up.

Bloody typical. Hanratty held Daisy back after work for an impromptu *Ask Eliza* meeting.

Taking pity on Daisy's single-life struggles, he released her from the shackles of *Ask Eliza*. 'But just because your *Ask Eliza* column goes, does not mean your challenge does too. Oh no, no, no,' he smiled and shook his head. His genuine care for her made him uncharacteristically assertive.

Je-zus, get on with it! begged Daisy, taking another sneaky peak at her watch.

'I still want you to find true love by the end of the year, and – if successful – which I am sure you will be,' he winked, 'you can still celebrate your joyous news with your readers on your page.' He smiled and scratched an orange tuft on the barren beachscape of his head.

'Enjoy your date,' he winked again.

'How do you know…?'

'It's not rocket science, Daisy. Your hair's brushed, you look exquisite, and there's a sparkle in your eye.'

Outside *Sainthill Publications* Daisy hailed a cab. *Fifteen minutes to get home, dump bags, check for unsightly bits in teeth, change pants, refresh mascara and deodorant and leg it to Toad and Tankard...* She might only be a little late. She checked her wallet. *Shit. No cash.* In the back of the taxi, she felt the murmurings of a panic attack. The butterflies in her stomach surfed the sudden sea of adrenaline that coursed through her veins. *Breathe woman, slowly, slowly.* Tingles dived all the way down her body, to nibble the ends of her fingertips and then her toes. Feeling dizzy and nauseous, she clutched the taxi door for support. *Not now* – she reasoned with her butterflies and willed them to behave.

She had to cross the Westbourne Grove to reach the cash point.

Breathe.

Feeling a release of clarity in this half-way state, she twisted her woozy head to glance blurry eyes at the oncoming traffic, got out of the cab, slammed the door and stepped into the road…

Daisy lay there in her pants, bra and shoes. Marcus's training came flooding back – A – B – C. He checked her airway and breathing – clear. She was alive. Pulse – thready and racing. Pupils – equal and reactive. *What beautiful cerulean eyes.* No external signs of trauma, she was groaning and moving all four limbs. He felt along her cervical spine – no step or midline tenderness – clear. Checking the traffic, he calculated that by the time an ambulance had reached them, the taxi could have got to Chelsea and Westminster Hospital. He called Dr Oliver and forewarned him: 'Female, twenty-something…might have been hit, not sure… We're on our way now. Her name is Daisy.'

The cabbie opened the passenger door to release the scarlet tie of her dress. He handed it to Marcus, who shrouded her in dignity.

Cries of alarm from witnesses had preceded the ricochet of car horns. All cars had come to a standstill, bar the one that Marcus presumed had hit her. *Or had it?* He had seen the black Mercedes there when she fell to the ground, before it revved away, through a red light and out of sight. But he had not actually witnessed the hit.

Marcus had noticed her immediately. The scarlet dress on the other side of the road had licked the corner of his vision. He had sensed a presence, and turned to see her slam the taxi door on the scarlet bow around her waist, before witnessing both the dress and the scene unravel.

Oliver arrived to meet them at the hospital entrance. 'Ah, it's *this* Daisy.' Her last visit to the hospital had lingered in his mind. He inspected her body in white bra and black pants. *Who would have guessed the earplug girl was so hot beneath her clothes?* 'I poked around in one of her orifices with my crocodile tweezers not long ago,' he grinned at Marcus.

'For fucks sake, mate,' Marcus was furious and hoped Daisy had not been corrupted by Cranston. The nurses, anaesthetised by Dr Cranston's years of inappropriateness, handed the scarlet dress to Marcus with not so much as a raised eyebrow between them. They covered her in blankets and wheeled her into the hospital.

On a plastic chair in the corridor, Marcus waited. He checked the time. *Eliza. Fuck.* He was now over an hour late for their date. Why hadn't they exchanged numbers? That was a shitty oversight. He could have made contact by now, explained, apologised...

His mind wandered to *The Toad and Tankard* and his eyes scoured the room but she was nowhere to be seen. He pictured her arriving at the pub, ordering a drink and waiting whilst minutes evaporated along with her already dwindling faith in men.

But what could he have done differently? Leave Daisy lying on the road? He couldn't and wouldn't have done that to anyone – Daisy or not Daisy, for anyone – Eliza or not Eliza. *Bollocks.* Daisy and Eliza. He felt he was two-timing with one girl he hadn't even met, and another he hadn't even spoken to. What was wrong with him these days? Age? Or self-inflicted solitary confinement? He was losing the plot big time.

He joined the cancer patients outside the hospital to smoke a rollie. He would apologise, of course, explain himself. With words? Eliza was the writer, not him. She was the one who had the way with words. He could paint an apology? He returned to the bleak hospital corridor, and as the evening wore on, he imagined suitably apologetic colours; yellows perhaps and blues. *Yes.* Soft colours, a moody painting. He could send it to her address... But he had just demolished her trust in him – trust he had painstakingly built, brick by brick. Why the hell would she give him her address now?

On Oliver's instruction, Marcus headed back to Notting Hill. Daisy was OK, he had said, but needed rest. He went via *The Toad and Tankard* to imagine the night that could have been. 'The usual?' bellowed Brenda. He noticed her large breasts sway and beer splash, like she was riding the waves on an old creaky ship. He thought of Daisy in hospital and hoped she would be OK. He saw her scarlet dress in his satchel as he reached for his wallet. *Bollocks.* He had forgotten to give it to Oliver before leaving the hospital; and since Daisy was still refusing to return the twin's calls, it looked like he might never get the chance to return it. He knew Eliza would say that was a good thing, *'Poor Daisy fainted at your exhibition wearing it, and then got hit by a car whilst wearing it, so good riddance to it, I say! It has bad luck sewn into the fabric.'* Yes, he pondered, that's exactly what Eliza would say.

Dr Oliver was curious as to the level of concern Marcus had shown towards Daisy, a girl he claimed not to know. He presumed Daisy had whispered her name to Marcus through short breaths before passing out.

Fresh young blood was just what the doctor ordered, since Tara Forsyth had failed to return his calls.

It had looked like Daisy, thought Max. A little, perhaps. He probably should have stopped, but he was late for Luise and their *Romeo and Juliet* date in the West End. He was not sure he had actually hit Daisy... Or even touched her... It all

87

happened so fast. He was sure she had fallen *before* he could have hit her. Perhaps she had faked it? Revenge for the "two-timing" debacle? Perhaps she was trying to frame him in a hit-and-run? Paranoia poured from his palms. Maybe he *had* hit her? He was quite sure he had not killed her at least. It had been less of a "hit" and more of a "knock". Actually, more of a "tap" than a "knock". Maybe even just a "stroke". Anyway, the main thing was, the Merc had escaped unscathed.

He relaxed his back into the theatre seat. Romeo, played by Floyd Clansey, was superb, if a little too camp and more in love with himself than Juliet.

Please don't be dead, Daisy...

'Pitiful sight!' rasping voice of *First Watchman* jerked Max back into the theatre.

'And Juliet bleeding, warm, and newly dead...'

Scheiße.

Friday, May 20th

Daisy had spent the week bed-bound in the country, being nursed back to health by her doting parents. Daisy's mother fed her an overdose of overdone boiled eggs and soldiers, whilst her father dressed her cuts and grazes with honey and natural yoghurt, which he insisted would prevent scarring. She left the eggs but licked the yoghurt and honey, like a cat licked its paws.

Against the hackneyed backdrop of daytime television, Daisy had time to think. Too much time, perhaps. *'You shouldn't be left alone with a mind like yours, that's asking for trouble'* – she recalled Lucian's words.

Her parent's Internet had been down the entire week. It seemed to spend more time down then up. Daisy wondered why they bothered having a computer at all. It was a redundant box that stole an absurd amount of space and offered nothing in return. They bought their ginormous computer from a car boot sale, having recently discovered the Internet (a couple of decades after the rest of the world), and were confident their daughters would finally think them "cool" and "with it". They continued to explore modernity with suspicion and trepidation. Her mother still struggled to activate her mobile, and her father only referred to the radio as a wireless, and wondered why Daisy never replied to the texts he failed to press send on. With regards to being "cool" and "with it", Mr and Mrs Hawkins still had a long way to go.

Things were always down in the country, Daisy considered; falling, closing and breaking – trees, pubs, cars and the Internet. 'The Internet is down,' Daisy's parents had said during the car journey from the hospital. She was momentarily mad at them for not telling her earlier. Neither knew what "the Internet" actually was, nor what it meant to be "down", and least of all what this meant for Daisy – with her disabled mobile sporting its newly cracked screen, an email apologising for standing Lucian up would have to wait until she returned to London.

They had forgotten to exchange numbers. *Stupid oversight!* She could have called from the house phone, explained, apologised. At least she had a good excuse, she reflected, as she looked at her bruised face in the mirror and rewound the events in her mind. But the more she considered how to deliver her story, the more she doubted whether she should tell him at all: *'I stepped out of the cab, shut my dress in the door (what a moron!), walked into the road without looking right or left (I know, I know), was hit by a car, my dress unravelled and I lay on the ground practically starkers, before being taken to hospital, where I fell again, head over heels with a familiar handsome doctor. Anyway... I'm sorry. Really sorry. How did your night pan out in the end?'*

She sounded like an airhead and floozy; falling in love at every opportunity, turning a hospital into a pick-up joint. Plus, she sounded unlucky; what man would be attracted to a beacon for bad luck? Who would willingly put himself in permanent potential danger, especially for someone they had never met? Daisy decided that the truth would most certainly jeopardise Lucian ever agreeing to meet her again. She considered trimming back to reveal just a portion of the truth – the hit-and-run – but she always struggled with that, being an all or nothing kind of girl. She was held back from work, she would tell him, by the boss. But how would she explain the bruises and scrapes on her cheeks and her hand? If she claimed that her boss beat her black and blue, Hanratty could get arrested. It was an ex? She dabbled in self-harming? Daisy decided to cross that bridge when and if Lucian agreed to give her another chance, and by that time the marks may have gone.

Who had knocked her over anyway? And why? She couldn't think of a single person she had infuriated to the point they would want her *dead*. Maybe it had been an accident. If so, what type of person would hit someone and then just drive off? Maybe they had gone for the brake but under pressure had pressed the accelerator? Maybe it was a case of mistaken identity? Maybe the driver had been aiming for a girl who matched Daisy's description? A mistress perhaps, or a wife, who had just discovered the mistress and was a thorn in the affair…

The motives and identity of the mystery driver had occupied Daisy's thoughts and runaway with her imagination throughout the week and well into Friday.

As did a certain doctor. First the earplug, then the accident. 'We really must stop meeting like this,' Dr Cranston had said. She could think of worse grins to come around to, but could think of better circumstances; a hotel room in the South of France, for example. Looking up from her hospital bed at that dirty grin and those chocolate-drop eyes, she had felt that warm, tingly sensation (*down there*), and almost drifted back to wherever she had just come from.

She was mortified that Dr Oliver had seen her in her underwear – *un-matching too!* – but it hadn't put him off, promising he'd call to check up on her during the week.

She envisioned a date with Doctor Fox. She would insist on buying him the first round, of course, because she owed him. And he would tell her again all about his heroic rescue, and she would swoon, again. He had been passing, he'd said, and had witnessed almost everything before rushing her to hospital, where he stayed by her side all night, administering various procedures and dressing her wounds. He was her knight in shining armour. Where would she be without him in her life? Still lying on the road with the earplug still stuck down her ear…deaf to the next oncoming car…

Dr Oliver had every intention of getting in touch with Daisy, but there was no rush. She was on his list. He knew he was worth the wait because women always waited. The English tended to like waiting. They were attracted to queues like bees to honey; the longer the wait, the greater the hunger, and the more grateful they were when they got to the front. And *oh boy*, how he liked a grateful woman.

His career was time consuming. He had chosen not to do gynaecology (to avoid mixing business with pleasure) and settled for a career in emergency medicine. It was much like his love life – fast paced, no lasting relationship with his patients; he was more of a one-stop-shop… *Wham, bam*, thank you, ma'am. He spent vast amounts of his time within the hospital walls. His male colleagues complained that the hospital saved lives but killed love lives, but Dr Oliver knew the secret was playing it right. 'Play the hospital,' he would advise, through the haze of disinfectant and death, 'smell opportunity.' Oliver was sensitive to the merest whiff. Nurses, physiotherapists, secretaries, radiographers, house-officers, orderlies and even the occasional patient; he saw his stethoscope as a fanny magnet, and combined with his cheeky grin, it formed a lethal concoction. Just last week there had been Sofia, the pretty hospital caterer, who had served him breaded chicken; 'I'm on breading duty,' she had said forlornly.

'Fancy that,' he had replied as he passed her his plate, 'I'm on bedding duty.' One wink, and the rest was sweet history. Women just seemed to fall for him.

Oliver liked to think he provided bespoke services to cater for all. He liked to think he approached his professional responsibilities with imagination and originality. He liked to think he sent hearts aflutter, that the entire hospital was in love with him and his dirty grin.

And often (but not always), he was right.

Like Tara Forsyth, Dr Oliver did not lend time to love. Sex yes (and lots of it), but love, no. Like Tara, he was sceptical of its existence. When and if he ever did want love, he would probe its existence then. Dr Oliver was in control of his life, and it ticked along obediently to his timetable. Right now, his time was too precious to waste on love; if and when he did schedule it in, it would be controlled and simple.

Marcus had been going spare all week, unable to get hold of Eliza and unable to apologise for standing her up. He assumed she was furious. When she replied to his *'Hi!'* that Friday evening, with amiability, he felt nothing short of immense joy and relief. He readied his fingers for apologetic action, but as it transpired he could not get a word in edgeways. *She* apologised. She had not made the date either apparently…held back late at work, she said.

There seemed little point in telling her about his accidental evening with Daisy and his journey to hospital; how Daisy had been his priority. He wondered whether he would have been able to resist telling Eliza how he felt about Daisy – the girl he had never even spoken to. Or resist telling her every minute detail of Daisy's solemn perfection, the graceful stride in the scarlet dress, how she reminded him of the art of writing, with her inky eyes, pencil-thin legs and calligraphy hair. And how, somehow, she reminded him of her, Eliza, his soulmate – the girl he had never even seen. And how he had been cynical of the existence of soulmates, being another bizarre ideal for the deluded, and how he had been converted.

Thankfully, he was spared – he need not mention it at all.

They rearranged their date for the following Friday. Behind poker-faced words, both were elated and braced themselves for another achingly slow week.

Marcus was both relieved at his good fortune and slightly confused by the venue of their rearranged rendezvous.

It was Eliza who had suggested the pitch-dark restaurant, *Eclipse,* in the East End of London, so Lucian would never have to see the lingering cuts and bruises on her cheeks. She didn't want to risk jeopardising another date.

'I'm still nervous about meeting you in person,' she wrote. Until now, they had only shared black and white words and she was worried about the sensory overload – sound, sight…touch? *'One step at a time,'* she suggested, *'one sense at a time, OK?'*

Friday, May 27th

'Knock, knock,' Beth's voice rapped on Marcus's studio door, before her nose nudged it open. She delivered two steaming mugs of tea to artist and muse.

Beth leant down to where Tara reclined, this time on a white sheet shared with a still life of lemons. She placed the tea beside the folded edge of the sheet, within Tara's reach but not disturbing the set.

That's odd, thought Tara, as she thanked Beth for the tea. The oddity was not Beth's gaze, which lingered a moment too long on her body – she was used to that – but rather the ring which dangled from her necklace. She had seen it before and hadn't liked it then either. She traced it back to Daisy's un-manicured thumb. She had noticed it during one of their awkward moments in the kitchen at work.

It was identical: the same thick circular rim of tarnished silver and the crudity of the capital letters. It *must* have been the same ring that was on Daisy's finger, Tara decided, unable to imagine two separate incidents of such misguided taste; the ring should have been buried along with the 90s. Such fashion faux pas must surely be unique. Daisy must have given it to Beth as a gift. She hadn't realised the two were friends... But then why would she? She knew very little about Daisy Hawkins. Was the silver LOVE ring a sign of a "special friendship", perhaps? She considered the sexuality of Daisy Hawkins.

'Dunk your tips in this paint here, if you would be so kind,' Marcus asked Tara. She leant her chest towards the tray. 'No, your *tips*, not your – here look,' he took her right hand and gently placed her fingertips in the tray of blue paint, before asking her to press them against his canvas 'wherever you wish.'

Marcus wanted to explain his thoughts behind the fingerprint experiment. He began by telling her about Degas's clandestine brothel monotypes. What most fascinated him was the relationship between Degas and his subject.

Yeah, whatever, thought Tara, trying to look interested. She imprinted Marcus's painting of her with her fingertips; pressing and dipping, pressing and dipping, until blue egg-shapes scattered over her feet and lower thighs. Aware that she looked mighty fine, she stopped there to ensure Marcus's eyes still had easy access to her body. On the top right of the canvas she pressed a few fainter prints in the background. He did not interfere once, letting Tara leave her mark as much or as little as she desired.

'OK, that's it,' she said.

'You happy?'

She hesitated before a final press. 'Yes. Done.'

To win favour, she mustered all arty-farty lingo and told him she liked the colour combination – 'baby blue, lemon yellow and a fleshy rose. *Monochrome* would've been so boring... *uninspiring*.'

But it was precisely the black and white of Degas's brothel monotypes that Marcus found so intriguing.

Oh. She was gutted. She had gone to town on her colour description and now had nothing more to offer.

He liked the mystery and sense of secrecy created by light and shadow, perfect for illicit scenes, like the brothels. He was drawn to mystery, he told Tara – a concept so foreign to his perception of her.

He opened a book from his bookshelf to show Tara the black and white images of women displaying themselves, on show in some for a mysterious top-hatted gentleman and the gaze of the anonymous voyeuristic viewer. She noticed the animalistic faces, the prominent black nipples and the inexcusable unkempt pubic hair amongst the shadowy smudges and scratches.

Marcus pointed at Degas's fingerprints, clearly visible on some of the girls' flesh. 'It's an intriguing intimacy, don't you think? How would you interpret these? The male desire to own women? To control? D'you reckon his presence is gentle or aggressive?'

She recognised herself in some of their barefaced positions. *Is he the gentleman and...* 'Am I your untamed whore?' blurted Tara. She remembered how disgusted she had felt after waking next to Dr Oliver Cranston's pile of money. She refused to let *anyone* make her feel that cheap again.

'Quite the opposite, Tara. Our painting is symbolic of the modern woman – like you – empowering and in control. Your fingerprints interrupt and control your body and the viewer's gaze. It's your body after all, do what you like. Anyway, an interesting experiment, I thought.' He watched her stifle a yawn. 'OK. Lecture over.' He smiled.

'So who wins?' she asked.

She was competitive – it was his turn to yawn. 'You do, Tara. Women win every time. Which reminds me,' he checked his watch, 'I have a date in about half an hour.'

'With the mysterious Eliza?' she snapped.

'How the hell did you know that?'

'It's not rocket science, whittling one down to…err…one.' Eliza was the only name he had ever mentioned *in that way.*

'Genius,' he muttered, as he left his studio with a handful of dirty brushes. He decided to call his painting *The Distance Between Us.* Fingertips or no fingertips, they would never be close. Himself and Tara. Always worlds apart.

Bloody "Eliza", thought Tara. She was sick of hearing that name. What did Eliza have that she hadn't? Such an *ugly* name too. She had felt some progression during the fingerprinting quality bonding session. It had been sweet and intimate. Marcus had valued her interaction, and he had *wanted* to teach her about mono printing, or whatever the fuck it was called. Unlike Eliza, Tara had painstakingly *earned* Marcus, through time and patience. She was ready to dunk her tits in blue paint for him, for fuck's sake! She wasn't displaying herself like an untamed whore for nothing!

Her eyes fell on his mobile phone, which lay on his brother's camp bed. Without losing a second to deliberation, she grabbed it and scrolled down to find *Eliza.* Then *compose text. Quickly, quickly!*

'Sorry, but I need to cancel tonight,' she typed, 'Something's come up.'

She could hear Marcus's footsteps mount the stairs. *Send. Shit!* She noticed flustered blue fingerprints all over the digits. As she heard him nearing the studio door, she flung the phone as far as she could under Jasper's bed. With any luck it would land in a hidey-hole amongst magazines, dirty socks, and whatever other sticky horrors festered beneath old public school boys' beds. She washed her guilty hands and buttoned her pounding heart in her coat, before making her way to the studio door. There she stopped and turned, and with one hand caressing the knob and a finger running down the frame, she cocked a knee seductively and said, 'You know, that's not the first time I've fingered myself during a boring History of Art Lecture.' She winked and disappeared down the stairs.

Daisy was gutted and so was Jude.

The girls were mid-wardrobe session at Daisy's flat, excitedly trying on dresses for the date in pitch dark.

'It's from Lucian!' shrieked an elated Jude, as she glanced at Daisy's phone after it beeped a text – the two had finally swapped numbers.

'I'm stuck, can you read it,' asked Daisy from inside a dress.

'Oh no…' said Jude. '*Bastard!*'

'What?' asked Daisy as she wriggled in claustrophobic irritation.

'Oh no…' repeated Jude.

'WHAT?'

'Oh n–'

'JUDE, for fuck's sake! He's cancelled?'

'I'm so sorry.'

'What did he say?'

'Something came up, apparently… Oh Daise, I'm sorry.' Five minutes of pushing, pulling and ripping until Jude helped her friend free from a cream Lycra straitjacket.

Determined not to let the entire Friday evening drown in a teary puddle, Jude made baby-sitting arrangements with Will and threw Daisy her jeans, before steering her to the Notting Hill Arts Club for music and shots.

The evening turned out to be memorable in a way Marcus had not predicted: being stood up in a blackened restaurant, drinking a bottle of wine on his own, and chowing down on God-only-knows, whilst listening to giddy couples explore sharpened flavours, smells and each other made for a remarkable evening, and one he would rather forget.

He had lost his phone. *Of all nights!* He berated himself. *What was the point of exchanging numbers when you go and lose your phone?* He was sure Eliza would have a good excuse. She was considerate. He presumed she had texted. Perhaps she had been held back after work again? He found comfort in the black surroundings of the restaurant. Bloody Internet dating, bloody Beth and Floyd for putting him on to it – he hadn't wanted to in the first place. Bloody Eliza, for not showing up. Bloody him for caring. Why did he? No one could see his cheeks burn with frustration and his eyes sting with disappointment. He burrowed into the dark and a second bottle of wine.

Had he been sober, he would not have taken a fairly circuitous detour via Heathrow on the tube, before finally stumbling home. Had he been sober, he would have been more perplexed to see Tara Forsyth, his life model, waiting expectantly on his doorstep. Had he been sober, he would not have gone to bed with her. In the darkness of his studio they probed the intensity of touch. Fingerprints battled for domination on each other's flesh.

Tara had known Marcus would drip home at some point with his tail between his legs. She had waited on his doorstep for longer than she would have for any other guy. But she wanted sex, that's all, she reassured herself as she felt an unfamiliar feeling bubble in the pit of her stomach. Sex. *Just sex.* She refused to entertain the fact that actually she wanted more, that somewhere she yearned for a lifetime of love from Marcus True.

Mistakenly, she thought one night of cold passion would be enough to knock the bothersome feeling on the head.

Jude felt uncomfortable, caught in the crossfire of flirtatious exchange between Daisy and Jasper True. Jude had recognised him immediately as the singer from Orlaith's wedding. His voice and arrogant swagger were unmistakable. Sadly, her best friend recognised him too, so a swift exit was not to be. The last time these two had been together, Jude recalled they had knotted in a drunken heap of spaghetti limbs, which had required enormous efforts from both herself and the pretty waiter to detangle.

But tonight, despite not drinking, and with her judgment intact, Jude didn't have the heart to interrupt Daisy's unforeseen smiles and the inebriated intimacy between the pair. She left them to stroke each other's skinny-jeaned thighs and drink vodka shots until the early hours of the morning.

There was undeniable chemistry between the two, thought Jude as she walked home, sober as a judge, to her husband and baby. She had noticed it first at the wedding. It was wired and intense, and for reasons that escaped her she didn't like it one bit. There was a sting in the electricity. She was sure she would be cursing herself tomorrow for leaving Daisy alone with Jasper True.

Marcus passed Tara Daisy's red dress. As usual, she had arrived naked under her coat. Assuming it was Beth's, Tara took it. An extra layer was needed in the nippy morning air. She desperately wanted to stay, to wake together. But she had got what she came for, she told herself strictly, as she downed her glass of wine on the bedside table.

Through hammered vision and the haze of morning light, Jasper wandered home from Daisy's Warren, sniffing out any bars that might happen to still be open.

He noticed a woman walking towards him. She looked like a king penguin with a scarlet plumage. The sides of her black coat were like wings. Was he in the Antarctic? Was she swaying or was it him?

'Hello,' he said, trying his luck.

'Hello,' Tara replied. She didn't usually talk to strangers, but alcohol slackened the rules and fuzzed her vision. She saw ten of the guy, vaguely recognised each but couldn't place any. She noticed his eye twitch frantically, like he had overdosed on speed. She felt his gigantic pupils pulsate on her breasts.

Sabotaged by boozy wonder, he fell to the pavement, leaving his scarlet plumed mate to continue her course home.

Friday, June 3rd

What better way to enter June than with a full heart, thought Daisy, as the train cut through the countryside, dividing fields and hamlets onto neat slices. Her head was full of thoughts of Jasper True, and an album of beautiful pastoral postcards slipped by unnoticed.

What was it about him? she wondered, as he disappeared down the carriage in search of the loos. He was magnetic. He was addictive. He was captivating. He was spontaneous. Last night, in a whirl of energy he booked "the honeymoon suite" at a luxury boutique hotel in the countryside (*How cool is that?*). He had grinned and twitched with excitement.

'I'm on a writer's salary,' Daisy had warned, as her stomach buckled beneath pound signs. But he insisted he would cover all the costs. *All the costs!* (The mini-bar bill would be enough to bankrupt her.) Then he had twitched and smiled again, the corners of his mouth lurched into his cheeks, as if controlled by a puppeteer.

The alcohol they had consumed during the past week had numbed the butterflies in her stomach. She knew they wanted to flutter with jubilation and ride the echoes of her heartbeat, but they were lightweights and had slumped, defeated at the pit of her stomach with heavy wings and thumping heads. She knew if they could, they would be fluttering like crazy. For she was in love with Jasper True! Even through the anaesthetising effect of alcohol, she felt its awesome might.

She had been out every night that week to his bar, *Jazbar*, and then onto gigs to watch him and other bands play in dark dens. She had rubbed sweaty shoulders and drunk with children of famous 60s rockers in grimy bars, and ex public school kids, too cool for school, rebelling against their privileged upbringing. The week had slipped by in a gluttonous haze of licentiousness and lasciviousness. Money was poured like alcohol. She drank beyond intimidation, burnt the candle at both ends and had the time of her life. *Old Daisy* would have shied away from all this, but now she liked the griminess and seediness of these lairs and those who partied within; it was raw and real. It was cool, and so, she felt, was she.

She felt dejected by the lies and pretences of life. She thought of Max, Floyd, and *Sainthill Publications* with their stream of glossy covers, the airbrushing, the vanity, the bullshit... And she thought about what it meant to be 30; diamond rings, marriage, babies – her womb could rot for all she cared – the pressure of it all... The bullshit of social conventions, brainwashing, consumerism, materialism, crooked expectations... She felt ashamed for allowing phoniness to fester in her life.

A new perspective clotted the air of this underworld and she breathed it in. She drank through the layers of crap with Jasper True.

Together they made electricity. He lit matches of energy or bonfires of spirit, and she sizzled and burnt with ecstasy. She was Bonnie, and Jasper was Clyde, and their motto was "fuck you"; it felt incredible to be on his arm.

There and then on the train, as Jasper wobbled back from the loos sniffing and wiping white powder from his nose with the back of his hand, she had a sudden urge to strip and embrace him, to feel flesh on flesh, to feel nature at its purist, to feel free and alive.

She sat opposite him. Her feet rested on the seat next to him. An elderly man in the adjacent seat noticed and frowned. She saw his forehead scrunch but she kept them there in defiance. *Fuck you.* Defiance felt good.

By nature, she was neither rebellious nor attention-seeking. Her views were liberal but shrouded in conservatism to control potential embarrassment of anarchy. Now, she felt ashamed of her old self and cursed her cowardliness. She had been a subordinate to society for too long. What had she gained from being such an exemplary cog in the social machine? *Fuck all, that's what.* Looking back at *Old Daisy*, she saw a pawn in the social structure, who sacrificed identity and freedom to abide by rules and expectations. *Pathetic! Loser!*

Without Jasper, she realised, she might never have experienced *real life*. His energy was everything. It resisted restraint. He lived in a world of his own, where he was free, and she was grateful he took her with him; there she was thriving.

She knew she was caught in his dynamic web. She begged him to spin through every nook in her body. It was a strange feeling, she considered, to feel so trapped yet so free.

In a week Daisy had changed. Not only physically – she wore blacker, tighter jeans and thicker eyeliner, and a raven lipstick, which matched her newly dyed black hair. But mentally too, she had hardened, due perhaps to lingering heartache and all the messy feelings involved: loss, hurt, betrayal, inadequacy. She was building her walls of defence. Her cocoon against the world.

As the train began to slow, Jasper leant forward to lick a trace of wine from her lips, before bounding up to grab their luggage from the rack.

In her emptiness, she felt full; in her insecurity, she felt secure; and in her weakness she felt strong. In tipsiness she felt the reality of these illusions. She needed no one but Jasper. It was themselves – and their nocturnal friends – against the world.

Jasper sucked the final drops from the bottle as the train ground to a halt. As they alighted, Daisy stuck two fingers up to the world for its greed, ingratitude and disloyalty. The idyllic English countryside was the undeserved scapegoat. As the train left the station Jasper hurled the bottle. Daisy watched the sharp shards litter the tracks. *Fuck you!*

That night in their honeymoon suite Daisy had a nightmare.

There she was, on the train of life, where she had been an obliging passenger for thirty years. The driver was a government official. His big belly housed life's rich pickings. The train chugged through the years of school and university, and when it reached dating, it began to choke and Daisy fell and landed on a dirt track. But the train did not stop. After all those years! It abandoned her. Just like that. *Fuck you!* She watched the government official at the front of the train shake his head with disappointment. She watched her friends, some waved and others looked ashamed that they had been friends at all. Some were successful businesswomen, some successful mothers, others successful jugglers of the two. The train snaked on before curving a corner and disappearing into the future.

That's when Jasper came along. Her Samaritan. He rescued her from the dirt track. She looked up at him in awe. Then she saw his flesh turn into paint and his eyes hollow, blacken and swirl around and around. They engorged with every rotation and grumbled thunderous hunger. She watched as they greedily sucked in the entire surroundings: the dirt track with its clumps of mud and stone, the grasses, fields and houses, brick by brick, then the contents, mothers breastfeeding babies, men reading books in the bath… Until entire hamlets had vanished. Then he turned to the whole of Britain, and his eyes unpicked with ease. Next he fed the entire universe down those insatiable black holes, until there was nothing left but him and her. They walked on nothing, for the dirt track had gone. They walked to nowhere, because the future had gone. They could not turn back because the damage had been done. She was scared.

He turned to her, with those big black eyes, swirling hypnotically like a carousel on speed. *No. Not me*, she pleaded. But it was too late. She was sucked towards one eye. She resisted and spanned her arms outwards as far as they could reach. Her gripping fingers curved around at the corners of his eye. Her legs stretched as far as they would go. She was like a starfish straddling the nozzle of suction. But she touched paint rather than flesh, and the longer they were there, the drier she felt his skin become. Drier and drier until bits of paint began to flake away. His face eroded. Then the suction stopped. Daisy fell like a fragile star-flake. She looked up at a familiar painted face of an eroding boy with hollow eyes. Jasper was the boy in the painting *Echo*. He was the boy on the walls at that exhibition. He was the brother of the artist, Marcus True, whom Tara Forsyth was fucking…

She woke.

Only a dream, she reassured herself, trying hard to stave off analysis. She was scared that analysis might spew up unwanted suggestions that she was in a "dangerous relationship" or something equally absurd. Besides, she thought, Lucian never analysed dreams, and he was pretty much always right. It was they, Jasper and Daisy, Bonnie and Clyde, together always against the world, and nothing else mattered. *So fuck you all.*

She took the bottle from the bedside table and wet her mouth with whiskey.

Friday, June 10th

Daisy insisted she was "finally herself", which was odd, thought Jude, who had not recognised her friend for a fortnight. Along with everyone else, she had noticed the changes; her permanently hung-over state, her weight-loss and black attire from top to toe. It looked like she had shovelled the grime of London's streets into her eye-bags. She looked tired and dirty. The wrong Daisy had fallen in with the wrong crowd and the wrong bloke.

Daisy said she was happy, which was odd, thought Jude, who had not seen her friend smile once as she awaited Jasper's texts with nerves gnawing her weight.

Daisy said she felt "alive", which was odd, thought Jude, who had never seen her friend look so lifeless.

Jude hoped that this was just a phase – one that most girls rid from their system during teenage years. This anarchy, this rebellion, this "playing the field" with "dangerous" guys…just a phase…

'She's lost, isn't she?' said Mrs Hawkins, that evening from the other end of the phone. Jude had had a difficult day at work followed by a difficult trip to the supermarket with a bawling Millie. She had a headache and didn't feel up to distributing empty reassurance about someone she loved. *Not tonight, please.*

'Yup, I'm afraid I think she is,' she replied. On hearing Mrs Hawkins's heavy sigh, she added, 'temporarily though.' She caught sight of her heaving supermarket bags. 'Imagine she's in a supermarket, lost in a bad section…like the frozen section where she's getting cold, and err…' Both Jude and Mrs Hawkins wondered where she was going with this. 'Well, whatever section she's in, and however bad it may be, it's temporary, as the exit is just a few aisles away. Don't worry Margot, she'll be found very soon, I'm sure, and we're all here to steer her in the right direction.'

'And that boy. Her *friend*. That Jasper. I don't like the sound of him one bit. She's been drinking a lot with him, hasn't she? Talks like he's *everything*. Oh what's wrong with her? Perhaps I should frog march her to the doctor's to re-test that funny heart of hers? Maybe they'll find something this time? She says she's *in love* with him! She's only known him two weeks, for Pete's sake!'

'Just lust, Margot, or infatuation. She's not in love. I've seen it in her a lot since Jesse. And that feeling is pretty shallow and can't survive. Honestly. Just a matter of time 'til she'll be back to her good old self, I'm sure.'

Jude calmed Margot but failed to calm herself. She had said Daisy's work had not been affected, but the truth was, it had – in both a positive and a negative way. On the negative side, Daisy had turned up late over the last two weeks. Every single morning. On the positive side, she had watched Hanratty congratulate Daisy for her increasingly 'raw' and 'un-frilly' use of language in *Musings of a Pisces*. Jude had read some of her fan mail earlier that day. *'It's refreshing that you're honest with us about love and life,'* said one. (*Refreshing* was a recurring word.) *'Your direct approach is enlivening, Eliza,'* said another. *'Thanks for the absence of patronising preaching,'* and, *'Thanks for your friendship in a time of loneliness.'* There were heaps.

Just a phase, Jude prayed, as she unpacked her shopping. Three times she threw a lemon into the back of the fridge; three times it rolled out in defiance. Just a phase, she hoped, hurling it back in again and knocking over a bottle of wine.

That piss-head-waster Jasper True, she thought bitterly, was seriously bad news. She unscrewed the bottle and uncharacteristically took a generous swig to calm herself.

It was an unusually chilly evening for June. The month began on a sunny note, but unable to agree on a tune, had become increasingly unsettled.

Marcus looked up to the sky before lighting the BBQ in his backyard.

Floyd opened a bottle of Pinot Noir, a gift from a love-struck fan to her Romeo. *'You grabbed Romeo by the balls,'* wrote a lady called Luise, *'and I fantasise about doing the same.'* This was one of many adoring notes and bottles of wine that Floyd had received for his acclaimed performance in the West End.

In a bowl Marcus made a marinade, using any bottle from the fridge that took his fancy. Beth checked on the potatoes, which were boiling away, and popped the broccoli into a pan. Floyd fumbled in the music cupboard and rifled through his party lists. Tonight he was in the mood to celebrate his outstanding reviews, but the current atmosphere was far too sombre. He hoped he might get Marcus in the mood to celebrate too.

None of them had been particularly delighted with the news that Jasper, of all people, had got together with Daisy Hawkins. The irony was rather amusing really, Floyd thought. He had been pissed off, Beth had been heartbroken, as had Marcus – to a far more worrying, and curious, degree, considering he had never even spoken to Daisy. Marcus was indeed perplexing. He was an archetypal artist: mad, aloof, eccentric and mysterious. He knew Marcus better than most, but sometimes he wondered if he knew him at all.

'Daisy?' Marcus repeated, after Jasper broke the news earlier that week. *'You* are madly in love with *Daisy?'*

'Yes and yes, bro! I actually met her months ago at that country wedding. She's a good person!'

I know!

'I'm happy, ecstatic in fact!'

So you fucking should be.

Marcus's heart felt the enormous punches that each word delivered, and his vision became blurred as the tears welled.

To get Marcus off his back and to give himself a break from the increasing pressure to go to rehab, he lied, 'I don't drink with her. She's like therapy. But way cheaper!' Jasper had chuckled then. 'She's an angel, mate,' he added.

Marcus had known she was an angel all along, from the first moment he had seen her at The Gemini Gallery... *Or was it on Elgin Avenue, or at Jazbar, or the funfair?*

'What do you do together?' Marcus probed, curious.

'You know. Normal stuff. Stuff that couples do.' *What the hell do normal couples do?* Jasper searched his mind blindly; he had long forgotten the protocol.

'Like watching TV on the sofa together. Old movies, massages, strolls along the Thames, stuff like that.'

Marcus tried to imagine Daisy curled on the sofa with his brother; the angelic sober not the demonic drunk. Two angels entwined together. But he was unable to do so. Was it jealousy alone that prevented him imagining them together in utopia?

Instead, he pictured his painting *Butterfly Echo*, showing Daisy in her scarlet dress standing before his brother's wildly inhaling wind-tunnel eyes – this image seemed more realistic and his heart felt another colossal punch.

'Look after her.'

'She makes me happy,' Jasper had repeated, 'and she's good for me.'

'Be good for her too. Do you promise?'

'Yes, *Dad*, I promise!'

After that conversation with his brother, he had turned to Eliza for comfort, for reassurance, for friendship – *for love?* But she never got back to him.

He seasoned the bloody steaks, spooned over more marinade and seared them in the frying pan.

He thought of them together again, and felt the roar of jealousy. *No!* He would not allow it. He loved his brother more than anything, and if Jasper was happy, then so was he. Simple as that. If Jasper was healing because of Daisy, then his happiness was complete.

He hoped Jasper would keep his promise and be good for Daisy. But he felt incomplete and anxious as he slapped the wet steaks onto the BBQ; from the frying pan into the fire, he thought grimly.

Friday, June 17th

That's a Boston terrier, thought Daisy as she walked into work that morning. She had become quite the connoisseur of dog breeds. She watched the dog turn to bite the handle of his lead, which was trailing behind, and give it back to his owner. With the knowledge that his master was holding his lead, he continued walking in confident contentment with a wide beam on his face.

Daisy listened to love songs on full blast and revelled in the burning sensation reverberating in her eardrum. She devoured every sad and angry word and each took on new meaning. She felt the cool air sweep her face whilst she watched the different breeds of dogs sniff, limp, wag and play. She loved the golden retrievers with their big soppy eyes and grinning faces. She watched the joggers, the roller-bladers and the power walkers. She noticed the leaves fall to the ground, and looking up allowed her mind to swim freely in the expanse of the sky. She savoured the beauty of today's face of nature. She was painfully reactive to all sensations, and she had never felt so dead and so alive.

She sucked like a leech on those fleeting moments of calm.

Again, she arrived to a pile of letters on her desk and a full inbox. Her readers' words of thanks comforted her. She did not realise this, but she had never needed them more than now. For the first time, she reached to her "friends" like they reached to her.

Concerned about Daisy's decreasing weight, Jude enquired what she was having for lunch; but her words fell on deaf ears. Daisy was unaware that she had zoned out to anything that did not resemble simple acceptance, outside of Jasper and his world. She avoided calls from all those who loved her. Some flaky friends from *Sainthill Publications* deserted her, opting to preserve their reputation. *'She had always been slightly odd; what's with the gothic phase? Tragically last season!'* Frenzied gossip scrambled the stairwell.

Jude longed to have her best friend back, to tell her the positive news. Twenty-four white pregnancy sticks showing pink crosses confirmed that a growing baby was responsible for the last two months of apple munching.

What a sweet image! thought Daisy, as she walked back home through Hyde Park that afternoon. In the distance she saw a silhouette of a child with his mother. The boy held a balloon. Daisy watched as his mother kneeled to secure the balloon around his wrist, to stop it floating away. Daisy watched as the boy skipped and spun around, watching the balloon follow obediently and bop and groove like a puppet on a string. As she got closer, she saw the boy pick up a stick. At first he included it in his dance and seemed delighted with his two props. He yanked the balloon up and down in the air and wiggled the stick between his fingers. But soon he tired of this.

Three's a crowd, Daisy thought gloomily; one of them had to go. She thought of Jasper and his addictions.

The boy stabbed it with his stick, just as she was passing.

She jumped with fright. *Am I the balloon?*

But there were *not* three in their relationship, she reassured herself, so no one needed to pop. He *used* to be an addict. *Past tense.* Now he only *'dabbled'* in drink and drugs, so they were no longer a permanent feature. That's what Jasper told her anyway.

She wished her family and friends would lay off, particularly Jude. Lucian kept trying to get in contact too. She could do without his righteous words and nauseating wisdom right now. He could save the lecture for someone who cared, or someone he had actually bothered to meet! Who was he to pass judgement on her? Besides, Lucian was the one who had told her to wrap herself in a protective cocoon and look after number one, and that's exactly what she was doing – just with Jasper too, and the rest of the world could bugger off.

Daisy knew nothing about drugs. She had been offered various pills and powders but had only smoked marijuana, which obviously didn't count – *who hadn't?* Jasper assured her that his "problem" was dead and buried, and that dabbling was just a bit of fun – which was fair enough, she decided; you're only young once.

The past week had been detox week, 'to flush those stubborn toxins that refuse to budge!' Jasper had explained brightly. She had witnessed him withdrawing several containers at a time from his cupboard. 'These,' he had explained as he wolfed down at least eight rainbow-coloured pills with a clear liquid she hoped was water, 'help my hair re-grow!' He chuckled and twitched manically. 'And these ones cleanse the toxins.' Another glug. 'And these, my sweetness, my light, my life–' he checked the back of the bottle, 'make me look se-e-xy!' He pouted before a final glug. 'Da-da! Have they worked yet?' He grinned wildly at her; the puppeteer jigged at the corners of his mouth. She had laughed and nodded her head enthusiastically.

Daisy's heart fluttered at the memory. You couldn't fault him for trying, she thought with pride, as she neared the Park gates.

Tonight they were celebrating the end of detoxing. She wondered what dabbling lay in store.

Later that evening, Daisy lay in Jasper's empty bath and bathed in warm exhilarating bliss.

'I'm going to marry you, Daisy Hawkins,' he said to her.

She blew an imaginary bubble at him. 'You can't leave me alone,' she giggled.

'You're damn right!' He grinned and took another swig of vodka. His pupils dilated, swollen with passion and excitement.

In the unfilled bath, with Jasper's words, as hollow and fragile as bubbles, Daisy made herself believe that she was blissfully happy. She tried to blame her mounting jitteriness and agitation on the booze, but the rabble of butterflies in her tummy didn't buy it and flapped until they choked on vodka fumes and she thought she might puke.

Friday, July 1st

Hurrah, thought Max. It was July 1st, which was a very good thing indeed. It was the start of the stag stalking season in Scotland, and he was away for a week with his father and a much-anticipated week away from his fiancé.

He looked at Luise. It was early and she was still asleep. These were his favourite moments. She looked so angelic, so pretty...

The calm before the storm. The lull before the psychological massacre.

He practised moving with stealth and slipped out of bed. He hoped to make it out of the house before the gales stirred. He would vent his frustrations on a stag.

Daisy had not heard from Jasper in over twenty-four hours. Having become addicted to doting texts sent at least every hour, these post-binge waits were loaded with angst. She too felt the brittle ache of withdrawal. She left work at lunchtime, muttering something about 'Doctor's appointment' to Hanratty, whilst pointing to her ovary area, and got a cab to Jasper's flat. Her heart pounded.

On her hands and knees she collected the glass shards and carefully scrubbed white powder from between Jasper's floorboards. She washed a prostitute's greasy hand marks from the bed head and peeled the condoms from the sheets. She spring cleaned lovingly and rinsed away the vice.

She put him to bed and stroked his brow, and wiped the intoxicated apologies that dribbled from his mouth. His body shook familiarly with the pain of withdrawal.

'Don't ever leave me,' he begged. 'I need you.' He clung to her and fell asleep.

He needs me. Relief rattled her bones like chilly wind through a forest. Her heart trembled like a leaf before it falls to the ground. He was so childlike and everything felt so fragile. There was no place she would rather be and nothing she would not do for him.

Jasper had decided he didn't need Marcus. He didn't need him to care for him, because he had Daisy. He didn't need him to rescue him, because he had Daisy. He didn't need him to protect him, support him, cook for him or clean his flat after a binging session...because he had Daisy. He didn't need his brother's love either anymore. Daisy offered hers in abundance, and it came with added benefits. The best bit was that he did not need to apologise to Marcus anymore, or feel faulty, ashamed, humiliated, belittled...or feel like Marcus had won and he had lost. Because *he* had won Daisy. He knew deep inside him, with an overwhelming clarity and zero doubt, what she and Marcus could have had together and how perfect they might have been, but meddling with Life's plan gave Jasper a sense of empowerment.

At *Portrait of a Boy*, Jasper had witnessed that loaded look that shot between the two of them like a bullet in slow motion, so intense it would have annihilated anything in its path. He had stood there watching. Mesmerised. Jasper the voyeur, trespassing in the most precious intimate moment between two people. Then Daisy had fainted, before either brother had the chance to speak to her.

Threatened by their perfect match, and the chemistry he himself had witnessed, Jasper intended to do all he could to keep them from meeting, whilst tarnishing the good man's name until Daisy detested Marcus and refused – *of her own free will* – to ever meet him.

Daisy slid into a seated position to check her mail on Jasper's laptop, which lay next to the bed. He snuggled against her leg and generally slept soundly, but every now and then his body tensed, his teeth ground together, and his hands squeezed her thigh so tightly that she had to cover her mouth for fear of waking him with a cry.

Since Daisy had been with Jasper, she had neither time nor inclination to converse with Lucian. Jasper required her 24/7. But a new email from Lucian not only caught her eye, it held it, and her heart and fingers twitched to respond.

'I've just drunk the same wine I drank at our date in the dark restaurant. The bottle is as empty as your seat was, and how I now feel. From the moment I stepped into our dark date, I have not seen the light. I miss it. I miss your words, Eliza. I miss you. It seems like ages since our last conversation. I measure my emptiness by it. Sad, but true. I am a sad mad man writing to no one. Tapping on keys and hurling words into space. I wonder if you'll ever be out there to catch them again.'

'I'm here.'

[Pause]

'Eliza?'

'You went to meet me at the restaurant?'

'Hi! Yes, of course.'

'Why?'

'Because we had a date. And I wanted to meet you.'

'Then why did you cancel?'

'What?'

'You cancelled.'

'I most certainly did not. Why would I do that?'

'You texted me. Remember? "Something came up," you said.'

'No way. Absolutely not.'

'It must have been an unremarkable "something" if you can't even remember. Here, I'm looking at it now. Sender Lucian. I'll text it back so you can see for yourself.'

'I have a new number, new phone...I lost my phone the night of our dark date. Believe me. I didn't send that, I would never.'

'OK then. A mystery?'

'A technical hiccup...' Or did someone hijack my phone? *'I would ask you out again, third time lucky, but I'm guessing you're back in love with some hopeless bloke who doesn't deserve you.'*

Daisy looked down at Jasper, and felt his dribble against her thigh. *'He is NOT hopeless.'*

The disappointment was intense. *'Are you happy?'*

[Pause]

'I'm in love.'

No shit. 'And he loves you?'

'He needs me.'

'Are you happy?'

[Pause]

'Well, I'm in love, aren't I?'

'Only you know that. Anyway, I guess I'm just pleased he isn't hopeless.'

[Pause]

'It's not his fault.'

'What's not?'

And the barrier lifted and her words poured out.

'He drinks a bit too much, Lucian. OK, like a lot too much. Loads. Like in one night, more than the average man might drink if you crammed together a year's worth of Friday nights. It's happy hour almost every hour. But it isn't happy – not for me anyway. Not if I'm honest with myself. Which hurts by the way, more than I can explain. And drugs and stuff, there's lots of that going on; don't quiz me, I'm no expert. He's secretive, but I know he takes them. Then he detoxes insanely. Obsessively. And I stay to help because he wants me to. One minute he says he can't live without me, threatens to kill himself if I go, but the next minute he can't stand the sight of me, shoves my clothes in a bag and throws it at me, telling me to fuck off. I've seen scenes I never expected to see. Felt things I never knew I could feel. Good stuff and bad stuff and then on top of all that I might lose my job and...'

'OK, Eliza. I've heard enough and I get the picture more accurately than I'd like to be honest...I'll help you through this, I promise. I know someone very similar you see, suffering the same, so I can completely understand. He's getting better now though, so there's hope for everyone. Would your guy consider rehab? There are some great places.'

'Yes, he considers all the time, but refuses to go.'

'Why not? Money?'

She glanced around Jasper's plush pad. *'No, money's not the issue.'*

'So why won't he go to a treatment centre, so he can be helped by professionals, rather than use you, Eliza?'

'Why? You think I'm not good enough?'

'Too bloody good, damn it! Can't you see that?'

'His brother refuses to let him go.'

'Why? What's his problem?'

'He's that artist Marcus True. You may have heard of him. His most profitable subject is his brother, Jasper – my boyfriend. So if you are a selfish bastard, like Marcus, why send the source of your income to rehab for months on end and risk fucking up your career? And if you are a loving selfless guy, like Jasper, why risk doing this to your brother?'

Marcus's stomach lurched. His fingers froze. His head pulled together black pieces of a jigsaw puzzle he was fearful to complete.

[Pause]

'Exactly! You wouldn't,' she answered for him.

[Pause]

'Lucian? You still there?'

'Sorry. Yes. Here. Thinking.' Words spurted discordantly. *'That sounds bad. Bad situation. His brother, a selfish bastard. As you say.'*

'Yup. I don't ever want to meet Marcus True. Guess there will be awkward family BBQs and stuff, but I'll try to avoid them. I hate him.'

Hate lodged in his throat.

'Where are your words of wisdom, Lucian? I need them. Please. I need them.'

[Pause]

'Lucian?'

[Pause]

'I really fucking need you right now.'

But he had gone.

Offline or off their fucking head. What was it with the men in her life right now?

She looked down at Jasper and felt like a traitor. Some dark thought or deep discomfort made his body lurch violently, and he dug his nails into her flesh again. She smothered her mouth but welcomed the deserved punishment of pain.

In a rage Marcus picked up his new phone and began to dial Jasper's number. *The bastard!* His eyes blurred with water. He messed up the numerical sequence. On hearing his call had not been recognised, he threw it against the back wall of his bedroom. 'No, I'm fucking sorry my brother has not been recognised,' Marcus mimicked the fem-bots voice. *My brother? My brother spinning such twisted lies? Injecting himself with fuck knows what, and injecting her with lies and hatred. How dare he? What reason have I given for him to hate me? Lying to Daisy. Lying to Eliza! Daisy is Eliza.*

My God.

Daisy is Eliza.

That night, insomnia embraced a medley of curdling emotions into its chilly bosom and together they danced on Marcus's brain until night tapped into morning. It was a party from hell.

Daisy is Eliza.

Friday, July 8th

It was lunchtime. The office was quiet. It had been for a while now. If it wasn't for the generic office whir, thought Jude, you could hear a staple drop.

Daisy barely said a thing these days. She just floated in and out like silk-gauze curtains in a breeze. No one noticed that she was late anymore; one minute her seat was empty and the next it was full. Well, about a third full, Jude corrected. Daisy picked at food like a bird. Her mind, body and soul were full of Jasper.

Jude wanted to ring his scrawny neck, yank tufts from his feathery hair – or give him a damn good talking to at the very least. But Daisy had been far from forthcoming in initiating a meeting so Jude had not had the chance. Besides, she doubted whether Jasper was ever in an appropriate state to meet anyone. She had rifled through album upon album of photographs, showing him drinking and dancing like an idiot on his Facebook profile page – so self-indulgent, such blatant vanity.

Jude missed *Old Daisy* and their lunchtime laughter. From her desk she watched her sip black coffee and flick though an old issue of *Sabre*. Having offered Daisy a helping of last night's lasagne, which she brought in especially, Daisy shyly opted for another liquid lunch. What am I meant to do? thought Jude. Ram it down her throat? Is that what friends do?

Opening the latest issue of *Nimbus*, Jude turned to *Musings of a Pisces*; perhaps this might shed some light on her friend's state of mind? But she was disappointed. What writing Daisy did offer consisted of light words with no substance at all. They were abstract and whimsical beyond comprehension.

Her neglected *Ask Eliza* readers had grumbled in her inbox: *'Our problems can't vanish as easily as your column!'* Through desperation they forgave their Eliza and continued to write to her in droves, until Daisy was beaten into submission and opened the gates to her precious *Musings* space, to share with her *friends*. They bulldozed their way in; their issues were published. Daisy's own *Musings* became a breezy backdrop for their moans. In a nutshell, Jude surmised, Daisy was doing the minimum amount of work possible.

Daisy shared nothing of her own relationship and problems with her readers, perhaps, thought Jude, because she refused to see her relationship as a problem. Or perhaps to avoid feedback she did not wish to hear. Jude could only gauge how she might be feeling deep inside, by her change in appearance and nature. Daisy took the time to read their dilemmas; she sacrificed space for them to express themselves. In a sense, she listened, which is, thought Jude, ultimately what anyone troubled really wants. It was their own voice – their own words – they cared about, all they wanted to do was vent, and that suited Daisy perfectly. Advice falls on deaf ears to those who do not wish to hear it. Unable to offer judgment or advice, and resenting the thought of being offered them herself, she nurtured a friendship based on silent acceptance, and gave little of herself away.

Jude hoped Daisy found solace when she read her *friends'* tribulations; they offered a temporary departure from her own. She guessed it must be easier to embrace friends with no faces. Their fragile identity consisted of a cluster of black and white words, ingredients for an easy, disposable friendship. If they overstepped the mark, wrote things that touched a nerve, she could edit them in an instant.

Jude was grateful that Daisy had this relationship with her readers – even if, at best, it was flimsy. It was the only one Daisy had with anyone these days. She didn't even have one with Jasper. Not a real one anyway. How could she, with a phony character that wouldn't exist if it weren't for drugs and alcohol? Who was he underneath those layers of toxins? Did he even know?

She wondered if Daisy's other faceless friend Lucian was still there for her, or had she rejected him too?

Her stomach gurgled and she rubbed her little secret gently. She would tell Daisy, just as soon as she thought her best friend might listen to her. She crunched loudly on another apple as Daisy floated out of the room.

Entering the office from the kitchen with another black coffee, Daisy returned to the past issue of *Sabre* magazine. She looked at an advertisement of a Grace Kelly look-alike in dark glasses, a faux mink coat, and ruby stilettos, before sifting through more pages of jewellery and clothes she could never afford in a million years. She had never been so appreciative of her superficial interest in fashion since she began working at *Sainthill Publications*. The publishing house pulsed with a passion for fashion, and if fashion was your thing, she contemplated; it would be like working in a bar if you were an alcoholic. She shifted uncomfortably in her chair. Her point was, that she could easily be bankrupt by now.

She cast tired eyes over her unfashionable ensemble, her "high-street" black jumper and jeans. These days she didn't have the energy for even a superficial appreciation, let alone any colour.

She had never understood how other girls tottered in on a wodge of cash each morning. That's what Daisy saw anyway; the higher the heel, the more expensive the shoe looked. Then there was the oh-so-important issue of the colour of the sole, and what it revealed about your finances. And this was only the shoe. There was a whole body to go yet. Either Daisy had missed numerous pay rise opportunities over the years, or she just hadn't married a banker. *Fuck that.* She would never marry anyone who sold his soul.

She flicked to *RAH!*'s smug album of the British aristocracy. She usually looked at these with Jude, each rushing to find a lord with three ears, or a baroness with four breasts after centuries of in breeding. These days, however, Daisy could not find energy for much that wasn't Jasper related.

She yawned. Jasper was fuel for insomnia. *'One Jasper before bedtime guarantees a life of sleepless nights. In the unlikely event of symptoms persisting, see a doctor.'* Her flighty mind jumped – as was its nature – to Dr Oliver Cranston. She had never heard from him after her accident. *Another flake, another liar.* She felt so lucky to be with Jasper.

Mid yawn number two, a man stared back at her from the pages of *RAH!* He held her gaze and took her breath away. Her yawn collapsed in on itself. Her heart fluttered as she took him in – his shoulder length dark hair, his green eyes, which looked at her, his easy smile, which smiled at her. *Am I dreaming?* She shut her eyes, but when she opened them he was still there. Again, those green eyes took her breath away. Daisy recalled her conversation with Lucian months ago about love at first sight; she was so sure, as she was now, that it could exist. He was familiar…from the worn brogues to the paint splashed shirt and jacket cuffs. She knew she had seen him before, outside a photograph. She looked across at the black and white text which framed the photo, and she longed to know what he might say if that space was his. Another glance around the page confirmed coverage of the exhibition *Portrait of a Boy. Was he the reason why I fainted?*

She searched for a name.

Marcus True.

No way.

Please no.

But she *hated* Marcus True.

'Why is Beth wearing Daisy's ring?' Tara finally asked, as her naked limbs sprawled seductively from the chair and into the evening light that filled Marcus's studio.

Marcus's loaded paintbrush halted on the clean canvas.

'*Daisy?*'

'Daisy Hawkins. She's a colleague. Your lesbo housemate Beth is wearing her Love ring around her neck.'

'She is?'

'Yes, she insists on dangling it in my face when she hands me tea.'

'A colleague, I mean – Daisy Hawkins is your colleague?'

'Sadly yes, different magazine, same company – the only thing we have in common, I might add. She's the airy-fairy, nut-job whimsical writer; I'm the naughty bitch-face ad salesgirl – way more fun,' she flashed him one of her grins. 'Anyway, around the time I spotted the ring on Beth, it stopped appearing on Daisy's thumb, and my day at work has become considerably less offensive, so hurray for lesbians, that's what I say. *What?* The ring does say "Love" on it.'

'No, they're not *lovers.*'

'You know Daisy?'

'Yes. I mean, no. No, I don't. But I know Beth, and I know she never dated Daisy. They were just friends.'

'Small world.'

'Yeah. It really is. Smaller by the day, it seems.'

'Might not be Daisy's ring by the way, just uncanny similarities and coincidences.' Tara's eyes licked the room. 'Daisy possibly just shrunk out of hers.'

'*Shrunk?*'

'Oh she just looks a bit haggard these days. Have you not met her then?' Beth stretched a leg and wiggled her toes.

'No. Not really.'

'Well, I wouldn't waste your time now. She used to look OK, I guess, nothing to write home about or anything, but now she's rough, all withered and shrivelled like a little old lady. Smelly too. Alcohol, smoke…pretty gross really. I get a whiff each time I pass her. I'm sure I'd get high but she looks so downbeat it's sobering. Plus, she looks constantly shattered and only wears black… Goth went with the

80s, yet she works on a fashion mag, kinda ironic, don't you think? She looks like a liquorice stick.' She laughed alone. Marcus went pale.

'Did I say something? Liquorice? Not a fan?'

'Err no, I mean, yes, you're right. Hate the stuff, it's rank,' he puffed out his cheeks and made a puke face. 'Is that the time?' Marcus asked, without looking at his watch. 'Why don't we call it a night?'

'I've only been here ten minutes!' Tara had been hoping for a repeat of their steamy one-night-stand. She recoiled her limbs and waded around to peer at Marcus's canvas like a stork.

'Your brush hasn't even touched the canvas!' she scoffed.

'No. You're right. Again. Sorry,' he stammered. He touched his stomach. 'The liquorice thing. Just saying the word turns my stomach. I think I might be–'

'OK, OK. If you're gonna barf, do it in the bin. Here,' she handed it to him. 'I don't think even Tracey Emin would puke on a canvas. I'll go now, but you're still paying for a full session.'

With Tara's departure, Marcus welcomed peace. He lay on Jasper's camp bed and closed his eyes to think.

Beth entered to collect the mugs.

'You feeling OK?' She asked with concern.

'Yeah, fine. Thanks.'

Unconvinced, Beth walked over to the bed and placed a hand on his brow. Marcus watched the ring dangle from her chain. It glided directly in front of his face, up and down, across and around as if drawing daisy petals in the air. It was hypnotic.

'I think you might just see through until dawn,' Beth smiled as she withdrew her hand. 'There's some homemade soup downstairs if you want, carrot and coriander. Shout if you want me to bring some up, OK?'

She glanced at the blank canvas. 'Oooh, one of your better ones,' she teased, before closing the door on Marcus and his thoughts.

He remembered how upset Eliza had been when she lost her ring, *'my hollow silver disc bursting with sentimentality!'*

He cast his mind back to Daisy's car accident. In the taxi to the hospital, he remembered her thumb was as nude as her body, and he recalled the pale loop of skin where a ring had been.

He remembered Eliza telling him that an "actor" she had been dating had given her ring to his sister as an "incestuous gift of love". That night of the party Daisy had been Floyd's "date". *Of course!* Floyd and Beth were Eliza's weird siblings. Had this not seemed so...*fucked up*...he would have laughed out loud. And that would explain why Daisy had disappeared from the party and out of their lives. Marcus appreciated the difficulty of grasping the bond between the twins, and if you combine this with an over-eager imagination, and a penchant for jumping to wild conclusions, the result is, Marcus thought with amusement, incest, *obviously!* Typical Eliza, he thought, about the girl he had never properly met.

He remembered the ridiculous two-timing guilt he had felt the evening of his first date with Eliza, the same evening of Daisy's accident. Eliza had not been held back at work after all, she had been hit by a car. Had embarrassment prevented her from telling him the truth? He had thought he had feelings for *two* girls, yet there was only ever one; Eliza, like Lucian, was a figment, an online persona. For reasons that made no sense, Marcus felt like he had lost one friend and gained another, like one had died and another had been born. It was confused and bittersweet. Yet by all accounts, his living friend was dying – heart, body and soul – because of Jasper.

Friday, July 22nd

Eliza hates me, therefore, Daisy hates me. So without Lucian, I cannot help Daisy at all. Whilst he was not yet ready to let go of *Lucian*, he had zero control over the fate of the real one. Lucian Freud's death last Wednesday had caused Marcus sadness and another painting frenzy in his studio. He mourned his dead hero, whilst Daisy nursed her addict.

'I'm in love with a dying man,' she had emailed Lucian earlier in the week. He had felt the blow of weighty words of disoriented love.

As usual, she found therapy in writing. Over the past week she had written to Lucian every day. He was always there for her, shining light on dark days. She did not push him away.

She told him about Jasper's cycle of regression and regeneration, of hope and despair; the nonstop rollercoaster of highs and lows. Lucian's responses were measured – almost as if he had been expecting her words – and showed concern rather than shock.

Lucian had urged her to leave Jasper, but she had neither energy nor desire to liberate space for the concept to cross her mind. She was in love with him, she said, over and over again.

Daisy felt Lucian was her only friend in the world. He listened and he understood.

That morning, she sent a text to Hanratty: she could not make it to work today. She was almost entirely drained of energy – Jasper had left her mere scraps. She had not slept for days, for exactly how long she did not know.

That evening, Marcus revisited *Jazbar*, with Floyd, and Xander Waterman, one of Floyd's acting friends, who had landed the part of Othello at Shakespeare's Globe Theatre. Floyd, who was Iago onstage, was more like smitten Desdemona offstage – he had developed a bit of a crush.

During the past week Marcus had made several visits to Jasper's flat and called and texted, but there had been no answer. He had made numerous visits to *Jazbar* too, but the staff, used to their remote proprietor, had not seen him for a while. So it came as a great relief when Marcus spotted Jasper that evening, on the other side of Jazbar's dining floor, dishing out bowls of pumpkin ravioli and lashings of charm to two female dining companions.

'He-ey, buddy! I was just going to call you,' Jasper caught sight of his brother before Marcus got the chance to speak. This was probably a good thing, thought Marcus, as Jasper set a jovial tone that he would have struggled to achieve – he wanted to punch his lights out.

'What's happened? Where have you been?' asked Marcus, returning Jasper's shoulder squeeze, with more force than intended.

'Sorry, bro! I've been shit at getting back to you, I know. I've been meaning to, honestly. It's just been a crazy time.'

Honestly. The meaning was clearly lost on Jasper. 'How's Daisy?' There was so much he wanted to ask and say. But if he told Jasper he knew *everything,* he might risk losing him forever; losing this thread of fraternal love from which their relationship dangled. And perhaps lose Daisy. One misguided move, and Jasper could sever the two very ties that meant the most to Marcus.

'Daisy's great. She loves me, which is awesome. I've been as good as gold and feel grrreeaat! How do I look? *Pretty?*' Jasper cocked his head, grinned like a clown and fluttered eyelashes manically.

Me, I, I.... How did he look? Well, bearing in mind this was flattering light, he looked like a fucking disgrace. OK, he had showered; a step in the right direction, and had dressed himself, and not entirely badly. Or had Daisy dressed him? Showered him too?

'Daisy's my rehab, I'm telling you, mate! Bet you're relieved you don't have to bang on about that anymore!'

No, Marcus thought. *Things couldn't be worse. My brother is throwing me lie after lie from every fucking angle, and he's killing himself and the girl I love.*

The girl I love...

Jasper's hands moved wildly as he talked, and his fingers sliced the air like a knife thrower. His thin body shuffled impatiently, trying to cope with the overload of energy. On his face, crow's feet trespassed intrusively, cross-hatching a nest of lines on his 30-year-old skin, for the magpie perhaps, who had pecked the shine from his eyes. His yellow teeth were rotting gates to a cell of atrocities. His hair waved like feathers refusing to re-grow; they had lost all strength to push through the follicles. A network of acid-etched trenches scored his face – imprints of past smiles and frowns, of highs and lows – all triggered by coke and booze. His feet danced on red-hot coals, and his pupils inflamed with energy, refusing to rest on anything for longer than a second.

His empty vitality was full of sadness, thought Marcus, such wasted space.

But of course, his customers, many as phony as Jasper, adored him. His energy was exhilarating. They loved his dynamism, charisma, and charm. Many "happily married" women, from *Sabre's* society pages, hung around until the early hours, so he could screw them senseless in his office downstairs (if he hadn't passed out by then). Marcus had caught him at it often enough.

But he knew it wasn't Jasper they loved. For *that,* he looked at his brother clearing a table, was *not* Jasper. *That* was the drugs and the drink moving and talking. *That* wasn't real. *That* had stolen his brother and the girl he loved. Like all those other women, she loved someone who didn't exist.

Marcus still wasn't sure what to do. He just couldn't for the life of him find a solution to rescuing both Daisy and his brother. The rehab card was redundant and would only drive Jasper further away. His estranged mother continued to turn a blind eye, and Dr Oliver was tiring of this whole "escapade" too.

With the exception of Lucian, Marcus was on his own. Lucian was his only link to the truth and any chance of reverting damage. *It's you and me, buddy.*

At 2am Jasper made it home and immediately woke Daisy – the party *had* to continue.

'Thanks for staying over, sugar,' he said, pouring some drinks.

Daisy rubbed the sleep from her eyes, ''Course, babe. It's all for you,' She reassured him. 'Everything I do.' The flat turned into a pub and Dr Jekyll to Mr Hyde.

At 4pm, he stirred and demanded she leave.

He hated her. Her 'obsessive stalker-like' presence was 'totally freaking' him out.

She walked home, fatigued from the push and the pull. Early light stroked the city and stung her eyes. Her body yearned for sleep. *Thank God, it's Saturday tomorrow.*

After what seemed like hours, she fell asleep and dreamt: *Her heart only beat in his tight clasp. One day she saw herself amongst the shit on his shoe. She polished until her hands bled. A sad stranger stared back from leather walls. She set her free to walk into her future, wounded heart pulsing in the expanse of freedom.*

'*Which is weird,*' she emailed Lucian, who had been wide-awake all night. 'Because I love him. All I want to do is be with him and help him. It's not his fault.'

Nothing was ever Jasper's bloody fault, thought Marcus bitterly.

She heaved her fragile body out of bed and observed herself in the mirrored panel of her wardrobe. She had tried to avoid that reflective menace recently. It mirrored things she did not want to see. She stared at a stranger. *Who is she?* The feeble figure stared back. *She looks terrible. And that black hair...what's that about?* She put on her black beanie and a baggy jumper to cloak the stranger's shame.

Taking a step closer towards the mirror, she probed beyond the surface and saw Jasper. Her identity had become a reflection of his; his words, actions and greedy life had swallowed up her own. *I've lost myself in him.* Her heart quivered with fear, and she sat on the bed. She was nothing without him. She reached out, and as her fingers touched the cold glass Jasper vanished, and she saw herself. *She is me. She is me!*

She touched her hip. She felt the bone. Her hand cupped her shoulder... She thought back over the past weeks; she had stopped eating. She had watched people eat in slow motion and could hear only low prehistoric sounds of vulgar orifices opening and closing, and could see only dirty fingers licking gunk from the corners of hairy mouths. Greed, grubbiness and gluttony repulsed her. She was starving, but only for him. Her bones throbbed like sensitive teeth in ice.

Friday, August 12th

8am

Hurrah! thought Max. It was August 12th, which was a very good thing indeed. It was the start of the grouse-shooting season, and he was off for another week away to the country with his father, and another much-anticipated week away from his increasingly difficult fiancé.

He thought of Daisy.

He looked at Luise. It was early and she was still asleep. These were his favourite moments. She looked angelic and pretty.

The calm before the storm.

The lull before the psychological massacre.

He practised moving with stealth and slipped out of bed. He hoped to make it out of the house before the gales stirred. He would vent his frustrations on a grouse or two.

9am

Another bloody parcel damaged by bloody Royal Mail, thought Marcus, as he caught site of a messy lump on his doorstep. Moments later, as he left his home to buy tobacco and milk, he realised that the bloody parcel was in fact Jasper.

He had got into a fight. Jasper could only produce prod-triggered mumbles, but it was obvious from the ripe bruises, the still river of congealed blood down his face, and the brown sodden fibres of his clothing. His shirt was ripped too, and he was missing a shoe and a sock. The exposed foot had gone purple, after *hours?* of biting morning air.

'Where's Daisy? Is she OK?' Once inside the house, Marcus hurled questions at Jasper's sticky face. The words flicked one of Jasper's eyelids – the other refused to move under the gooey ruby crust. Jasper winced with pain and returned nothing more than incoherent grumbles.

Dr Oliver arrived as fast as he could.

11am

Will stroked his wife's hair and squeezed her shoulders tenderly. 'The ambulance is on its way, my darling. I'll clean up the blood.' He rubbed her back. Jude's face was ashen against the ruby.

'What blood?' she asked, confused. All she could see were fine red satin sheets where her baby had lain. Shock prevented comprehension. 'My baby's here somewhere... Please help me look.'

'I'm sorry,' said Will, biting back tears. 'The ambulance will be here soon. I love you. It will be OK.'

Midday

Daisy collapsed on the paving stones outside Jude's home on Ladbroke Grove. Her withered arm reached up to scratch the door with bony knuckles. No answer. *Scratch harder*. Still no answer. The arm slumped back to the body.

'I tried to stop it,' she whispered to no one. 'They just kept coming…there was nothing I could do. Is he dead? *Dead?* I tried to help him. It's not his fault…'

But Jude was not there.

Daisy was too tired to cry. The paving stones were too cold. Her mind froze and she sunk to sleep.

1pm

At Chelsea and Westminster Hospital, A&E medical staff attended to Jasper's scrapes and stitched him up like a rag doll.

In the gynaecology ward, Jude lay in bed. Grief had detonated within her. She looked as white as her sheet. Will was by her side. Jude had miscarried and was undergoing the cold aftermath of internal examination.

On Ladbroke Grove, Daisy slept on, too tired to dream.

2pm

Tara's phone vibrated between her legs. It was not unusual for her to set it on *vibrate* and sneak it between her thighs. She never actually felt anything, but got a kick from the idea of it, and hoped it might unsettle cellulite. When she saw a text from Marcus, she felt the kick; he always had that effect on her. Tara read his words of cancellation: no life drawing tonight, he was sorry, and would pay for the costs and inconvenience of short notice. She slammed her clammy phone on the table. *Fuck it. Fuck him.* No doubt he's with Eliza. Even her interference had not doused his flames of desire for Eliza. *Fucking Eliza.* Tara exaggerated the aural quality of each letter, and turning them into daggers, she spun them in her mind, until *Eliza* grated. She detested the name. Tara wanted to know what she looked like – the colour of her hair, shape of her body – the instinctive female fascination in a rival.

She looked at her reflection in the computer screen. *How could Eliza possibly look better?* It always came down to looks with men, after all, she thought, looks and sex. And she excelled in both. Or at least, she did.

Hanratty's two favourite girls were off work, so he felt he should be too. Daisy was absent, an increasingly frequent observation. Although today she hadn't even bothered to send an explanatory text. She was obviously having a tough time of it lately, he thought. *Best to avoid her, until her little "episode" is over.* The thought of the scraggy emotional mess beneath her black attire terrified the life out of him.

And Jude's husband had called in to say his wife was sick. No surprise there either, she'd been feeling unwell all week.

Hanratty put on his soft shoes and padded away quietly to avoid the few disdainful eyes of the conscientious and healthy, although no one had even noticed he was there in the first place.

3pm

In the hospital waiting room, Marcus again checked on his mobile. But nothing from Eliza. Where was she? Was she OK? What had happened? Had his brother hurt her?

The pile of hospital magazines on the table looked as dead as the flowers in the jar beside them. He did not want to get lost in those, so he thought of Daisy and lost himself in her eyes instead; he wondered again what it was about sadness that allured him so.

A nurse walked past, attacking space with her sexuality. She reminded him of one of Beth's friends called Alice. Beth had harassed him into taking her out on a date last year. Alice had looked like a bubble bath, all frothy and playful. But whenever she spoke, she blew airy words that did not so much as tap on the door of his soul. He knew he could never fall for a girl who bubbled over the surface of life, without ever pausing to look below.

He needed a girl with substance, whose eyes leaked tears from her soul. Sadness intrigued him and pulled at his heartstrings.

He rechecked his emails, but again, nothing. He wanted to find her now, and protect her. *Daisy? Eliza?* He fidgeted between the names, feeling disloyal to one if he lingered too long with the other.

4pm

Dr Oliver brought Marcus a coffee. Marcus followed him into his office; his brother's painted face peered down at him from the white walls.

An hour later, they had booked Jasper into a rehabilitation centre, one that Marcus had had his eye on for some time. This time Jasper had no choice.

5pm

Dr Oliver and Marcus told Jasper the news. Jasper remained silent. He hung his head in defeat and shame like a running child who had finally been caught. He slowly shrugged his shoulders in a way that implied that if he had less pain, he would raise his hands to say, 'OK guys, you got me. I give up.'

6pm

Will arrived home with his precious wife tucked under his arm. He noticed a parcel on the doorstep. *Please don't let it be a parcel of baby clothes.* It wriggled. He blinked. It was Daisy.

Will had never played "mum" like he did that night. He nursed three women of varying sizes: Jude with her sore stomach and soul, Daisy with her sore heart, and little Millie, the strongest of them all. He fed and bathed them (as appropriate), tucked them into beds, and distributed kisses (as appropriate).

The house slept like a baby.

Friday, August 26th

In an Arizonian rehab Jasper received £40,000 worth of therapy. Daisy had said she would wait for him; he needed her. *He had said so.*

She had called him each night. *'We cannot accept or deny he's here,'* came the robotic American drawl. She wondered if a bullet could travel down the phone line all the way to Arizona. 'I *know* he's there,' she protested, 'and he needs me.' *He had said so.*

Musings of a Pisces was now devoted entirely to her readers, who revelled in their new forum. They ranted and raged on every spare millimetre of column, competing with one another to be heard. They just wanted to let it all out. It was their therapy, they said. As Daisy looked at her recent pages, she pictured Jasper in Arizona, sharing his problems with his new friends in his own therapy group. She thought of Lucian. *Everyone needs a friend.* She blamed herself for not being a good enough friend to Jasper. She blamed herself for his incarceration but hoped he might find what he was searching for there, since she had so clearly failed him.

Did you see me as your angel, to heal, to save?
Then I failed you badly, despite the love that I gave.

She had told Lucian how proud she was that Jasper had committed himself to rehab, against the wishes of his brother. His words continued to comfort her as she struggled to cope with the void that had replaced Jasper.

On Lucian's advice she had spent the evening in her third meeting for victims of addicts' abuse.

'How did it go?' he asked, searching for signs of progress.

'Oh, it was crazy fun. Lots of blubbing over a soggy paper plate of chocolate bourbons and watching a box of tissues do the rounds, again and again. In a damp hall in World's End, me and fourteen strangers all needing help to move on.'

He knew what was coming. *'Apart from you?'*

'I don't want to move on, Lucian. I'm there to stop time, to revel in his memory and keep him alive. I need him. He needs me. It's my duty to take care of his brilliance, no matter how many miles lie between us.'

'Early days OK, be patient,' he advised himself as well as Daisy. Love gone wrong is insatiable for healing time.

'And how's the writing?' Lucian had been encouraging her to write to vent her emotions, and more often than not they took on the form of poetry. She didn't set out to write poetry but went with the flow. Lucian told her that sometimes he didn't intend to paint certain pictures and would begin work on a canvas with no idea of the outcome. When he allowed his brush to dip freely into feelings, he produced his best work and felt recharged.

'*Your paper is my canvas, your words are my brush-strokes, your poem is my painting,*' he wrote to her. '*Your writing is your therapy,*' he added.

'*You're my therapy,*' she replied, with fleeting clarity. '*Well, you and fourteen strangers – and not forgetting the soggy bourbons.*'

'*I'm touched.*'

'*Last night I wrote Jasper a four-sided poem.*' It was a 4am stream of disturbed consciousness. Four A4 sheets of cathartic crying: each word dropping like a tear onto the page.

'*I'm all ears – well, eyes,*' he replied, apprehensive of what was coming.

'*I'm exposing my soul to you, you know. I wouldn't do that for anyone else.*'

'*I know.*'

'*You won't judge.*'

'*Never.*'

'*You're not going to like it.*'

'*Try me.*'

'*Brace yourself.*'

'*Braced.*'

'*The devil's blood trickling through your veins,
Controlling your thoughts, steering your reins.*

*I know I came second to the drugs and the drink,
Fill the bath to the top, let me swallow and sink.*'

'*Bored?*' she asked timidly, trying to keep it light.

'*Carry on,*' Lucian replied, but he felt sick with guilt already.

'*What is wrong with me? Am I so weak?
Why is it your disturbed love that I seek?*

*The sinner, the saint, the Jekyll, the Hyde,
My friend, my lover, but the Devil can't hide.*

*Glass shards, stained sheets, condoms, coke;
My boyfriend, the Devil, red eyes, black smoke.*

*The Devil took possession of your soul,
Raped you, robbed you, filled your heart with coal:*

*Incinerate him, crush him, and freeze him on ice,
Kill the fleas, the disease, the rats, the lice.*'

He felt each candid word sting and struggled with the role of counsellor. Feeling responsible for Jasper's downfall and behaviour, he felt so indebted to Daisy. He concentrated on guiding her through her loss and heartache, and fuelled her healing process with gentle persuasion. He asked for nothing in return and was grateful for the strengthening thread between them.

'I'm always here for you too, by the way,' she reminded. But his untiring focus on her rendered her words futile. She felt like a thief in the night.

Later that evening, as she lay on her bed, a butterfly flew hesitantly into her stomach. It raised heavy tear-stained wings up and down. The rise and fall reverberated around Daisy's stomach. Sodden wings slapped the wall lining. The butterfly circled the vacuum and denounced it unfit. This hostile environment was once a flourishing breeding ground. Its departure dripped with melancholy. Daisy felt the emptiness reclaim the butterfly's space.

Deeply, emotionally bruised and battered,
I miss you madly, my heart is shattered.

She thought of Lucian and his soothing words. He offered so much reassurance in the way he saw the world. *Happiness is like a butterfly.* Colourful words. *It comes and softly sits on your shoulder.* She imagined her friend, the butterfly, settling on her shoulder. *Someone to protect me from myself.* She felt the soft tickle. She felt Lucian breathing with her, feeling with her, dreaming with her. She did not feel alone.

Friday, September 9th

It was a bit like living within the pages of a magazine that had been dropped into the bath, thought Daisy, as yet another week dripped past in a similar damp and depressing fashion to the last. But as time went on, and she turned each page into a new day, the turns became progressively less arduous, as the pages became drier, more distinctive and vibrant.

There was still no news from Jasper, not a word, and Daisy's attempts to contact him in Arizona continued to be blocked. Had she fallen for a fake, whose fragile existence had depended entirely on abusive substances? Who was the real Jasper behind the mask? It was eerie to think that she had been so easily duped. Would he even remember her after rehab? Had she shared the same shallow attraction as a bottle of whisky or a line of coke? Had she really been that disposable?

Did our love mean anything to you?
I hope and pray it was real and true.

Do you remember? Did you really love too?
Was the guy I fell for real and true?

Marcus worried about collecting a stranger from rehab. Who had survived beneath the layers of toxins? Who had survived the abuse?

When Jude had returned to work after her miscarriage, she had tried to avoid Daisy. She was hurt with her so-called best friend for being so consumed in her own woes that she had not been there in her time of need.

'Maybe if you stopped thinking about how other people have failed to live up to your expectations, then you might realise that *you* are letting people down too,' she had said on her first day back, when confrontation proved unavoidable.

Daisy felt the bite of truth and immediately lent overdue and overeager ears and a bony shoulder for Jude to cry on. There was much remorse. The girls were soon in warm dialogue once again. Daisy had forgotten what a good team they made, and both took strength from their rekindling friendship.

Daisy looked over at Jude that Friday afternoon, and felt those sharp pangs of guilt tease her emptiness; guilt at her own loss – so insubstantial compared to Jude's, whose came in the shape of a tiny unborn baby, which cast a vast shadow over Daisy's, which took the meagre form of folly. The more Daisy tried to avoid introspection, the more it absorbed her, which in turn fed those self-destructive feelings. The harder she tried to escape this vicious cycle, the harder it sucked her in.

'So how did it go this evening? Chocolate bourbons again or an upgrade to custard creams?' asked Marcus.

'Jammy Dodgers, actually. And by the way, that wouldn't be an upgrade,' typed Daisy, before making herself comfy on her bed; she had lots to tell.

'Wow, they're spoiling you. The killer question – with cream in the middle or without?'

'With. Has to be with. Always.'

She's eating. Progress! He felt some weight dislodge from his shoulders.

'There were only thirteen of us. Rob's gone back to Janice, she told him she was sorry, won't ever beat him black and blue again, and wants him back.'

'Please don't tell me you're envious?'

'I'm not.'

Progress!

'And, guess what? I stood up and said, "I'm a love addict," I said. I actually said that out loud, Lucian.'

'You did?'

'Wait, there's more. I then said, "I should have known from the start, spotted the signs. I need help."'

'Fucking GREAT on you!' In his home on Aldridge Road Villas, Marcus breathed a big sigh of relief for her recognition, a huge healing step.

'Then what happened?' he asked.

'Well, then we all cried, Billy even clapped, and passed around the tissues and what was left of the Jammy Dodgers. We all drank tea, then held hands and recited stuff from a booklet. It was quite fun. And then it was over.'

And then it was over. He relaxed into the sensation of pride and release.

Friday, September 23rd

Jasper was ending their relationship. He had been '*dangerously co-dependent,*' as had she, he wrote, with his newfound righteous wisdom. '*an end was necessary for them both*'... He must '*sever all ties.*'

Daisy felt paper-cuts on her heart. Her hands shook the letter, his childish writing quivered, but his message held firm; it was as clear as a mountain stream. It was over.

'*i've met someone else,*' he wrote triumphantly, in his final paragraph, beneath the insensitive cloak of afterthought. '*sophie*' was American, '*sophie*' was a model, '*sophie*' was an ex-alcoholic, and '*sophie*' *really understood.* They had a '*natural bond,*' he explained, with childish excitement. '*i'm sober daise, and I'm feeling real love for the first time!*' They were expectant, selfish words that demanded she celebrate with him.

And he loved her.

'*i love her.*'
'*i love her.*'
'*i love her.*'
'*i love her.*'

Daisy read the line over and over, until the words blotted and she could see no more. Her heart trembled and she blacked out.

She came around minutes later. Lying on the floor by her front door, she peeled away pages of Jasper's letter, which had stuck to her wet cheeks like bandages, beneath which the words had slashed her soul. *But he loves me! He said so!* Her defence was feeble, no one cared to hear it anyway; she wished she would drown in heartache.

Halle-bloody-lujah! Jude had been waiting for this day for what felt like centuries, and was discreetly thrilled to hear the news but nervous of the implications.

Daisy's sorrow made way for anger, as she struggled to accept it was over.

Jude busied herself making tea and caring for her friend as best she could.

Thank fuck for that! Finally, his brother had set her free. She told Lucian the news that evening.

'*Write it down! That's an order. Tell him how he's made you feel, even though you can't say it to his face, you can pretend at least. Write. You know it helps. Tried and tested therapy.*'

'*I don't feel up to it tonight, Lucian. Completely and utterly drained.*'

'*DO IT. Vent. Let it out. Hit me with one of your poetic lines,*'

'*All right! If only to shut you up. OK, here goes,*'

'*I used to mean the world to you,*
Then you cast me aside...' She paused to think.

'Like shit on your shoe!'

'Good! I mean, not good! What a bastard.'

'You jeopardised a love so strong,
Love used, abused, so fucking wrong.'

'Damn right. You're on a roll, keep going.'

'Love deserves care, attention and respect,
Feed it, nurture it, don't abandon or neglect.'

After they had said goodnight, Daisy closed her eyes to sleep and Marcus turned to his fresco *Fairground Frieze,* which sprawled across his wall. He turned a paintbrush upside down, dipped it into purple paint, and inscribed Daisy's words of upside down love across the fairground sky: *'Love used, abused, so fucking wrong.'* They hovered over the crowd.

Then he turned to his first painting from his *Eliza collection*; the silhouetted stooped girl and her friend. Across the top, like a rainbow, he inscribed *'Love deserves care, attention, respect.'* Truthful, simple words, he considered. It was really good to see.

Next, he scratched more of her words into the background of *Butterfly Echo,* and with each application of paint he embedded Daisy's heart and soul further into his canvas and into his life.

Daisy thought she had lost her identity in Jasper, but she was wrong. Marcus could see that her identity was right there, ingrained in each of her words, which he painstakingly secured on his beloved paintings.

That night Daisy had a nightmare; in her sleep she watched Jude drown. She heard the muffled sounds of her name as Jude cried for help; down and down she went, her hand reached upwards but diminished in size. Jude's eyes flashed blinding fear through dark salty waters. She flapped and gasped for breath, each time swallowing pockets of water. A final gasp and the erratic stream of bubbles stopped. From a big timber ship, Daisy stared down, and kicked at the ball and chain that clasped her ankle. She stretched an arm out into the water, but fingertips only skimmed the surface; her chains prevented her from saving her friend. Looking over her shoulder, Daisy saw a naked figure lying at the other end of the ship. The figure was long and slim. Her beauty was insulting in the shadow of Jude's ugly death. It was Jasper's Sophie. The two were entwined. His groans of pleasure shook the ship's hull and absorbed Daisy's cries. Jasper wore the key to Daisy's ball and chain around his neck. Sophie toyed with it with her tongue.

Beneath her duvet, Daisy tossed and turned in shame for neglecting her friend. As her mind collapsed into its dank hole, Lucian appeared. She could not picture his face, but she could feel his warmth. He spring-cleaned lovingly and rinsed away the evils. He stroked her brow. Her body shook with the ache of it all.

'Don't ever leave me,' she whispered. 'I need you.'

Friday, September 30th

The Story of My Life,
by Daisy Hawkins

Wading through critical red, I review the essay of my life; angry question marks, patronising exclamations, blunt crosses, rejecting erasure. Protagonist is stranger, friend and foe. I edit in the empathetic – often-patronising – expanse of hindsight and prepare blank pages for a climactic conclusion, heart stroking ticks, contagious smiles and fated disappointment.

***

After work that afternoon, Daisy treated Jude to a shoulder massage at Liberty's, to help knead away the lingering pain. Jude had booked Daisy in for a hair appointment in the hope she would return to her natural caramel-blonde and rediscover her old self.

Jude loved Liberty's; its legacy, luxury and timelessness. *So much history*, she thought, as she walked past the flower display towards the Beauty entrance on Great Marlborough Street. Absorbed in the swelling pride of patriotism, she smiled. *So much in life to be proud of*, she thought, as she looked up to admire Liberty's splendid Tudor building. She pictured the two ships sailing on expansive seas before their heroic contribution to the construction. HMS Something-or-Other and "HMS Impregnable" – one of her many useless and random pieces of knowledge. *Impregnable*. She pondered on the word and touched her belly – *the impregnable fortress* – but, she took a deep breath and pictured Daisy smiling and returning to her old self in the hairdressers; there was so much in life to celebrate. As she opened the door to the Beauty Department, the rich bouquet of aromas blew her away. A sense of femininity repossessed her, booting out those remaining feelings of malfunction. The masseuse kneaded away tangles and kneaded in tingles of femininity. Jude was not faulty; she was a woman and she felt alive.

Down the road at the hairdressers, Daisy was not smiling. She had gone from gothic to nursing-home chic, a look she had not requested. Having asked for a trim, "Fabien" sculpted a severe bob. Having requested blonde, Fabien opted for grey. She sat in the swivel chair, swamped in her black overall, and felt like a mushroom protruding from soil. She shrunk into the mud. Fabien reassured her that when she stepped out of the salon, she would feel like she had stepped onto the catwalk; which was odd, thought Daisy when she left, as she felt as if she belonged on a dog walk. She felt the cold September air claim her naked neck, and sharp ends of her hair scratch her earlobe. She felt like one lone mushroom, in a field of black soil, in the centre of mocking Mayfair.

If she was unsure of her identity when she entered the salon, she was even more clueless when she left.

'Like Gwyneth Paltrow?' Jude asked excitedly, but continued before Daisy had the chance to speak. 'No, I know, like Cameron Diaz! Ursula Andress! No, Brigitte Bardot? I *bet* you look like the beautiful Bardot!'

Daisy looked at herself in the bathroom mirror. 'Try Jones. Bridget Jones on a bad day.' Paltrow certainly didn't stare back, nor did Bardot. But an aged Worzel Gummidge did. He grinned like an idiot, in all his rustic glory. Daisy could not return his smile. She looked as scared as his crows.

Before bed, Daisy laughed as she accidentally caught sight of her reflection again.

'I'm laughing,' she wrote to Lucian.

Progress! 'What about?'

'Life, I guess. It's resilience. It's determination.' Her words were less angular now, like her body.

'Like a cactus in the Sahara,' he said.

Hair spiked Daisy's neck. *'It will continue and grow against all odds.'*

'Yes,' he said. *Major fucking progress.*

Daisy owed Lucian more thanks than words could say. How could she thank him for being her lifeline? For saving her from herself? *Through words?* She loved words. She played with them; stretching and distorting into incredible shapes to wring out whatever credible meaning she desired. But no matter how she manipulated words of thanks to Lucian, she knew they would fall short.

Daisy needed to see him. Desperately now. Again that night, she lay awake for hours imagining so many things about him – it had become quite a habit. She wondered about his voice, eyes, smile, hands, hair, height, shoes and clothes. Did he carry around his easel and paints wherever he went, like a peripatetic plein air prodigy? Did he bite his nails? Did he floss daily? Did his eyes sparkle when he laughed? Did he leave his boxers lying around or judiciously pile them in a laundry basket? Her questions covered every millimetre of his mind, body and lifestyle. She tried to picture him, but no image seemed to fit. She had thought about all the men she could, from friends to celebrities, and although she liked aspects of each, none satisfactorily represented Lucian.

'Expect nothing and you won't be disappointed.' Her mother's words rang in her ears, but Daisy could not hear a thing. She expected everything and had reason to believe this was justified.

Friday, October 14th

Jude and Daisy had taken the past few days off work, to visit Alderney in the Channel Islands, with Daisy's parents and Orlaith and Vinnie.

It was an odd destination for this time of the year, thought Jude, as she looked out of the window at the shivering seascape and took a sip of hot tea. But reading between the lines on the tourism website, there was absolutely bugger-all to do on the island, which was ideal; both she and Daisy needed to switch-off, away from the pressures of London.

Following Mrs Hawkins's mantra, the girls expected nothing and were not disappointed.

Daisy got out of the shower and looked in the mirror above the sink. A girl stared back; she was familiar. Daisy touched her freshly highlighted hair – as did the girl. Daisy rubbed moisturiser into her tummy and bum and the girl copied her once again, and neither felt the bones beneath the flesh. She was comforted by the familiarity. *Welcome back, Daisy Hawkins.*

From the table in the kitchen of their rented cottage, Mr Hawkins looked up from his newspaper at his daughter's shower wet hair. 'Just been for a swim, poppet?'

'You know me, Dad,' Daisy replied, plunging bread into the toaster; she had rediscovered the deliciousness of food. 'Just twice around the island, nothing too strenuous.'

'There's my girl,' he said, spreading a heap of marmalade on a wedge of toast and applying crispy bacon on the top. 'You take after your mother,' he smiled at Mrs Hawkins, who only ever put a toe to water if it was in a bath and close to boiling.

It was their last day on the island and it was freezing cold, just like the others had been. They wrapped up and strolled to the beach. Jude and Daisy lingered behind the others, taking care to absorb it all: the fresh air, the sound of the sea, and the open spaces without a *Nimbus* issue in sight, before their return to London. They laughed and chatted and practised stone skimming across the water. Impatient of waiting, the others wandered off to a pub on Victoria Street.

A girl appeared from the freezing cold sea with a snorkel. Daisy and Jude stood with their cold hands in warm pockets and eyes out on stalks; she looked like Ursula Andress in that iconic scene in *Dr No*. The enviable curves of her body were snug in a black wet suit. She shook water from long blonde hair; it was the colour of sand. She strolled towards them, to where she had left her blue and white striped towel. She wrapped herself up in it, before turning to her onlookers.

'Hiya,' she said, beaming a radiant smile.

Her eyes were like the clear blue sky, her hair was like the wind; her skin was shiny like fish scales and her fingers were like fins. She looked like the island. She pointed the girls in the direction of Victoria Street. Jude thanked her and asked her name.

'It's Michelle, but people call me Shell.'

Another girl wandered over carrying fresh towels. 'And this is Vivien,' Shell introduced, 'my girlfriend.'

Vivien looked uncannily like Beth, Daisy noticed instantly, before the group divided and went their separate ways. *Beth* – She wondered how she was and realised she had actually really missed her gentle company.

Further along the beach, as Jude picked shells from the shore, Daisy watched her own footprints disintegrate in the sand with each wash of wave. She thought of Jesse, Max, Floyd and Jasper; all momentary imprints washed away over time by the wave of life. Life saturates emptiness. It was a comforting thought. She looked behind her at her past – some shallow prints vanished immediately, whilst others stuck around for longer. If she could, she asked herself, would she rewind to rework some heavily indented heels and shrink the size? Or flatten some stubborn toe-prints that were taking forever to fade? No, she decided, she would not smooth the pits and falls from her past. She wanted to enrich her life with bruises and scars, because she wanted to *live*. She no longer felt the pinch of regret, or the urge to beat herself up for the stupid decisions she had made. She felt remarkably light. Looking ahead, her eyes washed over the length of the beach and her future walk of life. She saw another set of footprints accompany her own – precise, consistent steps. *Were they Lucian's?* She watched them walk together, fresh prints always side by side, until they disappeared off the beach. The moment glistened like the ocean, with excitement and melancholy; somewhere between the two she found peace, and it settled in for the long haul. Excited by the discovery and intensity of the moment, she felt the sudden urge to be in the sea, and without any warning stripped down to her pants.

'What the hell are you doing?' asked Jude, aghast.

'Embracing life, Jude!' she laughed. 'I'm grabbing it by its big old hairy balls. Come with me!' she yelled back as she ran into the water.

'You'll get pneumonia! You're utterly bloody bonkers…'

But Daisy was under the water.

Above the water she was drowned by noise from the screeches of Jude and the seagulls, and the roaring engines of the low-flying planes. They merged and echoed, and left no room for thought. She hastily inhaled. Beneath the surface all was quiet. She went deeper and felt the sandy bed with her fingers. Daisy thought of Lucian and felt buoyant despite the weight of water. He had reminded her recently that she always had a choice. Now she chose peace and quiet. She stretched her long limbs in freedom and it felt good – freezing, but good. Her body undulated like a mermaid, as she rippled with anticipation, for tonight after her short flight back to London, was her date with Lucian. *Fucking finally.*

Marcus had felt no guilt when he asked Daisy on a date – *third time lucky* – earlier that week. If Jasper had really *loved* her, like he claimed, it would have been an entirely different story altogether.

As his hand snaked its way through the festering horrors beneath Jasper's camp bed, his fingers found an object that resembled his missing shoe. He delved in again for its other half. They were his best shoes, navy with orange laces, and he wanted to wear them tonight. Pointless really, he thought, since he had suggested they try meeting again in the dark restaurant *Eclipse*, knowing that Daisy still detested "Marcus True", and guessing that by now, she would have a good idea of what he looked like. Eclipse seemed to brim with benefits. *'I want to see you in the dark,'* he had emailed her earlier that week and could have sworn he recognised disappointment in her response. His hand felt beneath the mattress, bypassing dirty clothes and magazines to find his other shoe and his fingers fell on something hard and compact with buttons: his old mobile phone…*suffering from a bout of blue-spotted measles, by the looks of things.* He glanced over at his painting, *The Distance between Us. Tara bloody Forsyth!* He recalled his *'boring History of Art Lecture'* and Tara's blue fingertips. So it was Tara who had sent the text to Eliza cancelling their date; Tara's text had jeopardised so much. Her crush on Marcus was blatant, even to him – usually blind to such things. Everything about her was blatant, he thought, from her confident sexuality to her wily ways. He should have known she was responsible! When he found his other shoe, he kicked himself for being so stupid.

Jude sneezed again and smiled with pride as she looked at her friend that evening. 'You look perfect. Very retro.' She coughed and furiously blew her nose – it turned out that stripping down to her undies and following Daisy into the freezing cold sea was one of her more reckless decisions.

Daisy had wanted to wear her scarlet dress, but after turning her wardrobe inside out and failing to locate it, they settled on another.

'I've got a good feeling,' said Jude again, looking incredibly serious.

'You said that before,' Daisy rolled her eyes, 'before it all went tits up, remember?'

'Yes, but that good feeling wasn't *in my waters*!' She pointed down. 'I feel this one in my waters.'

'And your water is after all The Oracle,' quipped Daisy, although she felt far more nervous now then she did a few moments ago: Jude's waters were notorious for getting things right.

On her way to the restaurant, Daisy received a text. *Please don't be Lucian cancelling.* But surprisingly, it was from Beth, *'Have fun on your date tonight.'* The little space between Daisy and the restaurant was occupied with questions – *How the hell did she know about our date?*

Daisy arrived first, as planned, allowing precious minutes to calm the rabble of excited butterflies that had gratefully flown home to the more settled environment in her tummy. She inhaled and exhaled deeply and felt her nerves subside. When she breathed in again, the smell of forest cut through the blackened restaurant: pine trees, tobacco, then the faint fumes of turpentine, canvasses and paint. The blend was wildly intoxicating, heady and sexy as hell. She smelt Lucian, familiar, she supposed, from her dreams of him. Daisy's butterflies wolf-whistled and flapped like crazy.

'Hello?' he said.

His deep voice cut through the dark, it was intense and gravelly, like thick dry paint on a masterpiece. Her senses collided in the thrill.

'Lucian?' But she already knew it was him.

Eliza not Daisy, Eliza… 'Yes, hi Eliza. It's me.'

He lent down from where he was standing and carefully kissed her on the cheek – his accurate aim averting any awkward fumbling around in the dark. He breathed her in – the fresh scent of brand new writing paper. She took his breath away.

Before he straightened himself to stand, his hand felt for her coat on the back of the chair. Inside a pocket he placed her silver ring, which he had retrieved from Beth's necklace. A pocket full of LOVE.

A brief exchange of words – lids to the universe – before he apologised and disappeared to find the Gents to wash the underground from his hands.

A mobile phone rang from the tabletop. It was Lucian's. It rang loudly and radiated light pollution onto irritated faces of diners. Daisy rushed to hush it, but her fingers worked slower than her eyes, which fell upon the photo and accompanying name of the caller; *"Tara"* flashed like a beacon. The flashes were hypnotic and revealed more each time: *Tara, legs, Tara, pink pants, Tara, thighs, Tara, breasts*...Daisy's vision blurred, and she felt the familiar thud of palpitations rise in her chest. Tara's pink pants went black, her peach flesh went white, her red-lipped scorn turned grey, and the restaurant turned a blacker shade of black. But Daisy resisted the drag of unconsciousness and hurriedly felt her way out of the restaurant.

Marcus was oblivious to his date's departure. After a brief and very one-sided conversation, he discovered he had been exchanging pleasantries with an empty seat. In the dark, Daisy was nowhere to be heard. As his date slipped into the cold London night, he slipped into icy déjà vu. There he sat, once again, confused and alone in the dark restaurant.

Perhaps Lucian and Tara were friends? Daisy rushed to get the tube home, still feeling woozy from her brief spell. *Just friends?* Daisy attempted in vain to console herself, as Tara Forsyth's image and name continued to flash in her mind. Each time it appeared, it triggered a fresh wave of deep disappointment. But if they were friends, her mind argued, why would he have a *naked* picture of her on his mobile? Naked, bar her skimpy pink pants. The face and body were unmistakably Tara's. And if the image had not been clear enough, there was the reappearing name to confirm. If you aren't sleeping with a girl – Daisy thrashed out the debate – then why have a naked picture of her on your phone? *Exactly. You wouldn't.* Plus Tara was a renowned slut – two-timing Marcus True with Lucian was entirely in keeping with her character. *If you can get your claws into every man on the planet, then why the hell not?*

Daisy's thoughts were bitter and she was painfully disappointed in Lucian – just another typical bloke caught in Tara's web of seduction. She had thought he was different, yet knew she had no right to feel let down. Lucian owed her nothing. He had been more than generous with his constant support. And they were, after all, only friends. Get a grip, woman, she chastised herself. Lucian was perfectly entitled to sleep with whomever he wanted. She only wished Tara Forsyth had not flashed up. Any other girl would have been fine. OK, not fine. Better. *Or would it?* She decided against taking the tube. She needed to walk. Her feet hurried: one step in front of the next, walking, walking, walking on, like her stream of consciousness. She tried to justify her heartache: perhaps she was dating too soon after Jasper? Perhaps she needed more healing time? Perhaps this knock came too early? Or perhaps she simply cared too much for a guy she hadn't even really met.

She felt her heart tremble and her head fuzz. Her eyes zoomed in on the paving, until the grey slabs glittered with blacks and whites. Some stayed within the confines of each slab, others danced outside. Her eyes were dazzled by the sparkling floorshow, until she could no longer see her feet. They walked her body and mind into the haze, and she slipped to the ground.

Minutes later, she came around. A dashing man was there, one hand on her elbow offering support, his other reaching sideways to grab whatever had rolled from her pocket.

'It's you!' Dr Oliver Cranston said, grinning.

Hugh Grant! 'Dr Oliver!'

Without thinking, Daisy hugged him and pressed her sodden eyes and snotty nose into his shoulder. Compared to having an earplug extracted from her ear, and being rescued half naked after a hit-and-run, this reaction caused only minor embarrassment.

'Hey, heeey, no need to cry,' he rubbed circles on her back before placing both hands on her shoulders to gently push her away and look into her eyes. With his gloved thumb he wiped tears from her cheeks before producing a tissue from his pocket so she could blow her nose. 'Whatever it is, Daisy Hawkins,' he said, 'it's nothing a stiff drink can't put right. The best medicine. I'm a doctor, *I* should know,' he winked and she smiled.

He handed her the silver LOVE ring. For a moment she looked at it with suspicion, before casting the same look at him.

'It fell from your pocket,' he said, flashing white palms towards her in mock defence.

But it wasn't there yesterday!

Back in Notting Hill, Oliver led her to *Jazbar*. Daisy was about to protest, but he said, 'It closes after tonight. Completely shuts down. Two for one cocktails. Bring it on, I say!' Dr Oliver opened the heavy doors to her memory lane and she went inside.

Over two espresso martinis, Daisy imagined Jasper flitting around *Jazbar* from table to table, buzzing, as he did, with contagious energy and lighting even the darkest corners of the room. Old Jasper, she reminded herself. She had loved *Old Jasper*. Now, they would be nothing more than strangers. She rubbed tired fingers up and down each eyebrow, stopping at the base to massage the tension away with small circles. Spotting the symptoms, Oliver dived into his rucksack and produced a bag of pills, from which he found painkillers for her headache.

'Pills for every occasion,' he said, grinning. 'We doctors are the biggest hypochondriacs of them all.'

Daisy washed them down with espresso martini.

'Now tell me what makes you so sad?' She looked exceptionally pretty tonight, so his interest peaked.

Dr Oliver prescribed a perfectly proportioned dose of empathy for her woes, and agreed that 'this bloke sounds like a player.' *I should know*, he thought. He advised her not to waste anymore of her time. On hearing all about this poor bastard's mobile-phone gaff, Oliver's hand scrabbled in his pocket to turn off his own phone to prevent a similar offence – over the years he'd collated a comprehensive gallery of tits and arse. Daisy also scrabbled in her pocket, finding familiar comfort in the slow rotations of her cherished silver ring. Out of their pockets, their two hands scrabbled to find each other beneath the table. Like the cocktails, their kisses were two for one, and Daisy's feelings for Dr Oliver Cranston were reignited. She felt her heartbeat quicken to a rate of silliness, and tried to blink away the encroaching fuzz – Oh *PISS OFF*, will you, she begged, *not again!*

Daisy woke up on Saturday morning to Dr Oliver and his dirty grin...*Had we...? Did we...?* As her eyes scanned the whitewashed cell, it became clear that she had not woken in his bedroom, but in a ward at Chelsea and Westminster Hospital. *Oh. Guess we didn't then.* She felt quite relieved – she would want to remember it at least. So, she had spent the night with Dr Oliver Cranston, but not in the way she had hoped. She had a bastard of a hangover and cradled her throbbing head. She felt a cut on her forehead and traced a distinct scabby arch with her finger. It was sore. In the mirror next to her bed, she observed the damage.

'You fainted into your martini glass,' Dr Oliver explained. 'That arch is the side of the glass – which broke incidentally – a nurse had to spend half the night plucking out the shards. Nothing but guaranteed entertainment from you.'

Bloody marvellous. She rolled her eyes before wincing with pain. 'I save the most embarrassing moments of my life for you, Doc.'

She had undergone several medical investigations. It was news to her. Oliver perused the squiggly lines of her ECG, 'This is your heart trace,' he informed her. 'Looks normal to me. Strong as an ox. Must have been the martinis.' He shoved her scan on the pile of traces and X-rays to give to Marcus for his art. 'Still,' he continued, 'I've arranged for you to have a chat with the cardiologist, just to be sure all's tickety-boo on the heart front. Tickety-boo, get it? Tick. Heart tick? Yes? No? Anything?'

'Hilarious.'

'Well, it's a winning line with the grannies – they're clearly easier to please then you,' he winked, and she felt a rush of heat from between her legs. He was a very mischievous doctor indeed, and this was a most inappropriate place to be getting *that* feeling, she decided. She had a good mind to bend him over and give him a good whipping with his stethoscope, and had absolutely no doubt that he was thinking exactly the same.

Friday, October 21st

Hurrah! thought Max. It was October 21st, which was a very good thing indeed. It was the start of the doe-stalking season in Scotland, and he was off for another week away with his father, and a much-anticipated week away from his increasingly difficult fiancé.

It was early, and Luise was still asleep. These used to be his favourite moments, but now even in sleep she unsettled him. He turned his back on her, closed his eyes and pictured Daisy.

The calm before the storm.

The lull before the psychological massacre.

He practised moving with stealth and slipped out of bed. He hoped to make it out of the house before the gales stirred. He would vent his frustrations on a doe.

From her desk, Daisy re-lived the significant highs and lows of her last week:
On Monday...

Quizzed by cardiologist Dr Frampton, they discussed her fainting history.

'Yes,' she replied, 'I see fuzz and black-out a lot and faint regularly.' She gave him specific examples that he recorded on his notepad.

Dr Frampton was about seventy years old. He had lips like sausages, eyes like gravy, and hair like mashed potato; he looked and smelt as comforting as home cooking. (Given the choice, she would've opted for croissants and coffee first thing on a Monday morning, but nevertheless, he was someone she could confide in.)

'You see,' she said, as she shifted forwards in her chair in his empty office, and placed her thumb and forefinger beside her mouth to shield her secret, 'The thing is, doctor, I have a vulnerable heart.' Daisy watched his glasses fall an inch down his nose, and his eyebrows climb in interest...*or amusement?*

'My stomach is full of *butterflies–*'

His eyebrows reached the summit. She continued. 'I know this might sound peculiar, Doctor, but sometimes they flap like crazy, like when I fall in love they flutter uncontrollably. When my heart breaks they tremble, and in extreme circumstances, they all fly elsewhere and leave me feeling empty. They send me into a spin, and dizziness often leads to fainting.'

His glasses fell to the tip. He pushed them gently upwards, whilst keeping eyes on Daisy. He opened his mouth to speak, but she had not finished.

'This would not be such an issue, if it weren't for the fact that...'

'Yes?' he urged.

'If it wasn't for the fact that I frequently fall in love.'

'You do?'

'Yes. *All the time.* Sometimes more than once a day.'

'And these butterflies,' said Dr Frampton, 'have they appeared on a scan?'

134

Confirmed: he's taking the piss. FFS. She took a deep breath. Yet again she found herself at the fart-end of someone else's hilarious joke. She had hoped for more sincerity and sensitivity from a daddy-like doctor who represented home cooking. 'I *feel* them,' she said with grit, bravely holding eye contact.

'OK...*butt-er-flies,*' Dr Frampton stretched the word as he scribbled on his notepad. Looking up, he fixed her with his gravy eyes before returning to his notepad. She shifted in her seat, excited that *finally* she might be offered an explanation as to her curious heart.

'Now,' he said, 'I was hoping to see your ECG but it must have got lost in transit as it's not with your notes. But Dr Oliver Cranston said it looked normal, and he's usually got his head screwed on.'

As she got up to leave, she stole a glance at his notepad; instead of medical notes, her eyes fell on doodles of butterflies. Her heart sank as she felt the surge of humiliation; her stomach hurt as her butterflies felt the blow.

On Thursday...

Oliver took her to dinner. In a tapas restaurant on the Fulham Road he had dished out the news, that there was no news. Having been ready to sacrifice her life for Dr Oliver's medical research into her life-long cardiac mystery, she was somewhat disappointed to discover that her heart was normal. They had found nothing out of the ordinary. *Oh, the bitter anti-climax!* In shock, she flung a bit of tortilla down the wrong hole and choked in a most un-lady like fashion, until Oliver expertly performed the Heimlich manoeuvre.

Embarrassing maybe, she considered after the episode was over, but in line with their previous liaisons, so totally expected. Understandable too: who the hell wants to be normal? She was adamant her heart was different.

Daisy wanted to see Oliver tonight but he was on call – again. This dating a doctor business certainly had its downsides. Nevertheless (out of convenience), she duped herself into believing she was in love with him. The truth was, the more she persuaded herself that this was the case, the more wrong it felt. But intimidated by how perfect the relationship looked on paper, the truth shrunk in significance, and she was able to ignore it. Tonight she wanted to snuggle into his white coat because the more time she spent with him, the less time she had on her own to contemplate how the evening with Lucian last Friday might have panned out, had she not left the restaurant, had she ignored the picture of Tara, had she simply asked him about it, teased him even, or just remarked on what a small world it is. She wondered whether he was cross with her for vanishing, and if he had spent the evening alone in *Eclipse* like the last time, or if he had gone running to the comforting generous bosom of Tara Forsyth. *Probably. A guy like Lucian, who gets girls like Tara Forsyth, would never waste time with girls like me.* But she persuaded herself that she didn't care anymore, because she was in love with a handsome doctor. Oliver was like antiseptic cotton wool, absorbing thoughts that were painful and distracting.

But tonight he was on call. Her paper-perfect love of convenience was neither perfect nor convenient at all.

Instead, Daisy sought alternative distractions at Jude's home on Ladbroke Grove.

Jude, who had abandoned her Daisy Dating file when the friends had stopped communicating, blew the dust from the cover and wrote *Doctor Oliver Cranston* in neat letters along the tab of a fresh green divider. It felt good to be back, she thought, crossing her legs ever so tidily; she hated leaving jobs unfinished. *This time, I'm going to nail it.* The other tabs in the file showed past potential lovers – Max, Floyd, Jasper – beneath heavy crosses. It was like a dating cemetery. Daisy asked Jude to add Lucian to the pile. She was tired of the nowhere relationship with the faceless man. No true love or soulmate of hers, she said, would sleep with Tara Forsyth.

Jude proved a hopeless distraction; her kind face and empathetic nature left no choice but to vent all:

'The thing that hurt most,' continued Daisy, as the evening wore on, 'was that I put my trust in Lucian, shared everything. *Everything.* Heart and fucking soul. Sometimes I felt, he knew me better than anyone.'

Jude looked injured suddenly.

'Apart from you, of course. I just feel a bit despondent, that's all. Stupid really. A bit let down, you know? Embarrassed too. I told him so much about myself, it's like I put my life in the wrong hands. Like he abused my trust. Stupid, really.' Daisy took another gulp of wine to fuel the second leg. 'Don't laugh, but I thought he loved me. He led me to believe it anyway; what guy is so generous with their time if they don't feel anything for the other person? And I love him. Now there's a surprise,' she rolled her eyes. 'Well, *loved* him, I guess. And all the while he was probably shagging Tara slut-face Forsyth. And now I feel like a massive dick.'

Jude sighed. Her pen hovered over Lucian's name, ready for some punitive crossing-out action, but she couldn't bring herself to do it. 'I always said I had a good feeling about him, didn't I? Sorry, Daise.'

'Yeah, in your waters too.'

'Maybe I have an infection down there!' she looked horrified.

'I could recommend a doctor,' replied Daisy, and conversation inevitably flowed to Oliver. Well, Daisy surely could not go wrong with a doctor, Jude encouraged. Especially one who looked like Hugh Grant.

'Say no more. He sounds perfect!' Reliability, care and protection came with the package – *didn't they?*

…It was the perfect package down Dr Oliver Cranston's boxers that nurse Stephanie was after. Unlike Jude, she was well aware that the rest of him was far from perfect – a fact she found uncontrollably arousing. She happened to like naughty boys, and one exceptionally naughty boy very much indeed. She entered his office and closed the door behind her.

Dr Oliver liked his sex hassle-free. His one-night-stand with Tara had been exemplary. Whenever there was a hint of a string attached, he usually went nowhere near. But Daisy Hawkins was the one and only exception. She looked like a ball of string, loose parts frayed all over the place. The girl had major love issues, but she was *intriguing*. There was something about her he could not fathom. Was it just that she was fit? Or that he found her clumsiness endearing? Things were usually clear: he liked some girls for being kinky, others for being dinky, some for their lips, hips, bums, or mums, and Daisy Hawkins, because she was…*intriguing*. It was most odd. There was something about her – something more, something different.

At midnight, as Daisy wandered home down Ladbroke Grove, Dr Oliver's hands wandered down nurse Stephanie's pants, and Marcus's mind wandered down memory lane…

So odd, thought Marcus again, why Daisy had left the restaurant last Friday. Had he smoked her out by his stench of rollies? Had she fainted and fallen under the table? He knew all about her repeat fainting spells from his conversations with Eliza. He had not heard from her all week, no explanation, nothing. Should he have checked up on her? He blamed his silence on his manic work schedule, but deep down he knew it was foolish pride.

'Grab those, would you mate,' asked one of the removal guys.

Marcus had been distracted, yet again, by thoughts of Daisy.

He apologised – 'miles away' – and grabbed the stack of chairs from *Jazbar* and took them to the removal van parked outside. *Jazbar* was closing in order for Jasper to survive. A bar laden with booze offered no career for an alcoholic. *An ex-alcoholic.* So many memories, thought Marcus nostalgically, the good, the bad, the downright ugly. Life and death had occurred behind these doors, he mused, as he heaved them closed for the very last time. *Bittersweet.*

He wandered home with thoughts of Daisy.

Friday, October 28th

'i'm sorry for the pain i caused since dad died. i've been doing a lot of thinking in rehab – there's a tormenting amount of time to soul-search. i know i've been selfish. the guilt is more excruciating than the comedowns were and there's no booze to smother the pain. not after sympathy though! i know i deserve every bit.

i've been working on a song for you. these lyrics sound even cheesier without music, but hey, here goes a snippet:

"you took my hand, walked me through life, rain or shine. you never watched the clock. Tick tock, tick tock. then my strides fought yours. yours never fought mine. i won't let the drunken fool stumble beside you in your memories. now i watch the clock – i long to take your hand, tick tock, tick tock, and walk you to the future, pace finding peace with yours. You are my rock, you are my rock."

anyway, it's a lyrical pledge I guess – i'll put things right. i'll make you proud.

a favour – yes, another! – can you check up on daisy for me. the truth is from the moment i saw her, i knew how perfect you two could be together. it was a weirdly strong feeling, i can't explain. but i refused to lose to you again, so i took her for myself despite never loving her – addicted, maybe, but nothing close to real love. all i really want to say is, i'm sorry bro. sorry.'

Marcus read to the end; Jasper wrote of his mixed feelings over the death of *Jazbar*, shed more remorseful words, but never asked for forgiveness or trust, knowing such treasures had to be earned. Jasper continued to neglect capital letters. Marcus noticed how each looked needy and small, like a child imploring parental care. As usual, they tugged his heartstrings; he wanted to wrap each letter in muslin and protect and nurture, as he did the dying child in Jasper. Marcus ran his hand through his hair. It felt greasy. He had been so absorbed in Jasper's letter that he had quite forgotten that his shower was running and waiting. The wind chimes chimed. He searched for a towel. Christ, he thought, as he glanced at his watch. 6pm. *I'm late!*

Ten minutes earlier, as Daisy wandered the streets over to Marcus True's house that Friday evening, with the bulging envelope of ECGs and X-rays from Oliver, her eyes fell on the trees, the early evening sky, the strollers and anything that calmed her mind. This was not a journey she wanted to be making. But she had agreed to do Oliver the favour, and he had given her Marcus's address. She had no idea the man she loathed lived so close! Oliver was busy on call again, and since she had convinced herself that she was in love, there was little she would not do for him, even on a precious Friday evening. She saw her heart thumping through the trees. Below, her hesitant feet moved at a much slower pace. When Dr Oliver had mentioned the name *Marcus True*, shock caught her tongue. Old friends, Oliver had said, so for fear of offending, Daisy chose not to disclose her associations or sour feelings towards Marcus True. There seemed little point. Besides, Oliver

138

mentioned that Marcus would be out – 'Leave the envelope with his housemates if they're in; otherwise, post it through the letterbox. Worst-case scenario, leave it on the doorstep.' Loving the sound of worst-case scenario, Daisy agreed to go. Having never been invited to the Aldridge Road Villas home by the twins, Daisy remained oblivious that they were Marcus True's housemates. If she had, she would have recognised the address and made excuses to avoid the house altogether.

As she turned into Marcus's road, she looked at her watch. 5.50pm. She was early. So keen to get this favour for Oliver over and done with, she had mis-timed her departure from her Warren and now had time to kill. She did not want to arrive before 6pm and risk catching Marcus before he left. She had no idea what she would do or say if she had the displeasure of meeting him. By the time she had dragged her feet and pigeon-stepped down his road, avoiding the cracks between the pavestones OCD style, she approached his door at 6pm. *No need to ring the doorbell, or draw any attention whatsoever… opt for worst case scenario and leave envelope on doorstep, then get the hell out of there – Run! Just like that. Easy.* Her head struck some wind chimes hanging from above his door – *bollocks! So much for the stealthy getaway.* She cursed herself. The eerie high-pitched fluty tones made a right racket.

At the same time, Oliver wandered a hospital corridor and winked wickedly at nurse Stephanie. It was indeed a risk, sending Daisy to Marcus's house, he thought. It was a risk because he had lied: he had told Daisy that it was he who had rescued her from that hit-and-run, but the truth was that Marcus was her hero, not him. If Marcus slapped eyes on her, he would recognise her – for they had shared the cab journey together to the hospital – the truth would be revealed and Oliver would lose both Daisy and his Victoria Cross. And he was growing rather fond of her… Really rather fond of her indeed. He wasn't ready to ditch her or her admiration for him just yet. She did wonders for the ego. Plus, he hadn't slept with her yet… *Plus* – the plus of all plusses – she possessed that alluring *je ne sais quoi* which he hadn't yet managed to put his finger on. And boy did he want to put his finger on it – *on her, up her, anywhere, anyhow, in fact* – ever so much. She made him feel like a teenager again.

But Marcus had said he would *'definitely'* be out. So it was a calculated risk, Oliver reassured himself – *as is this* – he threw eyes down the corridor before joining nurse Stephanie in an empty theatre and unzipping his fly.

As the seconds ticked past 6pm, Marcus had still not found a towel. As expected, Oliver's latest squeeze was on his doorstep – Beth and Floyd's hideous wind chime was going bonkers – with a package of medical tests for his artwork. He should have left by now for his dinner meeting with a gallery owner. *Damn*, he thought, *damn, damn.* 'One second, sorry! Coming,' he yelled, as he approached the door, still naked.

Daisy recognised the voice immediately. It rang a bell in her memory, and she tried to place it. The chimes reverberated through her body, and culminated down *there…* Totally unprepared for a sudden sexy feeling, she gasped and almost dropped the envelope. Both voice and feeling were extraordinary and intense.

The letterbox flapped open and more of the familiar voice escaped. They took Daisy to the forest, beneath that pine tree canopy, where she had been before.

'You must be Oliver's girlfriend. Hi,' said Marcus, to a small section of skinny jeaned leg visible through the flap. 'I would let you in, but I was just about to jump in the shower, and I can't find a towel anywhere, so I am slightly indecent I'm afraid. But good to sort of meet you!'

She said nothing as she breathed him in, from the forest, to the paints, to the tobacco, to the turpentine. From the heart of the forest her mind flew her to the dark restaurant. *To Lucian?* Her heart curdled with love and fury – how dare Marcus True trespass on her precious thoughts of Lucian.

Interesting, thought Marcus, Oliver has a "mute" girlfriend. *Another case of style over substance.* 'Do you have a parcel for me, by any chance?' he prompted; he was already late and impatience was murmuring.

'Ah yes,' Daisy said, finding her voice. She had quite forgotten the purpose of her visit.

'Ah yes,' buzzed in his brain; he traced the voice to Daisy. His mind flew to accompany hers in the dark restaurant. He had to check with his eyes. He pushed open the letterbox as far as it would go, and peered out to breathe her in. He inhaled the familiar scent of fresh writing paper, before she took his breath away. His eyes fell on her slender pencil fingers and envelope hand, shielding so many mysteries.

As he kneeled down further on his doormat to widen the angle up towards her face, she bent down, and through the door-flap their eyes met. Both left the restaurant and reunited in *The Gemini Gallery*, the evening of his exhibition *Portrait of a Boy*.

An electric shock possessed her and her heart stalled in shock. She saw the encroaching tunnel in her vision and felt the butterflies in her stomach pause mid-motion. *Holy shit, those eyes...*

Marcus's heart leapt, but his head was determined to maintain composure. He cleared his throat. 'The envelope looks like it won't fit through the letterbox,' he said. 'Here,' he opened the door ajar and reached out his bare arm. The fish tattoo on his wrist splashed in Daisy's field of vision, ringing another big bell in her memory. Again, she felt the licks of culminating reverberations *down there*. Tattoos had never had this effect on her before. It was *HOT, HOT, HOT,* and she felt it – the palpable heat ignited right there between her legs and spread into every square micro millimetre of her being, and as it grew in intensity, it far transcended any chemical feeling she had previously experienced: the seduction sensation was primal and out of control.

She could not remember handing Marcus the envelope. Neither could she remember saying goodbye, nor leaving Aldridge Road Villas, nor arriving back at her Warren, nor climbing beneath her duvet. It was 9.40pm by the time she came around. *Shit.* She was late for Jude's birthday dinner. Was there no end to the number of times she could let down her best friend?

It was around that same time that Marcus came around to the fact that Daisy was dating Oliver Cranston, his friend, the notorious player. His meeting with Emerald Carter, curator of the highly acclaimed Emerald Gallery in Mayfair, had led to dinner, drinks and more drinks. Between his furious sips, Emerald heard Marcus's love story. There was something maternal about her, and Marcus felt the unfamiliar compulsion to confide.

'No wonder you're a successful artist,' she told him. 'Clients throw vast sums into brooding eyes and deep souls like yours. Quarry souls, I call them. Tortured souls produce greater art, and greater art produces greater profit, *thank you very much!'* She rubbed imaginary notes through her manicured fingers. 'Go complete your love story, Marcus True,' she commissioned, investing in him and his destiny, before offering him gallery space.

Jasper had also written Daisy a letter – her second from Arizona. Inside the envelope were similar sentiments to those he sent to Marcus; further remorse and gratitude. But the words remained in their paper sleeping bag, having fallen beneath a photocopier at Royal Mail's sorting office. There they slept undisturbed from prying eyes.

Friday, November 4th

It was lunchtime. Daisy was in a café with an old acquaintance, Kirsten, who was visiting London for the day. The girls had been born into friendship but had grown out of things to say to each other. Chumminess no longer flowed off the tongue, so they peppered their words with formality whilst searching for a topic that enthused them both. Daisy bombarded awkward silences with random words she hoped would form sentences. But before long, her mind bucked beneath the challenge and wandered instead to Hanratty's: to find true love by the end of the year, and celebrate it on her page. *How might my page look? White and organised, like a hospital: a nod to my love for Oliver?* But its glowing spotlessness refused to look right, and she bored quickly of the minimalist design. Her eyes drifted outside the café window to London life and its fleeting stills of colour and diversity: the red of buses, orange circles of traffic lights, green crosses of pharmacy signs… Her eyes relished the charming haphazardness in the heart of Mayfair. She wanted her readers to be as captivated by her page as she was, right there, in that moment…

'Miserable day, isn't it?' remarked Kirsten, resorting to the safety of the weather.

'Oh,' said Daisy, 'I think it's lovely.'

Back at her desk, she doubted whether a page that looked as sterile as a hospital could convey the vivacity of true love. Her idea of everlasting love was bright.

She thought of Lucian. She had always pictured his black text in all colours of the rainbow. If her bland page showcased love with Dr Oliver, perhaps she could introduce a bunch of Lucian's words to visually and verbally uplift. They could be arranged like flowers in a stark ward – a gesture of love and life. Lucian was integral, Daisy realised, to help convince her readers that *Eliza* had, against all odds, found *true* love.

A pair of green almond-shaped eyes flashed in her mind. *Marcus's eyes.* Their brilliance was blinding, and for a moment she could see nothing but the luminous shadows of where they had appeared, as if she had been staring at the sun before closing her eyes. Marcus's eyes were haunting. She felt flutters, before irritation stole the show. Why did she have to be reminded of him – *of all people!* – whilst contemplating true love?

Ever since Daisy had delivered the envelope of medical tests to his door, Marcus had been troubled by thoughts of Oliver taking advantage of her. That evening, as he had every evening that week, Marcus pictured Oliver's clean hands and dirty mind, with Daisy trapped somewhere between the two. It made his stomach flip like a pancake in a frying pan, until he could bear it no more. First, he turned to his canvas, dividing one into rigid geometric shapes, he cordoned off each with masking tape, like individual crime scenes. He painted each space various shades of white, each differing subtly, but none venturing too far from the whitest of white. When the masking tape was peeled away, the edges were neat and clean like the edge of a surgeon's scalpel. The painted areas of canvas represented Oliver and his calculated mind that always got what it wanted, and the hospital in which he was so entwined. Then Marcus incorporated the long abstract figure of Daisy in her red dress, as he had seen her at *Portrait of a Boy*. She appeared on the stark white canvas like a bloody gash. Marcus knew that Oliver would make her bleed. Unsure as to how much blood she had left to donate, Marcus knew then and there that he must intervene before the inevitable consequences of yet another heartbreak.

After telling himself to man up, he turned to his computer to disturb the silence that had lingered between them since their second unsuccessful date in the dark. Daisy was there. She had just returned from work, she told him. Thinking fast, he prompted her to mention Oliver; Marcus said he needed a good GP, and could she recommend one. He knew this was a ridiculous request, since he was an ex medic and knew more doctors than your average Londoner, but she took the bait and proudly recommended *'Dr Oliver Cranston. He's a hospital doctor though.'*

'Dr Oliver Cranston!' Lucian's deceptive words showed the surprise he did not feel. *'I met him at Medical School. Be careful, Eliza, he's a player. Don't get hurt. That's all I'm saying.'* He planted the seed of vigilance.

As their conversation drew to a close, Daisy offered a belated apology for her sudden departure from their date at *Eclipse*. She felt faint, she explained, and had to leave. She would have apologised earlier but had been *'feeling really shit all week, basically bedridden,'* and incapable of dealing with anything. He seemed to buy it.

Obviously Marcus knew she was lying. She had been up and about delivering the envelope of medical tests directly into his hands. He hoped his words made for more convincing lies.

He was, however, familiar with Daisy's fainting fits, so that part at least was plausible, and was pleased to learn that Oliver had taken the uncharacteristically selfless decision to organise some tests – despite the results, which Daisy said, failed to highlight a diagnosis.

'He's a player.' Strangely enough, Daisy recalled, those were Oliver's exact words for Lucian, after she had described the naked girl on his phone. 'This bloke sounds like a player,' Oliver had said.

'Be careful.' Lucian's advice itched her brain.

So she called Oliver at the hospital, but he said, 'I've never met a Lucian in my life.' Then he added, 'Gotta go. The whole of London's in A&E tonight; it'll be a long one. I'll have to skip dinner again.'

Lucian must have lied. Oliver was far too much of a workaholic to have time to be a player. Perhaps Lucian was jealous. She wouldn't have guessed Lucian was the type of guy to have a jealous streak, but then neither would she have guessed that he was the type to like shallow girls like Tara Forsyth. And *those* guys were used to getting what they wanted: hot girls and hot sex. Since Lucian had failed to get *her*, then why, she presumed, would he want anyone else to? He was your textbook jealous narcissist: proud and possessive with only one thing on his mind. *Just like all the rest.*

But her conclusion had no roots and floated like a virus – Lucian was anything but textbook.

An hour later, Daisy took a bus to Chelsea and Westminster Hospital to deliver Oliver his dinner in a Tupperware box. Guilt at having pondered too long on Lucian's warning, and consequently having questioned Oliver's fidelity, had driven her to make a very large heart shaped sandwich filled with cranberry sauce and brie. She frowned at the realisation of quite how cheesy the heart shaped offering really was. Beneath the guise of love, she wanted to check up on him. Glancing down at her big heart for Oliver in the Tupperware box, she wondered if she should have cut it in half to save him the bother.

Having walked for some time around the hospital, she finally admitted to herself that she was lost in the white labyrinth. She wondered if corridors led to life and death, and stairways to Heaven and Hell. She poked her head into an empty operating theatre. She felt it breathe to the rhythm of life and death; in the face of death the theatre pumped with life, when empty it died a death. It was a pulse that beat continually. She took a step inside and the doors swung close behind her. She felt herself breathe naturally to the same rhythm, finding her air on the periphery of two extremes. It was quite a shock, and her free hand reached for her heart. Jasper, she thought, had nearly killed her but she had never felt so alive.

Daisy panicked and stepped further into the empty theatre. It lacked heart and soul and was cool and sterile, physically, emotionally and visually. Large round articulated spotlights poised like giant stick insects on the wall and ceiling; long metal necks craned and unblinking eyes cast light on the surgical table. She saw light rest on blues, turquoises, greys and whites of clean geometric shapes. She smelt the air, heavy with disinfectant, and swept eyes over the steel and plastic surfaces: microscope, ventilator, monitor, pumps, tubes, taps and drapes. All was on standby. Anticipation stirred, like a windowless theatre before the opening night.

All of a sudden the wide double doors burst open in Daisy's mind. She stood aside as the scene unfolded. Tension entered, silence escaped. A bowel cancer patient was wheeled in. The theatre resuscitated and beat with life and Daisy's heart beat in unison. The surgeon scrubbed up. Tap water ran. Lights twitched; their metal necks bent into position. The theatre throbbed with expectancy. Daisy's heart pulsed and sweat pierced her pores. The gowned anaesthetist, surgeon and nurses switched onto autopilot; slick, swift, accurate movements, retractors and scalpels passed from gloved hand to gloved hand. Daisy took it all in hungrily. She watched the abdomen sliced cleanly with a curved knife to expose the bowel. The surgeon cauterised the flesh to control the bleeding. *Tsssssk.* Daisy jumped as the smouldering tweezers burnt the tissue. The rubbery stench of burnt flesh filled the room. The bowel flopped onto the patient's chest like an octopus washed up on the shore with purple tendrils flailing wildly. The surgeon extracted the tumour from the patient's abdomen. It was like a decaying grapefruit in size, appearance and touch: browns, pinks, yellows, all fleshy and soggy. He dropped the lump on the tray. Its body slumped sulkily. It smelt of shit. Blood trickled down the sides of the patient onto the polished blue floor. Daisy's wide eyes watched the abdomen fill and spill with blood. In the wake of climax, the beat of the theatre picked up pace, as did Daisy's heart, and looking down to her Tupperware box she saw her breaded heart had swollen with energy too; the lettuce quivered and the cranberry sauce glistened with beads of sweaty excitement. Movement, noise and emotion congealed. Alarms cried. Monitors vibrated. Lights flashed. Blood pressure plummeted. The nurse vacuumed the blood as the surgeon worked frantically to control the bleeding. Then flat-line on the monitor, as her heart pulsed with life. She watched the rise and fall of the chest as it compressed and released, and felt the rise and fall of her own. One heart stopped whilst the others raced. In the shadow of death, the theatre inhaled deeply and convulsed with life.

Daisy gasped. *Like me.*

'Excuse me, can I help you? Are you lost? Miss? Are you lost?' The nurse's voice jogged Daisy back to reality.

'No,' her epiphany had been vivid and enlightening. 'I mean, yes. Yes, I am lost. I'm looking for Dr Oliver Cranston. A & E. Do you know him, by any chance?'

'You could say that,' said the nurse, casting judgemental eyes up and down and resting sneeringly on the Tupperware box.

'Follow me.'

Daisy followed nurse Stephanie towards the A&E department, as her mind spun with the intensity and possible significance of her vision. She was disturbed by her warped reaction; she had shuddered with life as she witnessed encroaching death, and her sensations had climaxed on its arrival! Two-timing Max, incestuous Floyd and addict Jasper had made her feel the same... *Do I get off on the feeling of pain? Death even? Am I a danger to society?* She inhaled deep breaths in an attempt to keep it real, whilst words from her poem about Jasper sprang to mind:

What is wrong with me; am I so weak?
Why is it your disturbed love that I seek?

She was attracted to a disturbed love that would make her heart bleed. With love she associated pain, and with pain, adventure and excitement and the sensation of being alive. If she deleted the pain, then a bland stagnant love was all that was left. She thought of Jesse. Since then, she had embarked on a misdirected mission for a flimsy, fleeting, phony love that promised extreme erratic emotions, and drained her dry. But she had witnessed enough of her parent's marriage and Hollywood romances to know that *true* love offered steady satisfaction and endurance, but not devoid of ecstasies and drama. True love was *not* the fragile love that she had been searching for. Her theory of love was dented. She had got love wrong. She recalled Lucian's words: *'You always have a choice.'* She had chosen to *feel,* but had chosen the wrong paths and found the wrong feelings. She had been clogged with confusion, but now the hospital had flushed her system. She had had enough and was tired.

Her butterflies flapped in celebration – *she finally understood!* She realised she was yet to experience a love that was both painless and exhilarating; she was yet to experience true love. Then Marcus's eyes flashed in her mind once again, and she felt that awesome feeling engulf her. She used every ounce of energy she had left to push it away, but stubbornly it lingered, as it had done since the day she delivered the envelope to his door.

'Nearly there,' said the nurse, swivelling on the polished floor to throw another patronising glance at Daisy.

Daisy glanced downwards at the heart-shaped sandwich. She heard Lucian's words again, *'He's a player',* and in her mind's eye, the heart was already sliced in two. She stared suspiciously at the nurse's wiggly bum, then back to the sandwich. Was another epiphany in the Tupperware box? She did not want to waste her heart on yet another guy, so she tossed it into a bin, and turned in the other direction. Beneath the kiss-and-tell hospital lights, Daisy's theory of love was blown apart. In this whitewashed building of heightened emotion, she had stared directly in the face of true love. She understood now and the revelation made her feel alive.

Friday, November 11th

Marcus looked at the X-ray of a ringed hand that he had found in the medical tests Oliver had given him. He was working into the X-ray with paints and marker pens in the name of experimentation. He thought of Daisy, and hoped she had found her lost ring, which he had snuck into her coat pocket moments before she vanished from the dark restaurant. He scraped white paint from both sides of his pallet knife. It cleaned away like Camembert from a cheese knife. Next he scooped the tip into amethyst and dragged it along the side of the thumb's metacarpal.

Tara flashed up on his phone, but he refused to abandon his work. He had already told her he no longer needed her for life drawing, but she continued to call. A girl with her good looks could get any man she desired. *Just not this one*, he thought, wracking his brains as to what on earth it was that she was attracted to. Tara had looks to die for, but he had never seen her soul. He felt neither protection nor affection towards her. Besides, he could do without a model who took advantage of him when pissed, cancelled his dates, and graffitied his phone with fingerprints before hiding it.

Her calls were relentless. He had no idea a crush could be so persistent. He had only committed to life drawing to engage in subjects other than Jasper. But now his brother was safely in rehab, and he was preoccupied with his luscious muse, Daisy, and the medical media Oliver had given him for the Christmas exhibition, *Artopsy*. He had had neither the time nor the desire to add to his Jasper collection for months; the spell had been broken and Tara's services were no longer necessary.

Marcus was anxious about *Artopsy; Symbiosis of Art and Science*, which was to take place beneath the vaulted central hall of the Natural History Museum. The pressure was huge. He had been working steadily for weeks on a multitude of sketches, paintings and wiry experiments, from which he had produced four large canvases he was happy to submit. He pictured his work hanging beside the formidable Diplodocus cast which dominated the magnificent hall and was intrigued by the comparison the guests would draw between the dinosaur skeleton and his work, which drew from human X-rays and scans. Marcus pictured people pausing before his canvasses to contemplate life and death, and the ability of art to resuscitate a dying man. The exhibition would celebrate the continual evolution of scientific fact and artistic imagination. This was right up Marcus's street.

The envelope that Daisy had delivered the other week had been stuffed with inspiration, which now sprawled across Jasper's camp bed like a patchwork quilt. Blacks and whites dominated, but there were areas of computer-generated greens and purples, some so brilliant they resisted change. Then there were the fine red-checked papers carrying electrocardiogram (ECG) traces, lines graphing peaks and troughs. They looked like cracking strobes of horizontal light or a fracture down the centre of a breaking heart. He liked the crooked line for its electric energy and drama. That line alone down the centre of a canvas could say so much. Or, he thought, as his mind moved in a similar fashion, he could shrink it and scratch it's skewed journey multi-times across the background, until they looked like sea ripples. He could paint his standing man in the foreground. He wanted his viewers to *feel* the background beat, before they recognised the ripples as medical scans. He would paint his standing man red and incorporate sections of a real X-ray onto his chest, hand and foot. He would make his standing man breathe, *yes!,* until the viewers would imagine him stepping from the canvas and walking amongst the dead dinosaurs. *Yes, yes, yes!* He was excited, manic and focused.

He took a final drag of a dying rollie. From the bed he selected an ECG and traced the P wave and the peaked QRS complex with his eye. And again. He scratched his head and tucked lose strands behind his ear. Something was not right, which was peculiar, because Oliver was meant to give him X-rays and scans of patients who had not required subsequent treatment. Oliver held back those that highlighted abnormalities and required further investigation. Marcus returned to the bed and picked up another ECG scan to compare a normal trace with the one that had triggered his concern; it was definitely abnormal.

He called Dr Oliver. 'I know my medical skills are a little rusty, but this ECG smacks to me of Wolf Parkinson White Syndrome. The delta wave, the narrow PR interval and slurred upstroke. Hope you didn't miss it! I can leave it for you at reception this afternoon. I'll be in the area anyway. No problem, mate.'

Dr Oliver heard all this in horrified silence. *Shit*. He put down the phone. When Marcus had read out the date and time from the top of the scan, Oliver's diary confirmed it was Daisy's. *Shit*. He remembered dismissing the trace as normal and shoving the scan onto the pile for Marcus, even before Dr Frampton had had the chance to inspect it. *Shit*. He was entirely responsible for this oversight.

By 6pm Marcus had delivered the abnormal ECG scan to the hospital reception. On closer inspection, Oliver saw that Marcus was, as usual, spot on. That man had the eyes of a hawk. So Daisy Hawkins had Wolf Parkinson White Syndrome, a conduction disorder that affected the heart. And that, thought Oliver, would explain her intermittent fainting fits, dizziness and heart palpitations – her "heart flutters" as she insisted on calling them. These episodes were precipitated by stress, insomnia, caffeine and alcohol. *Hmmm, yup* – Oliver thought of Daisy – *sounds about right. Bollocks.*

At 6.30pm Daisy received a call from Oliver.

'Can you come into the hospital now?' he asked.

'Are you missing me?' They had not seen each other all week. She didn't miss him, but he was always fun to flirt with.

'Hell, yeah! Like crazy,' he teased, before realising that he actually did. 'Can you come then?'

'Well, I'm out with friends. I can't really just–'

'It's about your heart.'

'My heart? Hang on,' she rushed outside. 'What about my heart?' Neurotically, she slipped a hand beneath her shirt to check it was still there.

'I think I've discovered why your ticker flutters rather than ticks.'

Oliver met her at the hospital an hour later and handed her over to Dr Frampton. Oliver had managed to escape his blunder by continuing to wag his finger of blame; nurses and technicians were the easiest target.

Although Dr Oliver was notoriously dirty, Dr Frampton was satisfied that this time his hands were clean.

This time, Oliver thought, he had got away with it. But his career was unsympathetic to uncharacteristic oversights like this... *Something or someone distracted me.* Suddenly he contemplated love and Daisy...before shaking his head free of such nonsense.

Daisy was fitted with a 24-hour heart monitor, ECG electrodes were stuck to her chest and tummy, and a black box the size of an old-fashioned Sony Walkman was strapped around her waist. She jacketed her secrets and stepped outside the hospital onto Friday evening's lively Fulham Road. She felt like a suicide bomber.

Friday, November 18th

That evening, back at the hospital, Daisy was stripped of the electrodes and black box, so the technicians could print off the results. Dr Frampton looked at her scans. He was hard to read, Daisy decided. Were her results so peculiar that his eyes popped out on storks and pushed his glasses down his nose? When he pushed them back and looked at her through his lenses, it was as if he was about to say something very important. But he remained quiet. For a girl fixated on matters of the heart, and impatient for her own results, his demeanour was infuriatingly lackadaisical.

'Is all OK, Dr? Can I see?' Dr Frampton passed her the ECG and she traced her fingers along the craggy line, entranced by the peaks and troughs. *It's a letter from my heart!*

'You have Wolf Parkinson White Syndrome. All will be explained. Follow me, my dear,' Dr Frampton's words puffed from his sausage lips.

Wolf? She chewed on wolf. *Has an Arctic wolf been gnawing on my heart?* She imagined an entire pack running straight for her, howling, and flashing piercing amber eyes and white teeth. They picked up pace and her heartbeat fell in time with their quickening prints in the snow. She pictured them ripping at her heart, swallowing large chunks. *What next? The rest of me?* Would they crunch on her bones? Was her heart really as hostile an environment as the Arctic? She felt the claws of unconsciousness and looked at Dr Frampton to steady herself. From his gravy eyes, she looked to his mashed potato hair. She suddenly craved home cooking, home, her folks, security… She wasn't sure Dr Frampton was capable of killing a wolf, but she felt safe in his presence. She carefully placed her heart in his hands, and he passed it to the electro physiologists who explained the procedure.

'It's called an *ablation*. We'll put a catheter into your heart Daisy. Then we'll ablate your aberrant conduction pathways.'

'You'll what with my what?'

'Your broken heart will be fixed.'

Daisy fainted before the doctors had had the chance to anaesthetise her.

Two hours later she woke up to the grin of Hugh Grant. 'Dr Oliver, we must stop meeting like this,' she murmured, but her heart did not flutter. Again, she searched for the plush fittings of a hotel, but saw only white, sharp objects.

'Your special heart has been fixed,' he said, triumphantly.

She would, surely, fall in love with her hero all over again! She waited for the consuming flush of excitement. But it never came.

Weird.

Her emotions were all over the place, and she reached for the sides of the bed to steady herself. Anytime now she would faint and the lights would go off.

But they remained on.

Weird.

Sad tears fell for the loss of a special heart. The tears fell and her heart pumped. Happy tears fell for her feelings for Oliver, and sad tears for the fact they did not feel right. For the first time she caught these waves of emotion and rode them all the way until they petered out on the shore. They took her breath away, but she was awake for the duration. She did not faint as she continued to explore her emotions and test the stamina of her fixed heart.

Tears continued to fall for the cancer patients and their heart-broken families who walked slowly past her ward; for their suffering and pain. They fell for the boy on crutches, the double leg amputee. They fell for the grandchild with the roses for her dying grandpa, for the husband sobbing into his wife's neck. They fell for all of life's sorrow, and they fell for life's smiles, miracles, recovery and resilience.

Oh, for fuck's sake what now? Dr Oliver wondered if the procedure had gone very wrong indeed. Daisy was more of a mess than when she went in. But to his surprise he found her utterly endearing.

When Daisy cried tears dry, she rested her eyes on the white of the hospital corridor outside her door. Suddenly, two amber eyes flashed at her. She heard a monster inhale and fear made her sit to attention. She could just detect the furry shadow of an Arctic wolf before it slunk into snowy camouflage. The hunter had become the hunted.

Her heart was fixed.

But it was no less special.

Friday, November 25th

Tara Forsyth felt alone. She expected neither comfort nor sympathy from her colleagues, for she never offered any herself. She had a heart. She discovered this because she felt it break. It was only in the pain of its sorry state that she fully appreciated she had one. She attempted to liken it to the time she broke her arm when she was ten years old, or the time the lift broke in her apartment block – it was only in their absence that she fully appreciated them. Or like last summer, which she valued only in the face of winter's biting frosts. Sometimes, she thought to herself, you have to experience the bad to realise the good existed at all. She tried to translate her broken heart into a language she understood, consisting of an underrated summer, and a broken lift – things that did not threaten or confuse, and things that could be fixed. But deep down, in a place within her soul where she had never delved before, she knew these efforts were futile, for she had never felt pain like it.

Tara only realised that she had been in love when Marcus True failed to reciprocate. Her lonely love had hovered humiliatingly in the air, offering itself whole-heartedly, desperately, before falling flat on its face. Rejection crushed.

Falling hostage to love was never a position Tara wished to find herself in. Love was a weakness, and having your heart broken revealed negligence and lack of foresight. It was ugly too. Take Daisy Hawkins, for one; she had failed dismally to pull off the heartbreak look. She had carried her black makeover under a black cloud for weeks. It was not a good look. Tara sourced her power from beauty and success; ugliness and failure petrified her. Not knowing whether she had had a heart enabled her to maintain control. But to her horror, she realised she had a giant motherfucker of one. It was a major burden, like an unwanted pregnancy. She wanted to scream.

Deep down, beneath her fortress façade was a human with the same dreams and insecurities as the rest. Deeper still, into the abyss, where her thoughts journeyed today, she knew she had been scared that no man could love her. Tara was always the *"Fuck"* in the drinking game *"Fuck, Marry, Avoid"*. No one ever chose to marry her. If it was renamed *"Make Love, Marry, Avoid"*, she doubted she would feature at all.

It was symbolic, she thought, that today she wore the blood red dress Marcus had given her. The dress was a bandage, shrouding her seeping heart. A tear dropped and blotted a darker shade of red. The second-hand dress was a meagre gift of compensation. She struggled to remember the last time she cried.

Marcus True had not only got under her skin but also trespassed into dark depths where no one had ventured before. He was different. He refused to follow the crowd. He concentrated solely on his art, producing masterpieces for which she was in awe. He revealed little of himself, other than through his art; every stroke of his brush brimmed with a passion that made her tummy turn. He was respectful and sensitive and as sparing with words as generous with aura. She had relaxed in his unobtrusive presence. She had felt at ease to drop not only clothes but defences too, and he artlessly coaxed the real Tara. *No* man had ever done that before. She had presented her naked body, limb-by-limb, session after session, season after season, yet he still looked at her with indifference. Her disbelief turned to shock, shock to infuriation, infuriation to rejection, and rejection to heartbreak.

She looked at her reflection in the computer screen. For the first time she saw something that resembled *ugliness*, before feeling her body tremor as bricks of her fortress started to crumble away. She bit her nails before running the corrugated ends down her side until they stopped at her waist and her fingers squeezed two fleshy handfuls; she squished the offensive lumps that represented an indulgence she felt she did not deserve. Taking her miso soup from her desk, she walked to the kitchen and poured the snowy tofu contents down the drain. She had never felt so empty yet so fat. On exiting, with head held low, she almost walked straight into Daisy Hawkins, who was heading for the microwave with her lunch. Tara felt invisible.

'Oh, sorry,' Daisy exclaimed.

'It's OK,' said Tara, raising heavy eyes towards Daisy. She liked Daisy's hair. She had never before noticed that Daisy Hawkins had pretty hair. But she did. Daisy looked *content.* Back at her desk Tara ran her hands through her own raven hair. She felt the nips on her scalp as split nails deracinated some strands. Usually, her hair felt like silk. Today it felt like horsehair. Usually, her nails were polished and pristine. Today they were broken.

'Are you quite *sure* Tara was wearing your scarlet dress, Daise?'

'*Yes!* One hundred percent. Firstly, I bought it in a random boutique abroad; secondly, it was a wrap-around – exactly the same style as mine; and thirdly, the ends of the ties were mangled, like – hmmm, let me think now – they had got caught in a cab door or *something,* not that I'm jumping to conclusions or anything!'

'Well, I did tell you Tara had your cream cardigan too. Maybe she has a Daisy wardrobe fetish. You're an odd choice, it has to be said, but–'

'D'you remember, we searched my cupboard high and low for that dress before my date with Lucian, and we eventually concluded I must have left it in the hospital after my accident.'

'Yes, I do. So from the hospital to Tara. How is that possible? Daisy? You all right? Daise?'

'I'm waiting.'

'What for?'

'My heart tremble, my disappearing act. Pinch me, could you. *Ow, Jeeezus, not that hard!*' The temptation to test her repaired heart had occupied her throughout the week.

'*So*...Oliver rescued you, so he would have had your dress. Yes? So only *he* could have given it to Tara? Yes? But do you know if Tara and Oliver know each other, Daise?'

'*No!* I mean no, they certainly do not.*'

'You *quite* sure about that? She is acquainted with most of London's male population, remember, and the last time you gave Dr Oliver a check-up, he was all man, I presume?'

'You don't think…?'

'Well…*no*, I'm not saying they are shagging each other. Maybe just friends?'

'I doubt it's possible for Tara to be just a friend to a guy. The temptation to whip her knickers off must be *HUOWGE*. So let's say they *are* sleeping together, that would mean that Marcus, Lucian *and* her clients aren't enough for her… So Fanny-Forsyth has to dig her talons into Oliver too. Bloody hell, that girl is insatiable! Where does she find the energy, let alone the time? Don't get me wrong, I'm *very* angry and *totally* disgusted, but a part of me's quite impressed too.'

'Why don't you just go and ask her. Oi, Fanny-Forsyth, what you playing at?'

'No way. She terrifies me. Also, she looks sad today.'

'Smug, you mean?'

'No *sad*. Depressed. Seriously scrawny too. And her usually perfect nails looked like a mangled edge of Edam rind, as if she has been chewing on them and bugger all else. I'll see what Oliver has to say for himself later this evening.'

'Let him speak first before you jump to conclusions, OK?'

'Of course. I thought you'd be delighted with evidence against Tara?'

'Everyone deserves a fair trial, even Tara.'

'OK, Jude. But if we're right about this, I give up on men. *What?* Don't look at me like that, I'm serious! Princes, actors, singers, artists, doctors… Tinkers, tailors, soldiers, sailors–'

'Rich men?'

'*They're the worst!*'

'And love?' Jude looked quizzical.

'Well,' Daisy scratched her head, 'I guess if I gave up on love, then I would be giving up on myself.'

'Finally, you speak sense, woman.'

'But–'

'Uh oh. What?'

'I give up on *searching* for love. I will turn my attentions to other things, like Lucian advised, and it will come and sit on my shoulder.'

'And on your face, if you're lucky.'

'That's gross, Jude.'

'Let love find you.'

'*Exactly.*'

'So give up on *all* men *apart* from the one who finds you and bears the gift of true love?'

'*Precisely.* I *would* help him with his task by wearing my red dress, to stick out from the crowd like a distress signal, *but* for some *weird* reason Tara Forsyth is bloody wearing it.'

'Love will find you without your scarlet dress, Daisy, trust me.'

'That's so sweet.'

'You've got a voice like a fog-horn.'

'Oi!' She chuckled and hurled a ball of paper at her best friend.

That evening at just before 8pm, Oliver's dirty grin welcomed Daisy at his door. He held a bottle of wine in one hand, whilst the other removed an oven cloth from his shoulder. 'Well hel-lo, sexy lady! Just in time, grub's nearly up,' he said.

His chocolate eyes swirled beneath the hallway light. Daisy had always had a soft spot for Hugh Grant, and resisted temptation to strip off and dive in. Instead, she remained focused on her mission: to extract the truth about him and Tara.

'Pumpkin and butternut squash soup for starter,' he said, as he led her into the main room, where all the delicious smells were coming from. 'Followed by a Tuna Poke Tower with avocado. Followed by,' he flashed his cheeky grin at her, 'a poke from *my* Tower…*Yes?'*

'No,' Daisy's forehead crunched and Oliver looked broken.

'OK, then. Maybe a chocolate panna cotta with peanut brittle is more to the lady's liking?'

She smiled and darted her eyes across the plush modern fittings of the interior. It was so clean and clinical, you could perform an operation in there.

'And then, if mood dictates, we can always return to that second helping of poke.' His chuckle was thick with filth.

Daisy accepted a glass of wine before her request to snoop around his house was granted. She stretched the grant to a warrant and the snoop to a full-blown search, and left Oliver in the kitchen. Her eyes were set on wide alert, for signs of Tara-related activity – pants (especially of the pink variety), bras, mascara, eyeliner, snapped acrylic nails… Daisy had evidence to collect to build her case. She hooked her neck into the study, which burst with medical books. From the desk, her eyes scanned the shelves, then the walls.

Jasper caught her eye.

And again.

And again.

And held it.

Over.

And over.

And over again.

My God! She stepped into the centre of the room and swivelled around on the same spot. The walls were a dissection lab and Jasper's body parts were distributed across each: his tongue – which did not crush her; his mouth – which did not swallow her; his hand – which did not squeeze the life from her; his foot – which did not kick her; his eyes – into which she did not fall; his tear – in which she did not drown… She felt the aggressive quivers and beguiling flutters but stood strong. Jasper, not abstract, manipulated or malformed, but Jasper, as clear as day. He consumed the wall space but failed to consume her. Stepping forward, she read the expected signature on the bottom of a painting – *Marcus True*. She knew Oliver knew Marcus but she hadn't dare ask if he knew Jasper too; were they friends too then, or was Oliver just obsessed with Marcus's paintings of him? She closed the door to contain her ex and took a deep breath before opening the bedroom door. Her wine glass nearly slipped from her hand as she came face to face with Tara Forsyth – naked, bar her pink pants. Beautiful Tara. Her web spun the room and there was no space for Daisy.

Back in the corridor, she leant against the back of the bedroom door. Her heart trembled. She had seen her before, that particular Tara, in *that* nakedness, in *that* pose, wearing *those* pants, with *that* expression – sultry and vampish. She sourced her memory to Lucian's mobile phone and their date in the dark. The *exact* same

Tara had flashed before her eyes from the screen of his mobile; but not the pornographic photo she had presumed, rather an exquisite, photorealist painting.

Lucian was a painter after all, and Tara, Daisy knew, modelled for Marcus True. So perhaps Tara also modelled for Lucian? Modelled, *not* shagged. It *was* possible. She imagined the London art scene was incestuous like that, and not necessarily in a sexual way.

Feeling fractionally uplifted, she re-entered the bedroom and kneeling on Oliver's bed. She eyeballed Tara, before searching for Lucian's signature. She followed Tara's pointy elbow to the scratched name, but it read *Marcus True*.

Back outside the bedroom, Daisy's mind wrestled confusion – *how and why would Lucian have a photo of Marcus True's painting of Tara on his phone?* She spilt her wine and cursed herself. Looking down at the puddle on the carpet, she took a tissue from her pocket and squatted like a dog on all fours to soak up the alcohol.

'Wehey! Already?' Oliver's voice reached Daisy from behind. He liked what he saw. 'The Tuna Poke *before* the starter, eh? Well, well, Miss Daisy Hawkins, I must admit I rather like your style!' He unbuckled his belt.

Swivelling her head, Daisy saw him unzipping his fly.

'God, *no!* My wine,' she rammed a pointing finger back and forth at the puddle.

Oliver went to fetch a cloth; he should have known it was too good to be true. Daisy stood up, brushed the carpet off her skirt and the cobwebs from her mind; the Halloween tour of the haunted house of horrors had misted her clarity.

Over orange soup, Daisy hit Oliver with question after question, like a ball in a game of squash. He batted back answers, finding some less challenging than others, and at times he looked quite sheepish. He appreciated the unfamiliar strength in her voice: who was this woman – powerful, fearless, in control – who exercised a right for truth and respect?

'I've been friends with the True brothers for as long as I can remember,' Oliver explained. 'Marcus has been flawless in his friendship, exceptionally loyal…and I owe him, basically.' He paused and cleared his throat. 'So err anyway, I've always supported his artistic career. He's now exploring new subjects, and for the first time, I buy his work not because I feel duty-bound, but because I *like* them.'

'His female nudes, for example?'

By the tone of Daisy's voice, Oliver could tell there was a right or wrong answer. *'Err, yes…?'* he replied hesitantly. The expression on her face made him feel like a pervert; he liked it.

'Like the one of Tara Forsyth in your bedroom?' she asked.

Daisy's mind swam with astonishing revelations. She mentioned seeing Tara in her red dress earlier that day, and asked Oliver straight out if he knew anything about it, and if he was sleeping with her. Oliver was taken aback by the candour of her question and squirmed in his lose-lose situation, caught between a rock and a hard place. If he maintained his lie, that it was *he* who had saved Daisy from her hit-and-run, and *he* who had rushed her to hospital, then he should surely be able to shed light on the whereabouts of her scarlet dress, and explain why it surfaced on Tara's body earlier that day. But he could not. His lie arrived with a revelation he had not predicted. The truth was, this was the first time he heard that Daisy had worn a scarlet dress on the day of her accident; he had only had the pleasure of seeing her in her undies – even if non-matching. But if he maintained the rescue lie, then Daisy would presume he was sleeping with Tara and that her dress had been a post-coital present – *because that's the fucked up way women think*. He might maintain his hero status, but be presumed unfaithful, and he did not want Daisy to think he was cheating, because for once, he was not (nurse Stephanie didn't count). He did not want to lose Daisy. Therefore, Oliver chose to pass the buck onto Marcus. Marcus must have given Daisy's dress to Tara, as it was Marcus who actually rescued Daisy. 'Hands up,' – Oliver had lied – 'but on a good note, I'm not sleeping with Tara,' *All cool? Make-up sex now?*

Daisy chewed on these fresh discoveries: Oliver the liar, Marcus her hero.

As their glasses were topped, so were her questions and his revelations:

'What? You're kidding, Daisy? No, no you've got it all wrong. Marcus did not *prevent* Jasper from going to rehab; he was the *only* reason Jasper went to rehab. Marcus spent years trying to persuade his brother to go. I should know – he got me roped in too. Jasper's a stubborn git at the best of times, and then, when addiction really took its toll, Jasper refused to listen to anyone. He had to get to death's door before he finally gave in. Marcus is a total Saint.'

All that Daisy knew was turned inside out. Jasper the sinner. Marcus the saint. Once solid facts uprooted and turned to water as revelations continued to flow:

'No, no Daisy! As if! Marcus *resented* painting his brother. But painting was his way of venting…his therapy, if you like. Counsellors, psychiatrists don't do it for him, you see. He's not that kind of guy. He's private and individual and does things his way. His numerous paintings of Jasper are evidence of his devotion. He cared so much that he had no head space for anything else.'

'But he still exploits his brother by profiting financially from them.'

'No. He donates a large portion of the money he makes from the Jasper paintings to good causes: rehab centres, of course, London art galleries, WWF… Wildlife not wrestling. I presume anyway.'

Jasper the liar! On the inside, Daisy cried tears of shame and found new respect for a man she had disliked. On the outside, to her surprise, she maintained composure.

Well, thought Oliver, over untouched panna cotta, what else have I got to lose? He had lost any hope for sex, and by the looks of things, he might have lost Daisy too. 'I may as well mention…' And Daisy learnt then that it was Marcus True – not Oliver after all – who had spotted her faulty heartbeat; that it was Marcus True – not Oliver – who had diagnosed her heart condition; that it was Marcus True – not Oliver – who had fixed her broken heart…

…Marcus, whose painting of Tara in the pink pants had appeared on Lucian's phone; Marcus, who had a fish tattoo which matched the description of Lucian's. Marcus, who smelt of tobacco, turpentine and forest. Marcus, who smelt like Lucian. Marcus, who had an intense, gravelly voice, like thick dry paint on a masterpiece. Marcus, who sounded like Lucian. Marcus, who was a saint, like Lucian. Marcus, who fixed her broken heart. Like Lucian.

Thanks for dinner and apologies for her abrupt departure failed to slip through the thick mesh of her thoughts. She was caught in a net that carried her hastily from Oliver's table to his door, to a cab and to her Warren on Sutherland Place.

She lay on her bed in the dark and wondered: *when do coincidences become suspicious? When do coincidences become something more? How many does it take? Four? Five? Six? How many until you know you're onto something?* Could it be that just as she is Eliza, Marcus is Lucian? Could it be that the man she thought she loved was the man she thought she hated? Had the licks of true love triggered her faint at *Portrait of a Boy*, and again on Marcus's doorstep?

Juliet blushed furiously as she swam laps of her fishbowl. She could feel her owner's troubles in her water and knew the implications, 'My only love sprung from my only hate!'

Daisy realised that if Lucian and Marcus were one and the same, then Lucian must have known her real name was Daisy and not Eliza long ago, from the moment she had mentioned she was dating Jasper. Her detailed descriptions of him and her mention of 'his brother Marcus True' would have exposed her real identity. Eliza had become redundant long ago. *Embarrassing!* Lucian had gently guided her through her troubled time with Jasper. If he had revealed he was Jasper's brother, then he would have exposed his real identity and killed their friendship, for he knew how much she despised Marcus. So by keeping *Lucian* "alive", he had kept them alive – Eliza and Lucian. Daisy and Marcus.

And on their first date, when she stood Lucian up because of the car accident…he had not seemed surprised or irritated *because* he had been with her in the hospital all along. So he must have known she had lied about working late. *Mortifying!*

Then there was Tara. If Tara modelled and slept with Marcus, then she must provide that same service for Lucian too. Fact. Tara had told Jude many times that she and Marcus were "together", plus, he had given Tara the scarlet dress. How could any man not help himself to a serving of Tara Forsyth, and then resist going back for seconds, thirds, fourths and goodness only knows how many more helpings. He wouldn't just want to paint a beauty, he would want to touch it, caress it, mould it, own it, fuck it… *Enough!*

Well, thought Oliver, Daisy had not said thank you, nor had she apologised for leaving her food untouched. He had slaved away to create a dinner worthy of a Michelin star, yet in return she had bombarded him with a barrage of questions and left before any jiggery-pokery. *Well*, he thought again, Daisy Hawkins was shaping up to be quite a challenge. She had been downright rude. He would never have guessed she had it in her. *Wow!*

Amongst the uneaten food, one hand cradled an elbow, whilst the other rubbed his chin in contemplation. *Wow, wow, wow!* He had answered questions obediently, like a prisoner of war. Thoughts to question *her* questions had escaped him; she never allowed him time to think! *Why the obsessive line of questioning? Why the True brother interest? And Tara?* Like an expert, Daisy had concealed all and controlled the conversation from beginning to end, before fleeing with all the power, leaving not a crumb for him. Well, he thought again, I like her style. I like it a lot. Daisy the dominatrix. He stirred and swelled at the prospect. Was she really the same blushing girl with the earplug stuck down her ear? The same emotional nutcase who had blubbed like a baby after her heart procedure? He was entranced by her dynamism. He took her untouched peanut brittle from her plate and snapped it in half. Daisy Hawkins was the type of girl who could break his heart; he only knew this because that evening he felt a powerful sensation rise from a place deep within him, towering over lust, like Phoenix from the flames. He felt true love for the very first time.

Tara could not remember the last time she had stayed in on a Friday night. As usual, she had not been short of offers, to which she had been bothered to decline some but not all. As she climbed into bed, she felt like she was climbing a mountain. She hadn't eaten anything for a couple of days and suspected she wouldn't be hungry for a while. As she turned off the light, comforting warmth and distractions were swallowed by darkness. She closed her eyes and saw Marcus True and braced herself for the familiar pounce of heartbreak.

Friday, December 2nd

All I want for Christmas is Daisy Hawkins, thought Oliver. But by day two of December, things were already looking bleak. He had called her throughout the week, leaving message after message. *Am I calling too much?* He had bombarded her with texts and sent flowers to her work. *Am I being too keen? Be keen, keep'em mean* – there seemed to be truth to the saying whichever way you looked at it. He had never felt so insecure. It was a horrendous feeling. As her replies became less frequent, the more mysterious she became, and Oliver was hooked.

In contrast, nurse Stephanie was anything but mysterious. He equated her advances to the launch of an armada. When she had come to him the previous evening, with her cannon-ball breasts ready for action, he had refused to engage and his love for Daisy was confirmed. With no warning, love had arrived and made a mockery of his life schedule. But to his surprise, he didn't mind – it felt exhilarating to be out of control. Daisy's refusal to retaliate blasted his heart, but he launched himself whole-heartedly into battle for reciprocal love.

Oliver's relentless attentions failed to distract Daisy from his deception and thoughts of Marcus. His revelations were all that the girls had discussed over the last week. 'In a nutshell, it's all pretty complicated,' said Jude, 'You couldn't make it up if you tried.' Daisy was flummoxed at the discovery that "Lucian" was Marcus True's pseudonym, and therefore must be Tara Forsyth's boyfriend – current, or more likely ex, given Tara's recent disposition. Either way, her makeover into a bag of bones did not bode well for bedroom activity. 'She would snap in half like a twig,' remarked Jude.

It was true. Daisy glimpsed a spindly Tara flinching in her crowded imagination. Tara Forsyth no longer looked like sex.

'If Tara was sex,' continued Jude, 'the planet's population would plummet and the world would be a very sad place indeed.' She rubbed her stomach secretly beneath the tabletop, hoping her young suspicions of pregnancy were accurate.

As the afternoon drew to a close, Daisy popped another red-rosed bunch of Oliver's unrequited love onto Jude's desk, before venturing to the hospital for an impromptu chat with the man himself, where she would end whatever it was going on between them. With his abundant calls, texts and flowers in mind, she felt that face-to-face closure was the decent thing to do. Her heart felt fixed, and she was able to approach love with a new sense of clarity and purpose, and Oliver was not what she wanted.

She stood tall, pushed back her shoulders, and inhaled deeply as she waited on Piccadilly in the December cold for the bus to Chelsea and Westminster Hospital. Her mind wandered, as it so often did, to thoughts of Lucian. She had not been in touch. She had been busy attempting to solve the riddles of her world, starting with her hospital procedure and her fixed heart, then the incident of Tara in her red dress, then Oliver's revelations and the resultant litter of curious coincidences and suspicions. Her mind had mulled over months' worth of word sharing with Lucian; she wondered when *exactly* he could have discovered that Daisy was hiding behind Eliza.

Who was he? If Lucian *was* Marcus, then was her online lifeline kaput? The name was made up, was the character too? She had been duped, but knew she was guilty of the very same charge. When was he planning on ending their little game of hide and seek and revealing his true identity? And wasn't it odd that he hadn't defended himself against her spiteful words and accusations? During one of their conversations about Marcus, she regretfully recalled writing, *'I hate him.'* Lucian would have read *'I hate you.'* What type of guy would put up with that? She would continue to avoid Lucian until her mind and her repaired heart offered clear guidance. She was swimming in murky waters with no idea where she was heading.

Thankfully, the bus driver had a clearer idea of his destination. She sat on the top deck, whilst her mind continued to march.

As she approached Oliver's office, she saw a nurse through the half open door and recognised her from the evening of the heart-shaped sandwich. All of a sudden, Daisy witnessed a kaleidoscope of bare limbs and garments; the nurse was changing, so Daisy held back, respecting her privacy. She hovered around a corner by the water machine, but still in sight of the door. Around her neck, the nurse placed a stethoscope that bounced between her bosoms. Daisy watched as she bent down to secure some stiletto boots – thigh-high in inappropriateness. *That's some uniform.* Then she witnessed Oliver enter the office, before slamming the door. Daisy made a hasty retreat and made for the hospital exit. *'He's a player'* – Lucian's words rang in her ear again – *did I ever really doubt him?*

Ever?

'For Christ's sake, Stephanie! I thought I made it clear last night – this *cannot* go on. Put your scrubs back on, would you please.'

But she was all over him like a rash. He searched his mind for a remedy… Some kind of repellent… Something to soothe the incessant itch…

'I'm in love with someone else!' he blurted. *Immediate relief!*

'I'm in love,' he repeated, doubling the dose.

'I'm in love,' he said, to really rub it in.

Crestfallen, nurse Stephanie took some deep breaths and mourned the sabotaged moment. She removed her hands from his chest and her stethoscope from around her neck. She placed it gently in his ears before resting the bell on her chest. Her watery eyes stared out at him beneath long eyelashes. She hoped he could hear the irregular beat of her broken heart.

'Have you closed the door on closure?' asked Jude over the table at a mutual friend's engagement dinner later that evening.

'Yes,' said Daisy across the clatter of plates and the to-ing and fro-ing of chutneys, samosas, onion bhajis and wine bottles. 'Oliver did actually – saved me the bother.' When he had closed the door of his office earlier that evening, having chosen, Daisy assumed, to remain on the porno side, he had shut Daisy out of his life. 'Locked and bolted, and it could not have gone better.'

As Marcus washed remnants of his painting *Resurrected Autopsy* from his paintbrushes, he listened to the now familiar moans and groans coming from downstairs; Floyd was rehearsing the same scene with Xander, his Othello. Always that scene, thought Marcus suspiciously. Iago let out a groan. Othello roared back. Marcus wracked his brains, trying to decipher which particular scene presented such a challenge that it demanded such regular rehearsals. He came to the conclusion that it must be near the end when Othello attacks Iago. Although it didn't sound like a tragedy downstairs. Marcus was confident that he would be pitch-perfect if one of them fell ill. But on hearing another revealing groan, he decided against offering to be an understudy.

Back in his studio, with his door firmly shut, he returned to the painting that he was currently working on for *Artopsy*. His collection was building steadily, and he was pleased with the progress. *Resurrected Autopsy* was nearing completion. Despite his red standing man's incised chest – which exposed part of an x-ray and an elevated wiry ribcage – he appeared to breathe with life. Marcus had likened this painting process, and the evolution of both his idea and collection, to an autopsy in reverse; after a body is systematically sliced open, and all organs removed and analysed, they are returned inside, before being put back together in preparation for a funeral. Marcus, who had witnessed this process during his medical training, incorporated aspects into his process, but with hope – he prepared his painted figures for the future not the afterlife.

Meanwhile, downstairs in the sitting room, Beth sat on the sofa with Shell, drinking whiskeys and ginger ale. It had been Daisy who had given Beth's number to Shell, during her curative Channel Island retreat. Daisy had bumped into Shell at the airport after their initial beach meeting. On hearing that Shell was an accomplished photographer, Daisy hoped that Beth would appreciate the introduction to a promising new artist. Plus, something in Daisy thought Beth and Shell might get on, but why exactly that was, she could not tell.

'This particular collection', said Beth, pointing to a sea of pink boxes, and enlarging one, 'is truly sensational, Shell.' Each photograph showed various women emerging from large pink balloons. One image pictured hands peeking through latex, like she was emerging from a womb. In another the woman was obviously naked, yet Shell had only captured one side of her body and her foot prodded the viewer's space, like she was stepping out of a vagina.

'I see some of Georgia O'Keefe in your work,' Beth smiled.

'She's my heroine,' gasped Shell.

'And this one…' Beth enlarged another photograph, 'is quite *magnificent*.' She noticed the girl's hair was the colour of sand, and her smile beamed like a lighthouse; her eyes were like the clear blue sky, her hair was like the wind and her skin glistened like a mermaid's. 'Your work is breathtaking, Shell. And the way you've captured this moment…well, it is exquisite.' Beth took a closer look at the model in the photo – *a contemporary Raphael beauty!* She turned to Shell, who looked back with blushed cheeks. Beth gasped. 'It's you!' she whispered, wide-eyed. 'I think I love you,' she blurted accidentally, 'you're work, I mean. I love your work.' She swiftly offered Shell exhibition space in her gallery.

So whilst Marcus polished off his artwork for the Christmas exhibition, Floyd and Xander polished off each other. Shell broke into Beth's life and the London

Art scene, and at around 2am Marcus messaged Daisy. It had been a busy night of art and love on Aldridge Road Villas.

Daisy arrived home bloated with curry. Through the lace of cheap white wine, she saw a mangled envelope on her doorstep. It stood apart from the brash white of the bills. Perhaps this one, she voiced in inebriated mumbles, might be a giver not a taker. She saw the Airmail stripes and the foreign stamp…*Jasper. Bastard.* Her clumsy fingers scratched at the taped opening, and she attempted to read:

'*...i lied. marcus never stopped me going to rehab, he only ever encouraged it. he is the opposite of selfish. i want you to meet him. he loves you – who doesn't love the girl of their dreams? I'm sorry for keeping you two apart and for interrupting fate...*'

Daisy's butterflies geared up for the sensational flutter into unconsciousness but her mended heart resisted. Alcohol failed to numb her excitement, and she tripped towards her computer. *Could Marcus / Lucian love me? But what about Tara?* Her mind jumped to Max and Miss Polo, to Floyd and Beth, to Oliver and the nurse; she was tired of sharing love. She returned her gaze to the letter: '*he loves you.*' The letter was potent with a frankness and integrity that even wine could not disguise, and she believed him.

'*Hi!*' she blurted to Lucian on instant messenger, hoping he was there. If she had not been tipsy, she would have invested more time in planning. She waited for his reply but sleep found her first. She woke an hour later at around 2am to the beep of a message and Lucian's kiss: '*Hi Eliza. Can I have your address? Something I want to send. X*'

Across the Atlantic and in the heart of rehab, Jasper bit his nails as he walked with burdened steps towards the post-box. He had never bitten his nails before; in moments of anxiety, he had always preferred refuge in illicit substances rather than shavings of keratin. His nails, he realised, looking at their wrecked state, were the only part of him that had deteriorated in rehab. Generally, he felt good, but he would have felt a damn sight better if he had remembered to unpick the final nail from his coffin in his previous letter to Daisy. Once again, he found paper, and penned the following facts:

'*i forgot to mention the truth about floyd and beth... you know i knew them... old family friends and housemates of marcus... the truth is the twins are gay... your assumption that they were in love with each other was better than i could have invented myself. facts would've destroyed everything... you would have continued your friendship with beth, and she was a bridge to marcus that i didn't want you to cross... floyd is a great guy, but he used you to please his ill mum... he messed up... he's sorry... we all make mistakes... granted, some more than others... he's mid-rehearsing for the part of iago at the globe, and has fallen crazily in love with othello... floyd finally found his own balls too and told his mum the truth... she's loving her son's newfound fame and all the media attention... her recovery is gaining pace... beth was in love with you daisy... it broke her heart to hear how i was treating you...*'

Jasper slipped the envelope into the post-box, and his walk back towards the common room felt lighter.

Friday, December 9th

Friday afternoon chugged along like an old steam train. Eyes glanced at the clock, which stubbornly refused to be rushed; adamant it would go at its own pace. Some worked away quietly, making up for time spent battling the Oxford Street crowds whilst sneakily Christmas shopping during the week. Others prepared hair and makeup for a Friday night out on the town, whilst several had already started work on cans of beer.

Daisy was worrying about Hanratty's two-fold challenge to find true love by the end of the year and celebrate it in her column. She knew she had stronger feelings for Marcus than for any other guy, but the facts remained: she had not properly met him yet, so how could she convince Hanratty and her readers of *real* love? In fact, how could she convince herself? Her dating experiences had only made her wary and cynical. She felt the promise of love and the hum of something truly magnificent, but she needed to be sure he felt the same way; a one-sided love was nothing to celebrate. However, she would never jeopardise potential true love for the sake of a challenge in a magazine by rushing a meeting between them. After all, they had waited a year already.

Jude came over to Daisy's desk to exchange make up and overdue chitchat. With two ears on Jude and two eyes on *Sabre* magazine, Daisy was updated on Millie's toddling progress. *RAH!* Burst with its usual colourful display of upper class tittle-tattle.

'*My God...*' Daisy exclaimed, under her breath, 'Jude! Look here.'

Jude peered over Daisy's shoulder. 'But isn't he...?'

'Yes!'

'But...didn't you two–'

'*Just kiss!*'

'But...you said he was in love with his sister?'

'*I know.* Oops. Oh Jude, I think I might just have got that very, *very* wrong.'

They looked at Floyd who grinned back at the girls' astonished faces. His platinum hair bobbed coils behind his elfish ear. His Scandinavian skin was complemented by the skin of a handsome black man who reclined behind him on the chaise long, with his arm looped over Floyd's waist; '*Xander Waterman,*' they read, '*who plays Othello.*' Floyd's ice-blue eyes sparkled with contentment, beneath his highlighted quotation, which loomed above: '*Seething with hatred for a man I love can present a real challenge in some of the scenes.*'

Jude and Daisy flicked eyes across to another photograph that showed a healthy and beaming Mrs Clansey enveloping mauve cashmere arms around her son. '*Now everything feels right,*' she was quoted as saying. '*And the truth is magnificent.*'

'Well, well, well...' said Daisy. She didn't quite know what to think, but the article certainly explained a few things. 'Oops,' she said again. She recalled the conversation she had overheard between Floyd and Beth at Mrs Clansey's party:

'You shouldn't be treating her like this,' Beth had said.

'But she's perfect for–'

'For your little lie?'...

The lie was embarrassingly plain to see now: Floyd had never been in love with Beth after all; he was gay, not incestuous, and Daisy's role as oblivious accomplice was crucial to cover this up.

'Shit.' Daisy's face contorted before settling into a guilty smile.

'The robbed that smiles, steals something from the thief,' said Jude, before adding, 'Othello Act I, Scene III...I know, I know, I'm a genius,' she chuckled, and threw on her coat. 'Right, grab yer coat, love, and let's go wander this weird and wonderful little world of ours.'

Later that night back at her Warren, two intriguing envelopes greeted Daisy. One was black with silver writing. *From Lucian?* Since texting him her address, she had checked her post eagerly each day, clueless as to what to expect. Her hands shook as she noticed the name on the envelope was *"Daisy"*, not *"Eliza"*. She felt her cheeks flush. Anxiety made her put it aside.

She looked at the other envelope and immediately recognised the writing as Jasper's. Each of his letters looked burdened and uncomfortable under the pressure of scrutiny. Jasper tended to shy away from joined up writing and avoided capital letters. The end of the 'd' for Daisy screeched like an owl to the 'a', which bucked like a wild pony to the 'i', which clawed like a tiger to the 's', which writhed like a snake to the 'y', which kicked its tail like a whale over to Hawkins, and so on, and so on. Each letter wriggled noisily in the limelight and shot forward, refusing to take responsibility and passing the burden to the next in line.

Inside, on white paper, Jasper confirmed the truth about Floyd's sexuality that Daisy had discovered earlier that day. As words continued to span the width of each tidy line, they exposed further truths, which could have prevented the muddle, if Jasper had only shared them earlier.

Next, she turned to the black envelope with the silver writing. Each letter settled comfortably into its allotted space. The capital 'D' stood bold and proud, refusing to dash over to the 'a', which sat content before chivalrously escorting her to the 'i'; the 's' swooned quite graciously, and the 'y' just chilled, swinging its long leg beneath the other letters. Each letter enjoyed its moment in the spotlight and each held its own, confident and secure. She looked again at her silver name; *'Daisy Hawkins',* and again felt her cheeks flush.

Inside was an invitation catalogue to an art exhibition. She read the cover – *Artopsy; Symbiosis of Art and Science,* to be held at the Natural History Museum. She collected information from each page. *Best of young contemporary British artists, a group exhibition...* She glanced at work from the exhibitors. When she turned the next page, tiny paper butterflies poured out, *loads of them!* An entire rabble, all colours of the rainbow. They fluttered to the floor like star-flakes, falling from the pages that displayed the work of *"Marcus True"*. His two paintings chosen for the catalogue were startlingly expressive: gory, figurative, medical... They reminded her of the paintings of Jasper she had seen at both the gallery and Oliver's study. But there was a clear difference; the stain of burden had been washed clean away. It was obvious, even to Daisy's guessing eye, that this work was born from pleasure not pain.

Looking down to the floor, she bent to retrieve one scarlet paper butterfly from the confetti heap, which was larger than the rest. Each wing had been cut into the shape of a heart. There was writing in silver pen again, as on the envelope:

'Please don't turn your attentions to other things for too long.'

He was referring to the Thoreau quote, 'Happiness is like a butterfly.' She turned over the paper butterfly and read, *'Lucian. X.'* Through misty eyes she searched through the other butterflies. On only one she found more words, *'I hope you found your ring, Eliza.'* She looked at her silver ring on her thumb, recalled its magical reappearance after their brief date in the dark, pictured it around Marcus's housemate Beth's neck and fitted together the final lose pieces of the jigsaw. *Derren Brown, eat your heart out.*

Marcus had barely slept all week. The exhibition was in a week's time, and although Beth and Floyd agreed that his collection looked perfectly complete, he could see areas that still demanded hours of attention. He was a perfectionist, after all.

Daisy had, of course, been on his mind too. The invitation he had posted to her should have arrived by now. Jasper had assured him that he had cleared Marcus of any wrongdoing, and that there should be no outstanding reason why Daisy should harbour negative feelings towards him.

Marcus's mind was stuffed with a million questions that only Daisy could answer. *How did she feel? Angry? Betrayed? Relieved? Happy?* His note with all the butterflies...*was it too cheesy?* He had been carried away in the moment. They had taken him ages to cut, but had she cringed, as he was now, in the sarcastic glare of hindsight?

It's torture in the dark!

From years of practice, Marcus took advantage of his angst-ridden adrenaline to fuel the progress of his paintings. With thoughts of Daisy, he fired his work with passion.

Will she go to the exhibition?

He made small alterations to his collection for *Artopsy*. Whilst Marcus had control over his art's destiny, only Daisy had control over his own.

Will we meet properly in the light?

Friday, December 16th

Marcus mused on the word *"Symbiosis"* and lingered on its meaning: *a mutually beneficial relationship between two species.*

Would Daisy come tonight?

He stood beneath the 32-metre long cast of the Diplodocus skeleton in the central hall of the Natural History Museum. The hall was magnificent in scale and grandeur. He sipped on a coffee as the other exhibitors, curators, gallery and security staff, maintenance and transport guys, cleaners and caterers wandered to and fro, transporting various items: exhibits, labels, paperwork, bubble wrap, wooden boxes, tape, nails, security ropes, flowers, food, music equipment, all objects great and small required for an exhibition of this scale. Unusual sounds blared from the speakers, then screeched, before stopping abruptly. The intermittent dolphin cries for Carla Lightfoot's *Ascension of Man* was music to the ears in comparison, thought Marcus, as he watched candlesticks and plaques polished to bright and beautiful in preparation for tonight's Christmas exhibition.

Each exhibit was more or less in position. Rowena Mellow, head curator and museum dinosaur, had instructed Marcus and the other exhibitors to be present during the moving and installing of their work. Everyone involved had to be happy with the final results, considered Marcus, as his eyes coursed through the Diplodocus's ribs and up to the vertebrae. Organising an exhibition of this size was no mean feat.

Amongst the hustle and bustle, one man at least looked content: Charles Darwin, who sat on his marble throne at the top of the hall's grand staircase, casting watchful eyes on eleventh-hour kerfuffle beneath. *How could anyone dare put a foot wrong in his presence?* Marcus climbed the stairs to have a quiet word with the big man himself. Below, a mortal spilt a coffee. Marcus turned to witness a flock of people congregating with cloths and fuss. Looking back at Darwin, he translated a bemused expression on his face.

Marcus thought of Daisy as his eyes roamed across Darwin's furrowed brow and the setting of his lips in his beard. Marcus probed beneath in search of accurate translation: was Darwin concerned? Amused? Was there a hint of a smile? Was he trying to tell him something? To banish his high hopes and expectations? Would Daisy come tonight? He telepathised his questions through the air beneath the marble skull. Marcus had not heard from Daisy at all; had she even received his invitation? He imagined sitting on Darwin's knee, like a child sits on Father Christmas's knee, hoping for a gift. Suddenly, he felt small; telescoped into the boy he was. He wanted to be told good things; he wanted reassurance from someone he could trust. Then Darwin's great face turned to him and Marcus looked into his father's eyes. His father pressed his giant hand on his back, transmitting strength and support – such warmth from such cold marble.

Marcus watched Darwin's beard wobble as his lips moved with speech.

'Have faith, my son. She will come.'

And he noticed a careful smile and a nod, heavy with earnestness, broad and comforting. His eyebrows wiggled, in the way he remembered his father's would when a smile consumed his usual composure.

'Oi, Dippy!' shrieked Rowena Mellow.

Dippy?

'No, not you, Marcus. Him,' she smiled crookedly, pointing at the Diplodocus. 'It's his nickname. That said, despite yelling "Marcus" three times, strangely dippy seemed to do the trick.'

'Sorry. I was…elsewhere.'

'No kidding. No, you're all right you are. You're good to go. The other exhibitors have gone, apart from Buffy. We're struggling to squeeze her *Ticking Breasts* into their allotted space. Someone made a boob of the measurements. *Unbelievable!* Bit late in the game for things to be going tits-up!' She chortled, high on exhibition fever. 'Anyway, go-go, shoo-shoo…time's ticking on. Make yourself look beautiful, damn it!' Rowena hesitated, before her powerful hind limbs took steps towards him. Her large head first to prod new space, followed by Tyrannosaur-esqe forelimbs, which bore small, clawed digits. She looked appalled. 'My Gawd! Why, you look ghastly! Utterly exhausted,' she roared. 'Go get some rest and come back with your winning smile and some energy. It'll be fab. See you later.' She wiggled her stubby digits up and down in a fashion that resembled a prehistoric wave, before swivelling around to shake her tail in the direction of the big boob.

PR had done a sterling job in the run up to the exhibition. All of the Charles Saatchis of the world would be there, along with prestigious gallery owners and elusive private buyers. Everyone who was anyone in the international art scene would be present, in one way or another – if their feet weren't moving across the hallway, their eyes would be glued to the media coverage. Also expected, were eminent members of The Royal Society, The Royal College of Physicians and The Royal College of Surgeons. The media would be present – including *Sabre*'s notorious Weenie – capturing every moment to preservation. Like Archie, Marcus thought, as he wandered through The Darwin Centre on his diverted route home. He admired the behemoth of a giant squid in its huge tank. Archie, he read, was taken alive in a fishing net near the Falkland Islands in 2004. Apparently, the same team that provides tanks to Damian Hirst had constructed the tank. He considered Hirst's shark in formaldehyde: *The Physical Impossibility of Death in the Mind of Someone Living.* The words made him think again of Daisy.

Even the most frivolous, transient moments triggered thoughts of Daisy. She was everywhere. He saw her in the fossils and the bones of the River Thames Whale, in the Griffon Vulture and the Triceratops, and as he strolled outside he thought he saw her skating around and around the ice rink. He headed home, where he hoped to find a 'winning smile and some energy', but nerves skated on his body, slicing his confidence with their sharp blades. He doubted that she would come.

Two and half miles away at *Sainthill Publications*, Tara Forsyth was unaware that she was pushing her luck. She wore Daisy's scarlet dress *and* cream cardigan – or rather, the scarlet dress and cream cardigan wore Tara Forsyth, shrouded her, in fact. Tara was in there somewhere, like a hedgehog thrown into a bonfire, prickly on the outside, but small and vulnerable and destined for destruction.

Jude had spotted her first in the kitchen as Tara prepared another caffeine fix. Jude rushed back into the office laden with juicy tidings. Tara was not only wearing Daisy's dress *and* cardigan, but also a brittle-looking cascade of peroxide hair.

Daisy and Jude immediately dismissed their theory that Tara had pinched the cardigan from Daisy's chair, as surely no one in their right mind would repeatedly flaunt stolen goods in front of the robbed. What's more, the fresh knowledge that Beth was Marcus's housemate offered other possibilities. Daisy recalled leaving her cardigan at the picnic in the park with the twins earlier in the year... *Perhaps it all made sense?* Beth could have taken the cardigan home, and Tara could have borrowed it after posing for – *or sleeping with?* – Marcus. Either way, thought Daisy, she could overlook the cardigan. But her dress was proving tricky to ignore.

Tonight was *Artopsy.* Marcus had sent Daisy her bespoke invitation with the butterfly rain. She was desperately looking forward to meeting him properly and really wanted to wear her scarlet dress – Eliza and Lucian's story was sewn into its very fabric: Marcus would have seen her in it at his exhibition *Portrait of a Boy*, and again, when he took her to the hospital after the hit-and-run... *And how many other times that I don't know about?* With the growing feeling she might *at last* be playing the female protagonist in an enchanting love story, she wanted to direct and wardrobe-manage the final scenes, and felt it would be rather poetic to wear her red dress. Her last role was in a nativity play, so she was adamant she was not going to mess up this once in a lifetime opportunity.

That afternoon as Daisy washed her mugs, Tara joined her in the shared kitchen. Tara boiled the kettle and held straggly fingers above the steam like she was rubbing them over a fire.

'Freezing, isn't it?' she said quietly.

Daisy could almost hear Tara's shiver rattle her bones. *I always found that cardigan quite cosy, actually.*

'Lovely cardigan,' Daisy remarked, vibrating with words she wished to blurt, but Tara looked so sad.

'Yes,' replied Tara, wishing she could do it justice.

'Lovely dress too,' added Daisy – she couldn't help it. *Was it a post-coital offering from Marcus? Do men do that? What if I turn up tonight, only to find he actually loves you?*

'Thank you,' replied Tara.

'They look far better on you,' Daisy blurted involuntarily. *Did he cut out gazillions of butterflies for you too?*

'Sorry?' Tara asked.

'Err nothing. Great hair,' said Daisy, hoping to distract her and awkwardly pointing to Tara's head as if to remind her where her hair was. *Am I Marcus's back up, if things fail with you?*

'Really? You think?' Tara tugged her hand down her hair self-consciously. Strands snapped and weaved around her fingers like spun sugar. She shoved straggly ends behind her shoulders. 'Not so sure,' she said, downcast. Her dry lips joined and folded inwards self-consciously. She looked embarrassed and uncomfortable under the scrutiny.

In her mind, Daisy played out the scene: *Gliding across the museum's hallway, with my arms outstretched, only to find Marcus embracing you. He would turn to me and say, 'You really thought I could love you, Daisy?' before turning back to you and pointing at me, 'Daisy and me! Me with her? Can you imagine?' And you'd both roar with laughter and the entire gathering would do the same. Echoes would pluck the ribs of the diplodocus like guitar strings, until they snapped.*

The kettle shook.

Daisy boiled.

The kettle clicked, but Daisy heard the fire of a starting pistol, and unable to suppress any longer, words ran away with her in audible strides.

'Look Tara, that dress, well it's mine. The mangled bits are my mangled bits from my hit-and-run; I guess they got trapped in the taxi door before Marcus True rescued me. I don't mind, it's just a dress after all, but I really hoped to wear it tonight; it's an important night, The *Artopsy* exhibition. You're probably going for the same reason as me, to see Marcus? Anyway, the dress has sentimental value, you see. And this cardigan, well, it's mine too. Maybe Marcus gave it to you? You can keep it; it's just a cardigan. We were on the subject of missing clothes so I thought I should mention it too. And you're hair. Well, I lied. I don't like it–'

Daisy noticed a tear trickle down Tara's cheek. *Oh crap!* 'I mean I *loved* you brunette. Everyone did. You were beautiful. Oh no, I mean, you totally still are beautiful, drop dead gorgeous in fact, but you didn't need to change anything about yourself! Sorry – the hair thing – so not my place to say, dunno what I was thinking. *Crap...*' Daisy covered her mouth with her hands to plug her pesky words.

Tara was crying.

'Keep my cardigan, *please. I insist.* And my dress. Bugger sentimentality. It's high time I bought a new one anyway! I really didn't mean to upset you, Tara, truly.'

Tara slumped to the floor like a bag of bones. Daisy knelt down and placed a hand on her shoulder. Each tear was like a lumbering train, thought Daisy, as she tracked their journey down Tara's delicate cheeks. One station can take the weight of only so many trains, she thought, as Tara's face fell into her palms.

In the virtue of Daisy's sweetness, Tara's tears gained pace. And she cried because she imagined Daisy with Marcus. *Why not?* Daisy was beautiful and talented... She had won Max von Beck after all. And why else were Daisy's clothes at Marcus's house? She had presumed they belonged to Beth! Tara cried because she recognised love in Daisy's eyes – for hers were cursed with the same. In the presence of Daisy's warmth, Tara realised she actually liked her, and cried tears of guilt for her previous slanderous words and thoughts, and tears of guilt for the crime she was about to commit – she was about to break Daisy's heart.

'I'm sorry,' Tara said and sniffed.

'No, please, *I'm* sorry. All because of some *stupid* clothes!'

Daisy tried a smile.

'*No.* I am sorry.'

Christ, she knew Tara was competitive, but this was getting silly... 'Please, no need. I was a dick to mention it.' Daisy became aware of her hand rubbing furious circles on Tara's back, and was suddenly fearful she might bore a hole.

'*No.* I'm sorry because you have no chance.'

'Sorry?' Daisy looked quizzical.

'With Marcus. You have no chance.'

Woah, easy! Daisy was stunned by Tara's abrupt confirmation of her fears and swift dashing of her hopes. She removed her hand from Tara's back. *I understand. He loves you Tara.* 'OK,' she whispered.

'OK?' Tara looked surprised. *'OK? Is that it?'* She turned her head slowly to face Daisy's. 'But he's *besotted.*'

Daisy flinched. The message was already brazenly clear. Tara could have saved that final bullet.

'Look Tara, I know…I…' Her sentence collapsed with her heart. 'I understand, OK. I know all about it.'

'You do?' Tara was in awe of Daisy's strength. 'Tonight, if you see her, can you tell me what she looks like? What she has that I don't.' She corrected herself, 'Or that I didn't have before, you know, when I was beautiful.'

'Who?' urged Daisy, suddenly confused.

'Who?' Tara paused. *'Eliza, of course.'*

It was 3pm and the pubs were spilling with eager revellers. Hanratty had left the office for the day, and having felt the weekend tug at their fingertips, and the urgency to find alternative attire, Daisy and Jude had scheduled an afternoon retail blitz. Daisy buzzed around the shops with exhilaration, trying on dress after dress – Tara had said Marcus was *'besotted'*!

'You've had a delivery,' exclaimed Jude, as the girls returned to the office with bags of Christmas shopping. 'Let me guess, more inappropriate lingerie from the naughty doctor? Will he ever give up? How many bras can one pair of breasts need for crying out loud? Oh, why aren't we the same size, Daise? It's a cruel, cruel world.'

Daisy opened the lid of the turquoise box and pulled out her dry-cleaned scarlet dress. Beneath lay her cardigan and her latest torn out page of *Musings of a Pisces* emblazoned with the purple *Eliza* signature. Removing these from the box, Daisy discovered a sheet of *Sabre* headed paper, beneath which were words from Tara,

'Dear Eliza. Good luck.'

Tara tugged on her thick coat in the empty *Sabre* office. Downstairs she pushed the heavy revolving doors of *Sainthill Publications* and felt some Velcro from her coat lining snag her lacy bra. As she stepped out into the cold, she was grateful for her numerous rehearsals in wearing absolutely nothing underneath. For once, she thought, she had done the right thing, and it felt good.

The exhibition was going well. The Diplodocus looked as proud as Darwin and the exhibitors' achievement was rewarded with atmosphere and energy in the Great Hall. There were smiles on faces as words, laughter, canapés and champagne circled the magnificent atrium.

Standing alone, Daisy flicked apprehensive eyes across the crowd, from one face to the next – *could Marcus see her?* There were outfits of all sorts, a daring vibrant array of pattern and colour: futuristic shoulder pads, skewed necklines, ruffled Elizabethan collars, jaunty tartan and lace hemlines, tinsel boleros, barmy hats, and the heels! *How could ladies walk in those heels and still look like ladies?*

Some appeared to walk on wooden compasses, others on abstract metal staplers. Some bore no heal at all, just thick wedges scaffolding the feet.

Daisy cast her eye around the various paintings, sculptures and installations.

Suddenly, the hallway sang with dolphins. Attention focused on performance artist and illusionist Carla Lightfoot's *Ascension of Man*. Daisy had read about Carla's *'live birth as an art project'* in the catalogue Marcus had sent. She had thought *WTF?* then, as she did now. All eyes looked upwards to a naked Carla seated in water with legs akimbo, inside an open-topped illuminated transparent Plexiglas box, suspended from the floor. Suddenly, the canapés no longer looked so appetising. Daisy was as captivated as the other onlookers as she watched Carla's body work with her baby's movements, helping *'Rex'* – named before the birth – down the birth canal. There was something eerie and beautiful, thought Daisy (*and totally disgusting and unnecessary*), about blood seeping into the clear water like that, like swelling red smoke clouds. Outside the box, spare space was filled with probing dolphin cries, and whispers and gasps of the mesmerised crowds. *Holy shit!* Baby Rex was born into the red waters.

Daisy's phone vibrated in her pocket. It was Jude, desperate to get the low-down – *'Have you seen Marcus yet?'* And just as Carla had delivered her baby, Jude then delivered some special news of her own, *'I'm pregnant, Daise!'* The lights dimmed in the Plexiglas box. Creation hovered in the shady arched ceiling, emitting light from darkness. My God, thought Daisy, too much, too much... She felt giddy with elation at her best friend's news as anticipation continued to bubble for her meeting with Marcus. Her heart beat in her eardrum and she felt sick – admittedly, staring into a woman's vagina hadn't exactly helped.

She lurked nervously behind the huge Christmas tree. Casting her eye up candlelit branches, she noticed they were decorated with little gift bags. Each bag was black with silver trim, like the envelope she received from Marcus, which had contained the invitation catalogue. She peaked in one lower down and wished her fingers could probe beneath the silver tissue paper to see what Christmas goodies lay beneath. They were up for grabs, explained a jovial steward, who busted her peaking. 'One bag for each guest on departure.'

Marcus... Daisy could see him in her mind's eye and could feel his presence. She fidgeted self-consciously and yanked down her red dress with her wine-free hand. The feeling of being watched was unnerving. Had he spotted her through the thick crowds? For a better vantage point she darted through the sea of people and up the steps towards Darwin. There she mellowed in his reassuring paternal aura and contemplated sitting on his knee.

'Daisy.'

She stared at Darwin and froze. *Darwin?*

'Daisy.'

She noticed the voice had come from behind her. It was an intense, gravelly voice...*dry paint on a masterpiece*... She inhaled for clarity and breathed in the scent of tobacco and turpentine, paint and pine forest. *Marcus.* She felt a hand on her shoulder – the gentle touch of a resting butterfly. *Happiness.* She was frozen to the forest floor, unable to turn around.

'Hey,' he said softly.

She turned and there he was. One glance. They lost themselves in the truth in each other's eyes, but neither had ever felt so found. Their flesh became glass, their bones became crystal and their blood became water, as their hearts beamed out light that shone through all barriers. True love obliterated confinement.

Rabble upon rabble of butterflies burst forth from Marcus and made their way to Daisy – crossing flight paths with Daisy's, multi-coloured flutters, like Christmas glitter, filled the space between them. As they drew closer, Daisy noticed they were carrying colourful flakes – *fragments of me!* – that swayed as they moved through the air, like drying clothes on a breezy day. They flew into her soul and hastily dropped their loads in this final mission. They deposited not flimsy fragments but tough skin that could be stretched into sails, strong enough to endure even the harshest of sea storms, and shields that could deflect blows aimed at her heart. Then the butterflies found a comfortable place to tuck tired limbs and rest for a very long, undisturbed hibernation, happily ever after, to let true love reign supreme. Mission accomplished.

Part of him belonged to her, and part of her belonged to him.

They became one.

They felt complete.

'Ah, you two have already swapped notes, I see,' Oliver's unwelcome words tripped into their moment, 'and body fluids soon, no doubt.' Daisy and Marcus felt the interruption like blows to their chests that knocked them off course and severed eye contact. They looked over to see Oliver shifting uncomfortably. His feet juddered to a sad discordant melody. It looked a lonely dance.

'Of course, you have,' Dr Oliver continued. 'Suspected. Inevitable,' he waggled a finger back and forth from Marcus to Daisy, slicing the air chaotically, before dropping his scrunched face to the floor; he hadn't planned this. He specialised in rehearsed sophisticated movements, not these crude jerky gestures. He needed to get a grip – and a stiff drink. He yanked back his shoulders and swerved his head from side to side and up and down in search of a waiter with a tray, before ploughing on.

'Look, mate,' He turned directly to Marcus. 'I've been meaning to apologise, but I knew Daisy would get there before me… I'm sorry, OK.'

'For what?' Asked Marcus, perplexed by Oliver's unusual manner.

'Oh God, you're not *seriously* going to make me spell it out, are you? For stealing your crown, mate, you know. You can hardly blame me,' he glanced over at Daisy and inappropriately flashed his dirty grin, a feeble mask of happiness. 'I haven't had the chance to apologise for *mis-leeead-ing* Daisy, letting her believe it was me who rescued her from her hit and run, and,' he scratched his head and rolled his eyes in a manner that said, *what the hell*, 'that it was me who detected her heart condition.' Then raising his hands, he said, 'Hands up, Marcus mate, arrest me, I'm guilty as charged.'

No one recognised the doctor talking. Marcus looked bewildered, but Oliver continued to clobber the silence.

'Look. Why don't I make up for it and buy another artwork? Your male nudes are a little grisly, mind you. Any females? The ticking boob installation near the entrance, doesn't happen to be yours, does it? A nipple winked at me. Tickles my fancy, I must say. And baby Rex – don't suppose you had anything to do with it, did you? If so, well played mate, that Carla looked mighty fine from where I was standing, ha! and baby Rex is a little cutie. Name the price and I'll take him off your hands.' He practically choked on his empty laugh, but the jokes fell flat.

Marcus closed his eyes, pressed his hand against his forehead, shook his head to scratch away the image of Oliver tickling breasts and buying babies, and rewound.

'You mean to tell me, the ECG – the one I called you up about, was Daisy's?'

So Daisy didn't dob on me... Oliver's face reddened at the realisation that his humiliating confession was maybe not necessary at all.

Marcus turned to Daisy. '*You* had Wolf Parkinson White Syndrome? *Of course! Your heart flutters, your fainting...* It makes sense.'

'You fixed me,' she said quietly, suddenly overcome with shyness.

'You were never broken,' he replied.

Once again they were locked in the magnetic force between them.

Oliver wretched in the pot of a nearby Cheese plant, but for Daisy and Marcus, the rest of the world had vanished.

Friday, December 23rd

The office was quiet. Daisy was hurrying to tie up loose sentences for *Musings of a Pisces* before boarding a midday train to her parents' house in Hampshire for Christmas.

Hanratty had nipped in briefly to retrieve the *Iain M. Banks* novel he had accidentally left in the office – the thought of a Christmas break spent in reality rather than science fiction made his tufty hair moult. He spotted Daisy at her desk. 'Ah Daisy, I was going to email you. Tell me then, did you find it?'

'Yes,' she said, feeling pretty smug. 'Just in the nick of time. I always work best under pressure,' she smiled and Hanratty smiled back.

'Well, my congratulations,' he tipped an imaginary hat and dandruff sprinkled onto his shoulders. 'So what will your *Musings of a Pisces* column look like? How will you convince your readers of this delightful phenomenon?'

'Well,' she began, and shifted in her seat, 'this is controversial.'

'Go on.' There was a time and a place for controversy and preferably not one that encroached on his Christmas break.

'I want to place an advertisement as soon as possible. An electronic one in the form of an invitation, on the *Nimbus* website. It would be fitting, you see. It shouldn't cost the magazine and it might even improve circulation.' Daisy stepped into Jude's role of ad salesgirl – she knew Hanratty loathed advertisements, especially of the e-variety.

Hanratty staggered a little and furrowed his forehead in confusion.

'To advertise an afternoon of celebration at my new café *Tea and Sympathy*,' Daisy explained. 'An afternoon in celebration of love. And you must come too, Hanratty.'

He smiled bashfully.

'You gave me a two-fold challenge, Hanratty, to find true love and represent it on my page. Well, I have succeeded in the first, but failed the second. Or was it a test? You see, I've discovered that no matter how much I flex it, squeeze it, stuff it, it's no good, you simply cannot contain true love on a page. I adore words but they could never convince my readers of love. Not true love anyway. It's too…well, big. Enormous, in fact. I only know this now that I've found it.'

Hanratty's eyes sparkled with pride. *Maybe if you flex it, squeeze it and stuff it with love until it defies recognition, then maybe, just maybe, an electronic advert would not be so bad after all.* Daisy could sell him anything, he realised. The girl had a way with words.

Friday, December 30th

9.30 am

Outside *Tea and Sympathy,* a queue of *Nimbus* readers coiled down the Portobello Road, each gloved hand clutching an invitation, and all eager to meet *Eliza,* their Queen of Musing. The queue frothed with chatter, laughter, and an assortment of happy expressions. Each admired the blue façade with the turquoise-framed windows. Across the outside of the blue doors hung a red bow created from the snipped ties of Daisy's scarlet dress. Those near the entrance watched the figures inside hurriedly attending to last minute jobs, and admired the array of mouth-watering delights.

Inside Daisy tucked the keys to her new café in the pocket of her apron.

It was Rowena Mellow, the head curator, whose sharp eyes had spotted Marcus's envelope on the tree, as the exhibition evening drew to a close. *Artopsy* had been off-the-scale successful, and spirits were high.

'There's your envelope on the tree. There, see,' she wagged a claw. Marcus stepped forward and took the bag off its branch with the hand that was not clutching Daisy's.

'She's a pretty thing,' Rowena nudged Marcus.

'This is Eliza.' Marcus couldn't help but glow with pride.

'Actually, I'm Daisy,' said Daisy.

'Awkward!' Rowena laughed hysterically. 'Onwards and upwards, Marcus.'

'It's not actually as awkward as you think,' he muttered, as he opened the bag. Under silver tissue paper, Marcus found a weighty bundle. He took off the elastic band that held the contents together like a baton. There was a card, written in Jasper's writing. *Or was it his?* There were capital letters.

'A celebration of Marcus and Daisy, of art and writing, of understanding and forgiveness, of choice and resilience, of tea and sympathy. a celebration of two true arts, two true hearts and one true love.
Good vibes
Jasper x'

And on the other side of the card, a key was taped above an address. Marcus recognised it immediately.

Outside the Natural History Museum, Daisy and Marcus hailed a cab – cold and black and low on fuel. Inside they kissed a kiss so hot, so bright and so energetic, it could have taken them to the moon and back. But instead, they went to the address Jasper had given them on the Portobello road.

On the same site where Jazbar once stood, they found instead a charming café. Waiting for them on the doormat was another note from Jasper; once again it incorporated his fledgling capitals; his baby brother had finally grown up. *'My present to you.'* Daisy and Marcus held hands and took a gander. The whole place was like a Christmas tree, an expression of sheer joy. Shelves shone with packets of coffee and boxes of tea of numerous flavours from all corners of the globe. There was a silver coffee machine and an orange juicer, electric purple and green glassware, Art Deco cups and saucers, teapots and tankards, floral pottery plates and biscuit tins, and shiny cutlery with varying designs on the handles. The entire café clashed spectacularly. There was something that would appeal to every taste under the sun. Everyone would be welcome here.

They noticed that some tables were modified school desks with flat tops. Stout pink piggy banks sat in the centre of each table. Into the backs of the pigs, Jasper explained, customers could push their problems. *'A bit like when we used to write our wish list to Father Christmas, remember Marc? And we used to burn them in the fire, so no one actually read them apart from us.'* With one hand still holding onto Daisy's, Marcus lifted the lid of one of the old school desks to reveal clean pads of paper and polished pens. *'It's so customers can vent issues and get things off their chests. It's good to write them down. Really therapeutic. (I'm preaching to the converted, I know, ha!) No one else will read or judge them. Lonely Londoners can then get chatting over a cuppa and leave feeling a load better – with a take-away hot date too. If they get lucky.'*

Daisy gasped when her eyes fell on the walls. *'My God'* she exclaimed. 'That's *me*. And that one!' her eyes darted across the walls. 'And there with Jude. And there in front of that painting of yours... Yes, I remember standing there just like that.' Her voice was a whisper and her hands quivered. 'It's me...in my scarlet dress the moment before I turned and fainted...' But this time she did not turn; she just stared, fixated on this painted collage of her.

'What? How on earth...?' Marcus saw his entire *Eliza collection*, apart from *Fairground Frieze*, adorning the walls of the café. 'What the hell? How the h–'

'You mean these aren't your paintings?' Now she was really scared. He caught sight of her ashen face and was mortified.

'No, they are, they are,' he stammered and noticed her heave a sigh of relief.

'I just have absolutely no idea how they got here.' His cheeks burnt. This was beyond embarrassing. 'I know what this must look like, some weird Daisy shrine or something. Christ, I know, I know.' He massaged his forehead vigorously. *If I were her, I'd run a mile.* 'I don't really know what to say, apart from I'm a little nuts but I'm no stalker. Honestly.' He looked again at the walls; evidence was against him. He hung his head. *Balls.*

She squeezed his hand. 'Hey, if you weren't nuts, I wouldn't be here. It's OK.' Her smile was full of reassurance. 'It's more than OK, Marcus. It's the most amazing thing anyone has ever done. These paintings, I mean. All this time spent on me... And,' her spare hand did a mini loop of the walls, 'all this talent...wasted on *me*. They're all so incredibly beautiful. And well, I'm so incredibly flattered... And this, this whole thing, the paintings, the café, you, me, and...' She wanted to say *us*, but the word would take some getting used to. 'Well, it's all pretty amazing, don't you think?'

'Yeah,' he replied. 'I do.'

He noticed another note from Jasper, this time tacked to a wall. He read aloud, *'Hope you're not cross about this surprise exhibition bro. Know you didn't give your consent. And I appreciate a café venue is beneath you, but it would've been a crime to let all those masterpieces rot and fester in your studio. They're awesome. An inspirational – if a little offbeat – love story adorning the walls.'*

9.45am

'Are you happy with the position of this one?' Floyd asked Marcus, pointing to *Butterfly Echo*. 'I thought if I hung it above the kettle, the steam might damage it, so I moved it.'

Floyd congratulated himself once again, on both his handiwork and his ability to keep hush after Jasper had told the twins about his surprise gift. Since then, four elfin porcelain hands had been on deck. Confident that Marcus's attentions were focused on *Artopsy,* Floyd had stealthily snuck each painting from the *Eliza Collection* to the café.

'Absolutely,' replied Marcus. He looked at Daisy arranging the olive oil. *Everything's pretty damn perfect, my friend.*

'Are you going to sell them?' asked Shell, as she opened the jars of honey.

'Oh no, no. These paintings are priceless, to me anyway. Not for sale, I'm afraid,' said Marcus, disturbed by the thought.

'Floyd has pretty much padlocked them to the wall, Marcus, so have no fear!' Beth reassured from behind the coffee counter.

Marcus turned to Daisy. She was quiet. 'You OK?'

'Yup,' she looked at him, 'just a little anxious, I guess.' She scrunched the fabric of her checked apron and the keys rattled in the pocket. 'Is this pinny too Mrs Tiggy-Winkle? *Eliza*'s meant to be cool. I don't want to disappoint them.'

'Well, she didn't disappoint me. Besides, you pull off hedgehog-chic remarkably well. No, seriously, stop worrying, you look hot. And exceptionally cool.' Marcus gathered her into his arms and kissed her. 'It will be great. I'll make sure of it.'

She looked deep into his eyes and felt so happy.

'Urgh, get a room, kids,' yelled Beth. They'd been kissing all morning.

'That's love for you,' whispered Floyd to Xander. They caught eyes, and Floyd turned the colour of strawberry jam.

Looking out of the window, Jude spotted Will and Millie in the crowd. She waved and mouthed, 'Three minutes-ish!' Turning back to the chutneys, she popped the few remaining price tags on the jars before placing a tray of buns into the oven. Looking down at her own nicely rising tummy, she felt the rush of excitement. *So much to look forward to.*

10am

It was time. Everything was as polished and ready as it would ever be. Daisy unlocked the blue door and with Marcus by her side, she untied the bow of her scarlet dress and announced to the crowd, 'Tea and Sympathy is officially open! Come on in, guys, and let's get pouring!' The crowd cheered and waved their invitations like flags.

On one table Max von Beck sipped Earl Grey. After some consideration he picked up a pen and scribbled, *'Please help me to understand why I'm always in the doghouse. Married life must be an improvement? Things cannot get worse. Can they?'* He looked over at Daisy. She was chatting with an elderly man with a kind face. He clasped an *Iain M. Banks* in one hand and a coffee in the other. When Daisy met Max's gaze, he felt warmth and forgiveness pour into his own, before Luise's scornful stare scolded him from across the table. He jumped to her attention and buried his wandering eyes and scorched face in his mug of tea – *she terrifies me!* *'Please,'* he scribbled as fast as he could now, *'let me have chosen the right woman to be my wife.'* He stuffed his wish into the back of his pink piggy before Luise had time to intercept.

On another table Dr Oliver sat alone. On his piece of paper he wrote, *'Please fix my broken heart.'* He folded it carefully and popped it in his piggy bank.

On the adjacent table, Tara wrote the very same words.

Oliver noticed a delicate wrist creep into his field of vision to deposit a secret wish. He spoke to the pretty wrist. 'Let's hope the pigs don't sneeze our problems back at us. Some people's problems are contagious, and I've got enough of my own. And I bloody well hope they're not investment piggy banks, because I don't want mine to grow. They are meant to be very intelligent creatures, you know, so I wouldn't put it past the little swines.' The dainty wrist reached for her teacup. Oliver continued. 'Let's hope their stomachs make mincemeat of our problems and make our wishes come true,' he turned and smiled at the figure attached to the wrist. *Tara Forsyth?* – but a much thinner, paler version – *who clearly needed the urgent attentions of a good doctor!*

Tara gently replaced her cup on the saucer and they shifted their chairs to face one another fully. As their eyes met, a feeling ignited that had failed to ignite before. They found something that neither had been looking for when they first met; something that neither had believed existed then.

'You have to stand alone,' Tara said to Oliver later, over a slice of carrot cake, 'to prove that you can stand.'

'Yes,' replied Oliver, 'but it's far better to stand together.'

'Why stand when we could walk?' Tara said, 'There's a wonderful world out there to explore.'

Still taken aback by the ease in which their words strolled through unfamiliar depths, way beyond flirtation, they became two fixed parts of one component, like two healthy legs embarking on the marathon of life. They felt complete now.

As they got up to leave, they noticed a charity box by the café entrance. From Tara's handbag she retrieved a big wad of cash.

'No, no, let me donate from the both of us. Please,' insisted Oliver, reaching into his wallet.

Tara looked at him, 'Don't worry,' she placed the money into the box, 'it was yours anyway.'

He remembered the cash that he had left by her bedside and his face grimaced in apology.

'I'll forgive you because you look like Hugh Grant. For no other reason though.'

It suddenly seemed quite funny.

At close to midnight, the café had been returned to organised chaos. Daisy and Marcus had stayed after the last customers had left. Over tin mugs of Amaretto, they looked back on the day and forward to those yet to come.

Daisy locked the door and Marcus looked up at the starry canopy. It was beautiful.

In fact all he could see was beauty – not even London's thick canopy of smog could change that. Were they the only two in the world awake that night? It certainly felt that way. 'We've met here before,' he said. And they remembered the evening they had first made contact. From their respective bedroom windows, two stargazers had gazed as the rest of the world had slept. The faceless strangers had chatted unreservedly in a dreamlike space, free from expectations, pressures and inhibitions. They were the only two souls awake that night, and the only two that mattered.

'But now we're meeting here properly,' she said, and squeezed his hand. She felt emotional and willed herself not to cry. She waited for Marcus to speak, to pull her from tears. 'Come on,' she said smiling and nudging him gently, 'say something, please.' She wiped her cheeks with a gloved hand. 'You're useless. Lucian would know what to say, he's amazing with words,' she teased.

'Anyone would have thought you were trying to make me jealous,' mumbled Marcus between kisses. 'And I think you might just have achieved it. How weird is that?'

Daisy looped her arm in his, and they began their journey home.

In her mind's eye the pavement turned to sand. Looking ahead, her eyes washed over the length of a beach and her walk of life. She saw another set of footprints accompany her own – capable, consistent, brave steps. She *knew* now that they belonged to Marcus. She noticed that they walked together, fresh prints side by side, until they disappeared down the beach and towards the horizon. The moment glistened like the ocean.

Their conversation flowed like a stream of sleepy consciousness until morning broke quietly, not wishing to wake the magic.

'You know, I had toyed with the idea of calling it Shine on Wine; would've been a wine bar obviously, not a café,' Jasper had confessed to Marcus, over the phone earlier that week. *'You know, as a nod of gratitude to Shine Online. It played a pretty vital role in getting you two lovebirds together, wouldn't you say? And a part of me still wanted the site to flow with booze. To remind me of the good times. It's tough ending a love story, you know.'*

'Your love story with booze was hardly a happy one.'

'No. But the tragic ones are arguably the best. The ones people remember. You guys got your tragedy over and done with at the start. You wrote your love story the right way around. You're destined for a happy ending.'

Friday, March 30th 2012

Marcus had persuaded Daisy to move from her Warren to his house on Aldridge Road Villas. In fact, he had spent the majority of the New Year persuading her but Daisy was adamant not to rush it. Besides, she didn't want to look too desperate – according to *Nimbus*, desperation was *so* 2011 (she should know). 2012 was all about playing it cool.

Finally, at the beginning of March, she turned to Marcus and said, 'OK, I'm ready. You win.'

'*You* win more like, madam, I make a mean Full English, you'll see. Glad to hear you've finally realised you can't be without me,' he felt giddy with elation. 'I, of course, knew that well over a year ago.'

'Well, actually I need more space to write and I've had my eye on your studio for a while now,' she teased.

'Oh great. That's it?'

'No, no, the Full English thing too – I like my eggs fried by the way.'

'Anything else?'

'Yes, the mushrooms, I like them cooked with loads of butter, and I like my sausages and bacon practically burnt, and you can keep the baked beans and hash browns. I'm partial to a spot of black pudding too, just so long as you don't remind me what it is I'm actually eating at the time–'

'You're a pain, Hawkins. Ball busting, brain aching work. But that's what happens when you stray from the norm. And boy, the signs were all there.'

'You have only yourself to blame.'

'I'm fully aware. Any other reason why you've decided to move in with me then?'

'Hmmmm,' she looked ponderous. 'Nope. No I think that just about covers it. I did mention the eggs, didn't I? Sunny side up.'

'How about your heart? Which you'll find is permanently sunny side up now.'

'What?'

'Maybe, just possibly you're moving in with me because you are in love with me?'

'Uh-uh. Wrong.'

For a moment he looked crushed.

'I'm moving in with you because I'm in *true* love with you,' she corrected.

'Does that even make sense? Can you say that?'

'Well I just did. I'm crazily, truly, madly, deeply in true love with you Marcus True! True for true love.'

She grabbed his cheeks and planted a kiss.

'Woah, OK! I thought 2012 was about playing it cool.'

'Fair point.'

They laughed and kissed again. It was longer and hotter. A moment later their clothes were strewn all over the floor.

Daisy had packed boxes full of her things and remembered doing the same when she had left Jesse, but this time she had packed for an arrival not a departure. This time she knew where she was going.

Daisy's boxes squatted on his studio floor – a studio bursting with creativity hardly inspired something as boring as unpacking.

'Any music requests?' Marcus hovered by his gramophone.

She shifted her head from her pose to view his collection. 'I've gotta admit, "It Must Be Love" has been whirring around and around my brain recently.' She sang, 'I've got to be near you, every night, every day.'

'I couldn't be happy, any other way,' he finished.

'Bloody hell, you're shocking at singing! Maybe we should revert back to email communication only.'

He laughed. 'Well, I clearly don't have a Madness album. Anything else?'

'OK, a bit of Vivaldi's Four Seasons, please.'

'Another *very* odd choice,' he remarked. But without question, he put it on.

As Daisy listened, she recalled her old life, her daily walk to her old job through Hyde Park, her relationship with all the seasons, the relentless march of time, her development and her progress.

As he returned to his fresco, a crumpled piece of paper fell from the top of one of Daisy's boxes. Marcus picked it up and without thinking, began to read:

The Story of my Life, by Daisy Hawkins
Wading through critical red, I review the essay of my life; angry question marks, patronising exclamations, blunt crosses, rejecting erasure. Protagonist is stranger, friend and foe. I edit in the empathetic (often patronising) expanse of hindsight and prepare blank pages for a climactic conclusion, heart stroking ticks, contagious smiles and fated disappointment.

'Oh no, please don't read that.' Daisy jumped up to retrieve her writing. 'I wrote it ages ago.'

'I'd like to think you can edit "fated *disappointment*" now,' he said. 'And you shouldn't be angry or regretful. Never ever.'

'But what about all those mistakes I made?'

'We are living the result of your mistakes, Daisy, and I for one am quite enjoying myself. If we hadn't travelled down the specific roads we did and mess up with those exact people at those precise times, then our lives would've taken different directions and our paths would never have connected. See?' A splash from the fish bowl distracted his attention. 'And neither would theirs.' Marcus had returned Romeo to the sanctity of his studio – but this time with a pink girlfriend called Juliet in tow.

'I *appreciate everything* in hindsight,' Daisy corrected her writing aloud, 'and prepare blank pages for fated *happiness*. Because I know that it's you I need to take the blues away.'

'Perfect.' Now let's start filling those blank pages,' Marcus grabbed her around the waist, 'and I like the sound of a climactic conclusion very much…'

'Work, then play. Finish your painting,' she laughed and fended him off. 'I don't want to be faceless forever thanks.'

'This is a bit like *Titanic*,' Daisy mused.

'With one major difference,' said Marcus, taking her in once again, before returning to his painting to refine the features of her face.

'I'm not *completely* naked?'

'I'll see to that very soon. But no, not that. *We* end happily. As far as I remember, those guys weren't quite so lucky.'

'Happily ever after, like a fairy tale,' she mumbled beneath her breath.

She relaxed in the warmth of the notion and let her mind wander to where it had before; on the very evening they had exchanged their first words… *His brush strokes nude beige, then swells in blushing rose. Like a Renaissance master, his obsessive eye measures my body; painstakingly analysing forms until he sees nothing but perfection. I pulse harmoniously on the canvas. In the presence of a genius, I quake with rapturous humility. Vocal morsels of Italian deliciousness flow like frothy cappuccino from his cherub lips, whilst Vivaldi's Le Quattro Stagioni colours the background. I die in a haze of ecstasy as raw umber cups my breasts…*

Eliza was no longer faceless; her memories were frozen into *Fairground Frieze* and the fresco was now complete. Marcus looked at Daisy and smiled. She was so still but he could tell that her mind was racing – he loved that about her, so much depth and so much mystery.

The doorbell rang. 'Pizza time, m'lady,' said Marcus. 'I'll go, and I'll bring up a bottle of wine.' He paused by the record player, 'and enough of this classical stuff; it's Friday night after all, the night before the rest of our lives.' He removed the sleeve from a record and carefully placed it in position, before disappearing down the stairs to fetch the Four Seasons pizza. Vivaldi was silenced and The Beatles "Love me Do" sang out into the studio *'I'll always be true…'*

It was all a bit too cheesy and all a little too perfect. But they could no longer give a toss that 2012 was about playing it cool. They were deep in True Love, and wouldn't have it any other way.

The End